Wreck of the Royal Express and other stories

Robert L. Ramsay

Copyright © 2018 Robert L. Ramsay
ISBN: 978-1-79198-310-9

This book is a work of fiction. Names, characters, events, and dialogue are the product of the author's imagination or are used fictitiously. Any resemblance to actual persons, living or dead, is entirely coincidental.

First Edition

Table of Content

Wreck of the Royal Express

I wasn't thrilled to learn I'd be firing for Old Blister. He was known on the Great Northern Railroad from Spokane to Seattle as a miserable old cuss of a hogger, notorious for stepping over the line when it came to abusing his crew and ignoring company rules. However, firing for him would give me the chance to see a real live king and queen.

As a rule, we Yanks don't waste time on royalty. We left all that scraping and bowing behind in 1776 when we thumbed our noses at George III, but King George VI and Queen Elizabeth were making a tour of Canada. They would be in Vancouver, British Columbia on May 29, 1939, and the Great Northern Railroad, for whom I fired, saw a chance to make a buck. The company knew enough star spangled folks were royalty watchers to make it profitable to cobble together an Extra to run north of the forty-ninth. Canada Customs was gracious enough to send their agents to Seattle's King Street Station so there'd be no need to pause in White Rock for a border check.

The plan was to leave Seattle at six in the morning so the crown gawkers would arrive in Vancouver in time to take up positions along the parade route. I reported for duty at five o'clock, signed the register in the King Street Station, then sat down with a cup of black coffee to fortify myself for the ordeal ahead. About five-thirty Old Blister swaggered into the office. "You firing for me today, Kiddo?" he asked, banging his lunch pail on the counter.

"Yes, Sir."

He looked me up and down, took off his engineer's cap, scratched his bald head, frowned. "You look mighty skinny to me. Hope you got enough muscle on those toothpicks to heave some coal; no time for growing calluses on your butt when you're firin' for me, 'specially with the *fine* steed the company's assigned us today." He scrawled his signature in the register and aimed an angry looking wad of tobacco into the spittoon beside my chair.

"What've they given us?" I was hoping for a Mountain 4-8-2, one of the company's leggy greyhounds with sleek Vanderbilt tender, a locomotive fit to impress a king and queen.

"Quit asking questions, Kiddo. Get off your bony duff and go take a look. We're in for a rough ride."

I stepped across the hallway and peered through the window to the tracks below. The hostler was backing an eight wheeler onto our train of heavyweight steel cars. Old Blister was right about his forecast of a rough trip. The 2-6-0 Mogul was not known for the joy of its smooth ride. Even at moderate speeds it danced around on its 73 inch drivers like a ballerina, pirouetting and bowing to every mile post and signal tower.

I went back into the office, refilled my thermos with coffee, grabbed my lunch pail and headed trackside to check the beast's condition. I climbed onto the footplate, stashed my lunch in the cubby beneath my seat, then grabbed the oil can and made the rounds. Some wag in the roundhouse had coughed up two Union Jacks and stuck them on the front of the locomotive along with a sign lettered in red, white and blue: *Royal Express*.

Everything lubricated, I climbed into the cab, shook the grates, and built up the fire. I had the needle on 200 pounds pressure as Old Blister came charging out of the station. He paused to grab the orders from Conductor Stevens and read them. Then, grunting, he hauled his carcass up the steps, stashed his lunch pail, set his coffee on the metal lip overhanging the firebox door, and checked his watch. He handed me the schedule. I glanced at it—pretty tight, but if all the meets happened as carded, we'd deliver the royal watchers to the parade with half an hour to spare.

The cab whistle squealed twice. Old Blister yanked his goggles down from his forehead, pulled his cap firmly in place, turned on the sanders, and grabbed the throttle. By the time we exited the tunnel we were doing thirty-five along Seattle's waterfront. The speed limit was twenty-five, but speed limits never bothered Old Blister when he had a job to do.

We had clear signals all the way to Everett, but the track curvature prevented speeds any higher than the posted forty miles an hour. Not even Old Blister dared open the throttle any wider for fear of delivering the passengers black and blue to Vancouver, along with a trainload of lawsuits. When we got to Everett we had to sit in the hole while the westbound *Empire Builder*, running several hours late due to spring floods on the plains, slid down from the Cascades and headed south to Seattle.

At the green signal, Old Blister released the brakes, poured on the sand, and away we went, rattling across Everett Junction where the mainline heads east, then danced a bit too fast for my comfort across the spider-like bridges spanning the Snohomish River estuary. Then we were in tangent country and Old Blister notched the throttle as far as it would go, racing through Tulalip and Marysville. "We'll have them there in time to lay the red carpet," Old Blister chortled as we hit sixty whistling through Arlington.

We danced across the railroad bridge over the Skagit River at Mount Vernon and barely touched the high iron heading north, Old Blister maintaining at least ten miles over the speed limit. When firing, I usually had a couple of minutes to rest between standing to tend the fire, but with Old Blister at the throttle I was on my feet the whole time. Several times I had to hang on to prevent being thrown to the footplate, but we were making great time.

Coming into Bellingham, we hit a red signal that wasn't supposed to be there. The operator ran out to give us the bad news—a freight had pulled a knuckle trying to get up the heavy grade out of town. We would have to wait until the two sections of the broken train were brought back down the hill.

"Don't envy Stevens bearing this news to the cattle in back," Old Blister said, standing up to retrieve his lunch pail from beneath his seat. I did the same, biting into the thick egg salad sandwich my landlady had prepared for me.

"Nice going, Kiddo. Stink up the cab with them rotten eggs, why don't you?" said Old Blister, sticking his head out the window and spitting.

A half hour passed before the switcher appeared hauling nine cars from the rear of the stalled freight. Ten minutes later the front half crept down into the yard. It was eight-thirty—almost impossible to get our royal watchers to the parade route on time. I glanced over at Old Blister. His jaw was set, his goggles in place, his hand on the throttle.

I had the fire roaring, the pressure back up to two hundred, and at the green signal Old Blister gave two toots on the whistle, turned on the sanders, and we plodded up the grade out of Bellingham. The run to the international boundary was pretty straight forward with some good tangents. Old Blister had the needle tickling the big Seven-O, twenty notches over the speed limit as we roared towards Blaine, overtaking a short freight sitting in the hole.

Old Blister slowed for the curve at Peace Arch Park, though at forty miles an hour it felt like the Mogul was leaning far enough over to expose daylight between the rails and its drivers.

"White Rock," I shouted, pointing ahead. Old Blister nodded but didn't ease back.

"White Rock!" I yelled again.

"I know where we are, Kiddo," he hollered, opening the throttle as we bounced across the Little Campbell River bridge and started down the tangent fronting White Rock's beach. To beachgoers it looks like a smooth speedway, but it's one of the roughest sections of track in the system, built on top of loose beach sand that shifts with every change in the tide.

"Better cut the speed," I yelled, pointing to the needle nudging fifty. "Thirty along here."

"Kiddo, we're not stopping today," Old Blister yelled, yanking his watch from his pocket. "Can still make her if you quit your blabbering and keep that fire hot."

He yanked another notch out of the throttle. We raced towards the pier where a couple of strollers, catching sight of the insane dance of the approaching locomotive, fled from the crossing. They held onto each other and the pier's railing to brace themselves against the wind of the passing train. We whipped past the station, skipped over the siding switch, and galloped westward.

"Better slow down around the point," I yelled. "It's a tight curve." I had fired the route many times and you had to take it slowly around the high cliff that jutted seaward. If not careful, you could run into a rockslide, a fallen tree or simply fly off the rails. Old Blister just shook his head and gritted his teeth.

In all my years firing I'd never experienced a derailment, but as the Mogul heeled into the first curve it danced its way to freedom. There was a thunderclap from hell as the pony truck leaped off the rails, followed by splintering wood as the drivers made kindling out of the ties. The next moment the locomotive was heading for the sea that happened to be at high tide. I looked over at Old Blister. He still had his hand firmly on the throttle.

"Jump, Kiddo!" he yelled. I dropped my shovel, stepped to the door, gave a mighty push, and as the locomotive chewed its way down the rocky embankment I hit the water with arms and legs flailing, fully expecting to be crushed by passenger cars following our lead into the deep.

Seconds later all was still, except for the scream of venting steam from the Mogul, and the hiss of seawater dousing the fire. The engine was lying on its side in about five feet of water—I could just stand on the bottom. The tender had uncoupled and crouched helpless, half-way down the embankment. Somehow the passenger cars had all remained on the grade, though they had jackknifed into a pattern of crazy angles.

I swam-waded over to the Mogul, paddled right into the back of the open cab. Old Blister's leather glove was curled around the throttle but there was no sign of him. Had he taken a leap after telling me to jump? If so, where had he landed? I swam out of the cab and clambered up the embankment, peering beneath the tender, but it was impossible to see if Old Blister was trapped there. If he was, he'd almost certainly be dead.

By this time Conductor Stevens and some of the passengers had escaped the cars and were coming to have a look.

"Get back!" I yelled. "That boiler could explode."

Conductor Stevens ordered the people back, then came down the embankment. "What's that?" he asked, pointing to the locomotive.

"It's a runaway Mogul," I said, wondering if he was suffering from shock to ask such a stupid question.

"Not the engine. That!" He was pointing to the sea beside the locomotive.

The sand had been all stirred up when I'd been swimming around right after the wreck. Now it had settled and there lay Old Blister, his legs pinned beneath the side of the cab. He was lying face up, his engineer's cap gone, his goggles still firmly in place, his lips pulled back in a tobacco-stained grin. His right hand was stretched above his head, moving back and forth with the ocean's swells so that he seemed to be beckoning to us. Stevens and I waded in, dived down, grabbed his belt and yanked, but he was firmly wedged beneath the engine.

We turned our attention to the passengers. By some miracle, most had only minor injuries: cuts, bruises, a few broken arms.

None of us got to see the Royals that day. At an evening reception King George offered his sympathy to those who had been injured in the wreck and his condolences to Old Blister's family. Poor old cuss had blistered the rails for the last time, but he'd taught me an important lesson. When I became engineer and was tempted to bend the rules to make up time, I'd remember Old Blister lying in the sea. I'd see his arm waving a cautionary signal—not even a king and queen were more important than the safety of my passengers.

Natural Remedies

Dr. Angora Mallard was a shrunken, pale-faced man, and like many sub-standard males, he made up for his lack of stature by shouting. His credentials weren't stellar either—a degree from some no-name academy of marginal medicine. I wouldn't have attended his lecture, but my friend, Frank Slaughter, had been suffering desperately from a sore throat ever since he started work at the abattoir up in Brownsville.

According to the newspaper, Mallard could cure high blood pressure with beet juice, and banish migraine headaches by laying lemon slices on the forehead. I figured a sore throat would be a cinch, and sure enough, after bleating like a sick goat for ten minutes, Mallard said that gargling turnip juice would heal a sore throat. He promptly demonstrated the cure.

There was no affliction beyond Mallard's skill. Earache could be cured by stuffing pureed bananas into the ear canal. Cancerous tumors could be shrunk with a poultice of raw, mashed Irish potatoes. They were also excellent for shrinking hemorrhoids, not mashed, but carefully carved into a suitable shape.

This latter piece of information inflamed the crowd. There was a frenzy of hand waving and demands to know where Irish potatoes could be purchased. When it turned out they were the kind we eat every day, half the crowd slipped out the door. I chuckled to myself, imagining all the potato carving that would be going on that night.

Suddenly I had a brilliant idea. For several months my jeans had been shrinking. Each time I washed them they came out a size smaller. I had assumed it was something in the water until one night when we were showering at the pool. Frank grabbed me, marched me into the change room, turned me sideways, and ordered me to look into the mirror.

While I didn't see Alfred Hitchcock's exact profile, my furry belly certainly could have made the front cover of People Magazine if I had been a pregnant Hollywood starlet. Since that night I had been doing sit-ups, crunches and other irksome exercises, but if mashed potatoes would shrink a tumor, surely they would melt a jiggly belly.

After the lecture I stopped at Safeway, grabbed the last sack of potatoes, and hurried home to process a large bowl of white goop. I laid a couple of plastic garbage bags over the bed, stripped, lay down and spooned the sticky mash over my belly.

It was four in the morning when I awakened, cold and wet in a pool of potato juice. I tried to sit up, but the mash had hardened like cement. I picked at a corner, broke it away and pulled. "Ouch!" I screeched as a large clump of belly hair came off with it.

Half turning onto my side, I squiggled my legs over the edge of the bed and down to the floor. I stood erect, potato water dripping onto the rug. I hobbled into the bathroom, stepped into the shower and was about to turn the water on when I realized that the mash, when it came loose, would block the drains.

There was only one solution. I stepped onto the backyard patio, grabbed the hose and twisted the faucet. Cold water splashed against my potato belly and down my legs.

"Ooh, Ahhh," I screeched, dancing about as the icy water hit my toes. It was agony, but after several minutes the hardened mash softened, then began sagging in large chunks. My movements became more frenzied as more of my pelt was yanked away, and I danced out onto the lawn so I wouldn't have to clean the mash off the patio. Unfortunately, I'd forgotten about the motion-sensor light on the garage. There was a flash and I was bathed in its naked glare. Never mind, I was almost free of the horrible mess, and who would be watching at that hour anyways?

I was rubbing my now smooth but still jiggly belly when I was blinded by the beam from two powerful flashlights. Holding up my hands to shield my eyes, I saw two police officers, one male, the other female, standing beside my house.

I explained about Mallard and his lecture, but they didn't believe me, despite the pile of crusty, hairy, mashed potatoes I was standing in. Shaking their heads, they snapped cuffs on me and led me out to their car, muttering something about taking me to a shrink.

I hardly noticed the shadowy huddle of neighbours next door, because my mind was fixed upon revenge. When I caught up with that quack Mallard, I'd tell him where he could shove his potatoes.

On second thought, he was probably already putting them there.

Husband Material

Sunday-morning light seeps through the venetians. I glance at the bedside clock. Six-fourteen. I want to get outside while it's still cool. Weeds are taking over the rose garden. The beefsteak tomatoes need to be pruned and the scarlet runner beans are ready to be harvested.

I lie still for another half hour. I don't want to waken Parker. It was after midnight when he got home from work. As always, he undressed in the dark, trying not to disturb me. Still, I wakened as he crawled between the sheets.

"How was work?" I asked.

Before turning onto his side, he gave my hand a squeeze and muttered, "I'm worn slap out."

In the four-plus years we've been living together I've learned silence means a rough night. A week later, when the photograph of some ghastly accident appears in the *Peace Arch News*, he may say, "Timothy, you're lookin' at the man who pulled the mother out of that twisted hunk of metal. Drownin' in her own blood. And the baby. A wisp of a girl. So precious. So dead. I hope you'll never see anything like that, Husband."

Makes me nervous when he calls me *Husband*. I know he wants us to marry, have a proper church ceremony and a sit-down reception with a white cake topped by two grooms. He's always watching gay proposals on Youtube. I'm almost afraid to go anywhere with him in case he's secretly arranged one of those public displays of affection. I imagine us walking to the end of the pier where all his buds from work will swarm us. Parker will pull a little black jeweller's box from his pocket and drop to one knee while the gulls scream and the tourists point phones.

"Won't a wedding spell the end of our relationship?" I said to him yesterday when he brought up what's become a daily subject. "We both know couples who were doing fine until they made it official. Look at Callum and Pete."

"Callum and Pete's relationship was off like a herd of turtles from the get-go, so no surprise there," he said. "It would've taken more than a few sacred vows to pump life into their marriage. But you and me, we're too wise to split." He reached for my hand. "You and me, Timothy, we're tight as a day old scab and we'll not let anyone, or anything, pick us apart."

"Such a romantic simile, Parker, but how many lawyers have bought new BMWs thanks to couples who were too smart to muck up their own lives?"

In slow motion I lift the sheet and slide out of bed. I tiptoe into the bathroom, closing the door before I snap on the light. As I shave and brush my teeth my mind wanders over my relationship with Parker. I first bumped into him at the Model Railway Show in Chilliwack. My clumsiness caused him to drop a rare BC Rail wide-vision caboose. He could've yelled at me as he picked up the pieces. Instead, he flashed a smile and drawled, "Wipe that apology off yer face, young man. The fun's puttin' it back together. You can buy me lunch while I inventory the damage."

I'd about given up looking for Mr. Right, but Parker turned out to be husband material. He's gainfully employed with a real career, not just a glorified sales person pushing high-end purses at Nordstrom's, like the previous fellow I dated. Parker makes enough money as a medic to pay off his credit card every month and always pays his share of our household expenses. He doesn't snore or kick his dirty laundry under the bed.

We both enjoy gardening, though I do most of the heavy work in the summer since I have two months off teaching. Evenings, when Parker's not working, we hang out at Softball City and in the winter binge on movies from the '40's.

There's a lot to like about Parker, not least his husky build due to a daily hour at the gym, but of course he isn't perfect. I can't stand the sound of him brushing his teeth—like he's putting his teeth through a car wash, soapy spray all over the counter and mirror. Also, he's a bad one for putting the empty cereal box back in the cupboard and neglecting to replace the toilet roll when he's used the last bit.

Parker hails from Alabama, which he fled during the later Bush years. He brought nothing with him except his training as a medic and his deep southern accent. He doesn't talk much about his family, but when he mentions them, he calls them white trash.

"My momma's as shy as a lil ole catfish," he drawls. "After more than forty years married to my daddy, she still undresses in the closet. You ever heard anything so precious?"

I suppose it's a vestige of that conservative upbringing that drives Parker's desire to get married. He wants to make our relationship legit.

Some evenings, when we're sitting in the living room, me reading the latest political autobiography, Parker snuggled next to me watching gay weddings on his laptop, he'll look up and say, "This house is awfully quiet. Shouldn't we be filling it with the shouts of sweet little boys and girls?"

"You haven't spent your day in a classroom with twenty-five of those sweet little boys and girls," I say. "If you had, you'd welcome peace and quiet at home."

"You don't want children of our own?"

"It's not on my list of must-haves."

"I think you'd feel differently if we were married and they were ours."

Parker is too wise to lock heads with me over an issue like children or marriage. Instead he bides his time, stealthily seeding my brain until my thinking catches up with his. That's how Mr. Kazoo came to live with us.

I grew up on a farm in Langley where we had the full-deal menagerie: half a dozen cats, a Lassie-look-alike, a gentle Shetland pony and a couple of cocky peacocks. The animals were great fun to play with, but they were all outdoor beasts, free to roam our forty acres.

Shortly after Parker and I moved in together he started hinting we should have a dog.

"What would a dog do in this townhouse?" I asked. "He'd be by himself all day, howling his lonely head off and chewing the couch to bits."

"I usually work evenings, starting at four," Parker said, "and you're home by four-thirty, so he'd hardly ever be alone."

"Maybe not, but the city's not the place for a dog. They like to run free. Besides, I'm not crazy about being a little *poopie's* sanitary engineer."

Parker ignored the humour. Over the next few weeks our bike rides took us near the off-leash parks, the one beside Centennial Arena or the big one off 20th Avenue. While I'd have preferred to keep pedalling to maintain my heart rate, Parker insisted we pause to watch the dogs. The four-legged beasts certainly were entertaining while expending their boundless energy. I understood why a single person might want a dog for company, but Parker and I had each other.

And then it was my thirty-third birthday. Without the faintest blush of deceitfulness, Parker presented me with a foxy, copper and white Japanese Shiba Inu. Despite my reservations, I was soon devoted to Mr. Kazoo. Now I look forward to his cheek-licking greeting when I come home. Who cares that we lost a pair of leather shoes before we got smart and stashed them on a top shelf in the closet.

My morning ablutions complete, I pull on my shorts and t-shirt and my garden Crocs and head outdoors with Mr. Kazoo. He races around the backyard, re-marking his territory. Then he lies on the sun-warmed patio while I start the weeding.

As I dig out the buttercup, I wonder how serious Parker is about wanting children. He's got four brothers and two sisters, so he's used to being surrounded by a tribe. I was a single child so never had to compete with siblings. How would I feel if Parker focused most of his free time on a child and took me for granted? Marriages can break up when that happens.

I'm almost finished the flowerbed when I hear the neighbour's patio door slide open. Jack steps out with a brown bottle in hand. He and Flora are in their eighties, quiet neighbours until Flora has one of her bad days. *Madder than a wet hen*, Parker describes her, and today she's on a roll.

"You're not drinking already, are you, Jack? It's barely eight o'clock," she calls from inside the house.

"It's going to be a hot one so I'm priming the system. The doctor told me to stay hydrated."

"You're killing yourself with beer," she yells from the kitchen. "When are you going to stop? Are you listening to me, Jack? Are you listening to me? Are you listening to me?" She repeats it in a monotone, with each repetition louder, like one of those self-serve checkouts gone berserk.

Through the cracks in the fence I see Jack rise from the chaise lounge and go inside. He leaves the door open and I can see Flora sitting at the kitchen table. He stoops over her, puts his arms around her and rocks her like a baby. *Are you listening to me* grows fainter, fades away, is replaced with heartbreaking sobs.

I finish weeding the flowerbed and stand up to stretch the kinks out of my back. Jack comes back outside and walks over to the fence.

"Flora having one of her bad days?" I ask.

"It's the stroke talking," he says. "Never an unkind word from her for fifty-three years, then a ruptured blood vessel among the grey cells."

"I admire your patience," I say.

"You've heard the saying, *what goes around, comes around,*" he says. "A few years before you boys moved here, I fell off scaffolding. I was flat on my back for months. Flora looked after me without a complaint. She had a sense of humour before the stroke. She made herself a nurse's uniform—white dress, shoes, even a cap like they wore years ago. She'd come dancing into the bedroom, my painkillers and lunch on a tray—she almost made being an invalid fun.

"Now, it's my turn to care for her. I wish she didn't need it, but I find pleasure in calming her down, helping her get through the day, though I haven't got into nurse's drag yet."

We both chuckle and he goes back into the house. I start pruning the tomatoes, thinking about what Jack said. I realize my fears about marriage are based on selfishness, and that's wicked. I've got to prune it away just like I'm snipping off these sucker branches from the tomato vines.

Say I suffered PTSD after some lunatic shot up my school, I know Parker would be here for me. Even if I disturbed his sleep with sheet-twisting nightmares and screams, or refused to get out of bed to eat or shower, he wouldn't abandon me. Why am I so fearful of making a commitment to him no matter what happens?

The back door opens. Parker steps onto the patio. His ginger hair is still damp from the shower. He yawns, stretches, scratches Mr. Kazoo behind the ears, then pads barefoot across the grass. He hugs me, plants a toothpaste-fresh kiss on my lips.

"Didn't hear you get up, Husband." He brushes my forehead with his fingers. "You're sweatin' like an ole sinner in church. Want a glass of water?"

"No. I'll be in soon."

He nods. "I've been thinking we could have our wedding in Peace Arch Park."

"We're having a wedding, are we?"

"That's right. Lord willin' and the creek don't rise, we're getting' hitched. There's a real nice hall for rent in Peace Arch Park. We can cycle down after breakfast, take a look."

Without waiting for me to comment, he walks toward the house, then turns and says, "How be if I make your favourite breakfast: hotcakes with Saskatoon berry syrup?"

"Husband," I drawl, "that'd make me happier than a coon in the henhouse."

Marriage Vows

I envy guys who are conscious of their affectional orientation from day one. What an advantage to know such intimate details about oneself so early in life. What an opportunity to map out one's life, to plan how to handle one's deepest desires.

I wasn't so lucky. I didn't cotton onto the nature of my own affectional orientation until my mid-twenties, and by then it was too late to plan anything. This was a major disadvantage in my family where planning was a part of any undertaking.

Something simple like going to Clear Lake on the May long weekend required detailed planning. Mom was the planner in the family, so it was she who announced at the supper table, "We need to plan for tomorrow."

"Aren't we going to the beach?" Dad paused, a forkful of cream-soaked bread sprinkled with brown sugar in hand.

"Yes, Ralph, that's exactly what we're doing, but don't expect me to do all the work."

"What's to do?" Dad asked, pushing back his chair.

"Don't you go and leave me, Ralph," Mom said. "Just sit down, finish your dessert, and help me and the boys plan." Mom reach to the windowsill for a pen, a scrap of paper, and shifted into full planning mode. "Have you filled the car with gas?"

"I don't think you'd want gas inside the car." Dad frequently injected a note of frivolity into family discussions, hoping that it would excuse him from the planning process.

"You know what I mean, Ralph. I don't want the car running dry like the last time."

"That wasn't my fault, Marjory. We hit that construction zone and had to take that long detour. You may recall that I wasn't the only one hoofing it to the service station."

Mom turned to Freddie and me. "Now, boys, do you know where your swimming trunks are?"

We both pointed out the window. Our trunks were flapping on the clothesline, drying out after we'd spent the afternoon playing in the swimming hole.

"And Trevor, what about your inner tube? Is it pumped up? I don't want to hear two little boys fighting over one tube because you forgot to put air in yours."

"I'll run and check it right now." I was thankful for an excuse to avoid further planning.

When I got back into the house Mom was still going through her list. "What about the cows, Ralph? Are the fences in good condition? We don't want them getting out while we're gone. And boys, is their water trough pumped full?" And on and on until we all felt like yelling, "Forget it! Let's not go! We'll stay home and tear down that old chicken coop. We'll gas the rats out of the barn. We'll muck out the calf pens. We'll do anything to avoid this plague of planning."

Despite our annoyance, Mom's constant planning rubbed off on me, and I guess that's why I think what an advantage it would have been if I'd had some early warning that I preferred the intimate company of men to women. If I had known, I would have chosen a different university, perhaps the University of Quebec where handsomely swarthy fellows of French Canadian extraction would have whispered sweet things to me in their slippery *joual*.

I might have enrolled in Business Administration instead of elementary education. While studying economic theory, I could have snared myself a budding business tycoon. His earnings might have given me the lifestyle I yearned to become accustomed to living.

However, being ignorant of my innermost self, I blundered along with Mom and Dad's assumption that I would marry someone of the female persuasion. Dad was never very specific about the trajectory my life should take, but Mom had a list of must-haves. Freddie and I would marry good WASP girls, those with English, Scottish or Irish blood flowing through their veins. They'd be rosy-cheeked lassies with flaming hair like Mom's. Such girls would know that money doesn't grow on trees and would be capable of turning out a pan of golden scones and a pot of scalding tea at the first hint of company.

My brother Freddie followed Mom's plan to the letter and gifted the family with three ginger-haired young ones. However, I never met a lassie who inspired thoughts of marriage. I bumbled through those early years alone. Only after I graduated from college did I realize my preference for spending life with the male of the species. I don't know why it took me so long to understand this—there were clues I should have picked up on.

There was Yvan "King" Yacenko, my twelfth grade biology lab partner. He played hockey for the Greenfield Grandees. While he and I performed open-heart surgery on frogs in biology class I used to sneak downward glances at his hockey player thighs. The margins of my notebooks were festooned with our interlocking initials, sometimes engraved within hearts. You'll know how dumb I was when I swear that I never equated my feelings with lust.

I worshiped Yvan with a close-up, pure love, wishing I had body parts exactly like his. I happily dictated answers so that he could fill in his lab book when he'd missed a class after a grueling hockey game. I lent him my favourite mechanical pencil to complete his sketches. I was thrilled when he chewed up the eraser end. I immediately stuck it into my own mouth when he handed it back to me. Even today I sometimes reach for the leather-covered five-year diary I was keeping in those days. I flip it open to March 12, 1961 and caress the strand of his hair I snitched from the barber shop floor when I found myself getting clipped next to him.

My adulation of Yvan wasn't the only clue to my male-loving personality. Long before high school I fell in love with Brian Spikkel, a travelling evangelist who dropped by our sinful little corner of Manitoba. Like everyone else in our farming community, who had only one snowy television channel to watch, we were easy marks for every live entertainment that whistled through town. Along with our neighbours, we packed the community hall to see Pastor Spikkel's blood-curdling slides illustrating his theories about end-time events.

It was the fifties. I was four, maybe five years old. The Soviets had the bomb, and Pastor Spikkel had it all figured out that the battle to end all battles was about to erupt. Our quiet corner of rural Manitoba would be blown into an eternally burning hellfire if we didn't all shape up, and quick. If we wanted to escape eternal destruction we had to give up Agatha Christie's crime-ridden novels, movies like *Peyton Place,* and brainless television shows like *I Love Lucy.*

By the end of the evangelistic series half the community had been scared into the portable baptismal tank. I would have been one of them, but Mom and Dad thought I was too young to know what I was doing. I now realize that I was more attracted by Pastor Spikkel's wide grin, thick golden hair and tight trousers, than by the meek and lowly Jesus.

The summer I turned six there was another clue. This time, not only did I become helplessly infatuated with a man, but I shared my infatuation with the whole family.

It started with a letter from Dad's sister. Aunt Millie's weekly letters were deadly dull. She taught English literature in a private school in Calgary. She'd write how she'd gotten up at six to wash and set her hair before going to work. Then she'd report on some poem the girls were memorizing or a song they were preparing for the Spring Fling.

"Poor Sis. She's all alone in life," Father would say after reading one of her pedestrian epistles. "Not much chance of her catching a man either, not with that big boot."

It was true. Aunt Millie wore a big boot on her left foot. I don't know whether she was born with a defective leg or suffered some sort of accident. It was never discussed.

As a six-year-old I could see that Aunt Millie was no beauty. Her mouse brown hair was so fine that when she walked on a calm day it floated above her head like dandelion fluff. Her face was round and flat as a pancake. She had a tiny nose, a mouth that was too wide, a big gap between her two front teeth, and eyebrows that grew bushy if she forgot to mow them. It was almost as though her face had been cobbled together from leftovers after God finished making the beautiful people.

But as a six-year-old I didn't care about such things. I loved Aunt Millie and basked joyfully in the attention she showed me during her annual visits to the farm. On those too-infrequent Sabbath afternoons, she'd take my brother Freddie and me for walks along the rutted cow trails through the community pasture. We'd head down to Cottonwood Creek where the big steel trestle carried Canadian National trains across the valley. Freddie and I often walked that way on our own, heading for the swimming hole, but with Aunt Millie the hike became an adventure. She spotted wasps' nests we'd never noticed, or spied cottontails crouching beneath thickets of silvery wolf willows.

Mom, as well as all the girls I knew, screamed at the sight of a spider or a wasp, but the previous summer Aunt Millie had proved that she wasn't afraid of any living creature. Freddie and I had been helping her pick Saskatoon berries down by the creek. When our honey pails were full, we stopped to have a swim. Aunt Millie began to teach me how to keep my eyes open under water while I bobbed and breathed. I was just getting the hang of it when I saw this greenish yellow ribbon gliding towards me. Even before my head broke the surface I was screaming. "Snake! There's a snake. It's gonna get me."

Aunt Millie just laughed as she scooped the tiny garter snake out of the water. "Aren't you the cutest little fellow," she said, winding it around her arm like a bracelet. "Aren't you God's little jewel." She pointed out how the scales interlocked on its greenish-white belly, and how if you looked closely you could see the fork in its tiny pink tongue.

This particular summer Aunt Millie's letter contained startling news. *Some months back I met a man,* she wrote. *His name is Richard Toombs. He's a rancher. We have fallen in love and just last week he asked me to marry him.*

She went on to write that they'd like to get married in the little Anglican Church in Twin Meadows. Since Richard had no brothers or sisters, she hoped Dad would be the best man. She would write to her high school chum Gwen, to ask her to be her bridesmaid. Then she addressed a paragraph to Mom.

Marjory, I know you're good at planning. Could you reserve the church for August 12th and arrange for the priest to conduct the service and for Eadie Bellows to play the organ? I know it will be a lot of work but could we hold the reception on the lawn at the farm? I'll come out two weeks ahead and help get everything ready. Love, Millie

"Well, I never!" Mom handed the letter back to Dad. "I never thought I'd see the day your sister would walk up the aisle. You don't think there's something funny about this man, do you?"

"What do you mean?" Dad slathered butter onto another slice of Mom's homemade bread.

"Toombs is a spooky name."

"I don't think we should judge him until we meet him."

"No, I suppose you're right, though your sister is almost forty. That's a dangerous age for women. They get to feeling desperate and are liable to do something foolish."

"I don't think Millie is foolish about anything, and just because she was never 4-H Queen like you, Marjory, doesn't mean she can't find a husband."

"I didn't mean that. It's just that at her age she's liable to act on impulse. We wouldn't want her to make a terrible mistake. Still, I guess we should make some preparations." Mom reached to the windowsill for a pen and scrap of paper. "There'll be a lot to do, especially with the reception being held right here. We'll have to plan…"

25

Dad did his planning in secret. Three days before Aunt Millie arrived, he drove the '49 Chevrolet Deluxe over to Sprucegrove. Two hours later he drove home in a new '58 Chevrolet Impala, four-door hardtop, in Sierra Gold. It had a V8 engine, an automatic transmission, and twin raked radio aerials on the rear fenders.

Freddie and I thought it was the finest car we'd ever seen. Mom was upset. "I know you love your sister," she said to Dad, "but I think you've gone overboard—trading away the car you used to court me."

Dad just hugged her. "Hop in, Marjory. Roll down the window and enjoy the ride."

We all hopped in again three days later to drive to Greenfield's train station. We got there just as the throbbing diesel locomotives, brakes squealing, arrived with their string of stainless steel coaches. The conductor swung the door open, dropped the steps and reached a hand to help Aunt Millie off.

A big smile slashed her face in half when she saw us. "There they are! There's my big brother, his lovely wife, and my two favourite boys." She bent down and covered our faces with sloppy kisses. "Now, who is going to help me with these suitcases? Aren't they just the biggest old things you ever saw?"

Freddie and I each grabbed a case and struggled along beside Aunt Millie, her big boot clomp-clomp-clomping along the platform's pavement. When Aunt Millie saw the new car she dropped the little overnight bag she was carrying and took a step back. "Ralph! Is this really your car? I have never seen a finer looking machine. Is this special for me?"

Dad nodded. "A car fit for a bride, don't you think?"

"The Queen could not ask for anything finer." Aunt Millie hugged and kissed Dad and then he opened the front door for her.

"So, you really are getting married?" Mom settled herself in the back seat, sitting between Freddie and me so we wouldn't fight.

"I am indeed. Who would have thought it at my age?"

"Who is this Toombs fellow?" Mom pulled her compact out of her purse and studied her face, patting powder onto her nose. "You didn't say a whole lot about him in your letter."

"Now don't you be giving Millie the third degree." Dad shifted into Drive and we glided out of the station parking lot.

"I'm not giving her the third degree. I just think it would be nice if someone in the family made sure your only sister isn't making a mistake."

"Richard is no mistake," Aunt Millie said.

"Do you have a picture of him?"

"You'll see him soon enough," Aunt Millie said. "He'll be driving down a week Thursday."

"He's not one of these fellows I read about in the Ann Landers column, is he?" Mom asked. "You know, some lazy lay-about preying on single women?"

"I assure you he doesn't need to prey upon anyone," Aunt Millie said. "He owns a ranch in the foothills west of Calgary— runs a thousand head of cattle."

I leaned forward, sticking my head over the back of the front seat. "What does he drive, Aunt Millie?"

"Most of the time he drives a pickup truck," Aunt Millie said, "but he'll be coming down in the car. It's big and white. That's about all I know."

"Is it a Chevrolet like ours?" I asked.

Freddie leaned forward. "Is it a Buick or an Oldsmobile, Aunt Millie? Does it have power steering, and power brakes?"

Aunt Millie chuckled and reached back to pat Freddie's head. "I don't know. You'll just have to wait until Richard drives onto the yard and then you'll know all about it."

Back at the farmhouse, Mom shifted into high planning gear. There were dresses to sew: the wedding dress, a mist of snow-white lace, and two going away outfits. There was the wedding cake to bake and decorate, and a million other things to do.

For the most part Freddie and I stayed out of the house. We helped Dad get the yard cleaned up for the reception. We pulled weeds from the flowerbeds along the driveway and picked up branches after he pruned the lilac bushes. Freddie steered the rusty Massey-Harris tractor that hadn't run as long as I could remember, while Dad towed it out of sight behind the machine shed. Freddie and I whitewashed the fence and painted the chicken coop and even Rover's doghouse.

The Wednesday evening before Richard was to arrive, Mom came upstairs to tuck us in for the night. She sat down on the chair between our twin beds. "Now listen carefully. You boys have to promise me that you'll mind your manners when you meet Richard Toombs tomorrow. You must call him Uncle Richard. Remember to hold out your right hand when he reaches to shake your hand. When you're introduced say, 'How do you do, Uncle Richard?' Do you understand?"

"Yes. I've been practicing with Rover all week." I snuggled under the covers. "He lifts his right paw when I say, *Shake a paw*."

"It was me taught him that," Freddie said.

"Did not. I taught him first."

"Boys, boys, please don't fight. You don't want to fight in front of Aunt Millie or Uncle Richard, and whatever you do, don't laugh at Uncle Richard."

"Why would we laugh?" I asked.

"Well, I don't know, but just in case there's something funny about Richard Toombs, you're not to point, or laugh, or make faces behind his back. Do you understand?"

"Is there something funny about him?" Freddie sat up in bed, turned his head toward me, stuck his thumbs into the corners of his mouth and pulled down his lower eyelids. "Does he look like this?"

I couldn't help laughing.

"Boys, stop it! Stop it right now!" Mom wagged her finger at us. "It would serve you right Freddie, if your face stayed that way. Then we'd see who was laughing."

"Does Uncle Richard have a big boot like Aunt Millie?" I lay down and pulled the covers up to my chin.

"Hush. You must never say anything about that. We don't know what this Mr. Toombs will be like, but we have to be prepared to welcome him as Aunt Millie's husband—no matter what he looks like. Is that understood?"

On Thursday Freddie and I hung out in the tree house we'd built in the old maple tree at the end of the lane. Using field glasses Aunt Millie had given us one year for Christmas, we scanned the road to the south. Each hoped to be the first to see the big white car coming up the road.

That evening Freddie was in the barn, helping Dad with the milking. I was at the hand pump, filling the cow's watering trough, when the long white car with sharp tail fins like an airplane came zipping up the road. It slowed, then turned into our lane.

"Uncle Richard's here! Uncle Richard's here!" I yelled as I ran into the barn.

"Hush child. You'll scare the cows and they won't give their milk," Dad said.

"But he's here."

Freddie jumped up from milking our little Jersey cow. "What's he driving?"

"I'm not sure, but it's big and white just like Aunt Millie said, and it has huge fins."

"It must be a Cadillac. Dad, can I go see?"

"No, you may not," Dad said. "Finish your milking, and Trevor, you go feed the calves their chopped oats and close up the chickens for the night."

"But Dad?"

"Your Aunt Millie will want to spend a few quiet minutes with your Uncle Richard. Go finish your chores."

I usually lingered to watch the calves butting heads as they scrapped over their evening treat of chopped oats, but not that evening. I flung the oats into their manger, then scurried over to the chicken coop. I often made a game of chasing the hens. "Last one in gets the axe!" I'd warn while they looked at me with their stupid, button-like eyes. But that night they seemed to know I was in a hurry and they refused to cooperate. I was still struggling to get them inside when I saw Dad and Freddie heading for the house.

"Wait for me, Dad," I yelled, tears springing to my eyes. Dad handed his milk pail to Freddie and came to help. We soon had the chickens locked up for the night. Before going into the house we paused to admire Uncle Richard's car. "It is a Cadillac, Dad. See!" I traced out the chrome letters reading Coupe DeVille.

"So it is," Dad said. "Your new uncle must be a wealthy man."

While we were washing up at the sink in the back porch and changing out of our barn clothes, I could hear voices from the front parlour. There was Mom's nervous laugh, Aunt Millie's low purr, and another voice: lower and huskier and with a drawl that sounded sort of familiar.

Finally, Dad led us into the parlour. Aunt Millie stood up. She took hold of Uncle Richard's hand and helped him up, then handed him a cane with a silver horse's head for a handle. I glanced down at his feet to see if he had a big boot, but he was wearing ordinary shoes.

He wasn't much taller than Aunt Millie. His face and neck were the colour of strong tea, his cheeks reddish like a sun-ripened peach. He had light brown hair like Aunt Millie's, but his was thicker, bleached almost blond by the sun. He was wearing blue jeans, held up by a brown leather belt with a silver bull's skull for a buckle. His red cowboy shirt had black pockets. When he smiled, the skin at the corners of his eyes creased up like a paper fan.

Aunt Millie introduced Dad, then Freddie, and finally me. I was so entranced by Uncle Richard's smile that I forgot what I was supposed to do. Mom had to say, "Trevor, remember your manners. Uncle Richard wants to shake your hand."

I blushed and stuck out my right hand—at least I got that part correct. Uncle Richard took my hand in his. "Young man, you have a nice firm handshake," he said, crinkling up the corners of his eyes. "You must be a big help to your dad on the farm."

I nodded and retreated to the sofa. I sat down between Mom and Dad while Freddie dropped onto the hassock. Aunt Millie helped Uncle Richard ease down onto the love seat across from us.

Dad quizzed Uncle Richard about his Cadillac. How many cubic inches were under the hood? What kind of mileage did a heavy car like that get? Then he asked about his ranch.

"Runnin' over a thousand Herefords this year," he said. "Good rains. Lots o' grass. Should do well if the price o' beef stays stable." He spoke slowly, dragging each word out. I'd heard a voice like his on television: Matt Dillon on *Gunsmoke.*

"How does one person take care of so many cattle?" Mom asked.

Aunt Millie turned towards Uncle Richard and took his hand. "How many hired men do you have now, Honey?"

"Two right now," he said, "but I bring more on during the roundup in the fall. With this bum back o' mine I'd never manage without help."

"What happened to your back?" Dad asked.

"Thrown off a wild bronc a few times too many." Uncle Richard crossed his legs and settled back on the loveseat. For the next hour he entertained us with stories about his years on the rodeo circuit. "Course at my age—forty-three last month—I won't be doin' that sort of thang no more."

"I intend to hold you to that promise." Aunt Millie patted his hand. She started telling how she'd met Uncle Richard at the Calgary Stampede, but her voice kept fading away as I sat snugged against Mom.

"Do I see little eyes closing?" Mom patted my knee.

"No. I'm not tired."

"Well, it is bed time. Your Uncle Richard has had a long drive so he'll be heading to bed pretty soon, too. You boys get upstairs and use the bathroom before we come up." Mom pushed me to my feet.

"Freddie, I've made a bed for you on the cot in the basement."

"Aw Mom, it stinks down there."

"Shush, child. There's nothing wrong with that basement and I've had the windows open all day. Besides, it'll only be for a couple of nights."

"What about Trevor? Why can't he sleep in the basement?"

"Because we only have the one cot. He'll be in his own bed, that is if you don't mind sleeping in the same room with Trevor, Richard?"

"Not at all. We'll just pretend we're in the bunkhouse on the ranch." Uncle Richard winked at me. "If I start snorin' like some old cow poke, just fire up the branding iron and give me a jab on the you-know-where." He chuckled and winked.

"Away you go, boys," Mom said. "Into your pajamas, and Trevor, you get under the covers and close your eyes so Uncle Richard has some privacy when he comes upstairs."

We dashed out of the room. "I get to sleep with Uncle Richard. I get to sleep with Uncle Richard," I teased as Freddie and I raced up the stairs.

"So?"

"And you have to sleep downstairs with spiders, great big, hairy spiders."

"I'm not afraid of spiders. You're the fraidy cat," Freddie said, poking me in the ribs.

"Am not."

"Are so. You're just a big crybaby."

"Boys! Boys! Stop your scrapping." Dad came up the stairs two at a time behind us. "Do you want your new uncle to think you're a couple of savages?"

I obeyed Mom that night and closed my eyes when Uncle Richard came into the room. I listened while he took a shower in the bathroom next door, then pulled the covers over my head when he came back into the room.

I wondered what Mom had meant when she'd said he might be funny in some way. He didn't seem funny to me. Using a cane was different than most men his age, but if it helped his sore back that was okay.

I didn't wakened the next morning when Dad tapped gently on the bedroom door, opened it a crack and whispered, "Time for chores, Trevor."

I eased myself out of bed and turned on the bedside lamp so I'd be able to find my clothes. I looked across the room. Uncle Richard was lying on his side, facing away from me. The sheet and blanket were thrown back, exposing his backside—naked. I knew I wasn't supposed to look, but I couldn't help myself. What was that on his butt? It looked like someone had scribbled on his cheeks with a blue pen.

Holding my breath, I leaned forward until I could see better. Uncle Richard had a tattoo on his butt: a horse on one cheek, a chuck wagon on the other. Until that morning, the only place I'd seen a tattoo was on television: the anchor tattooed on Popeye's arm. Was this what Mom meant when she said Uncle Richard might be funny? Did she know he'd have a horse and chuck wagon tattooed on his butt?

As I ran out to the barn I was dying to ask Dad about Uncle Richard's tattoos. But I didn't dare say anything. I'd be admitting I hadn't kept my eyes closed. But did Aunt Millie know? What if she didn't want to marry a man with tattoos, especially one with wild west pictures on his butt?

I decided to say nothing. I wanted to avoid the butt-warming I would get from Dad for peeking, but most of all, I wanted Aunt Millie to marry Uncle Richard. If she learned about the tattoo and decided not to marry him, I might never get to ride in his Cadillac, visit his ranch, ride his horses, or see the Rocky Mountains.

The wedding was scheduled for two o'clock that afternoon. While Dad gave the lawn a final trim, Freddie and I helped Uncle Richard wash the Cadillac. "Good job, boys." Uncle Richard gave a final wipe to the roof. "Hop in, you cow pokes. We'll take our steed for a little ride."

Until that moment I'd thought Dad's '58 Impala was the finest car in the whole, wide world, but Uncle Richard's Cadillac was a zillion times finer. It had white leather seats, adjusted by the push of a button. It had air conditioning and a push-button radio. Uncle Richard started the engine and shifted into Drive. He drove behind the machine shed and parked in the shade beside the rusty old tractor.

"You cow pokes can help me decorate, but don't tell your auntie. We don't want her to see the car all fancied up until it's time to drive to the church." He unlocked the trunk and lifted out two cardboard boxes of paper flowers: yellow and pink. He handed each of us a roll of tape.

"Got these thangs in Calgary," he said, "and now you're gonna help me tape them to the car. We'll start on the hood."

When we'd finished, we helped Dad and Uncle Richard set up tables and chairs on the lawn. And suddenly it was one o'clock and time to get ready for the wedding. Mom had put our clothes in the basement so we could dress there and leave the bedroom for Uncle Richard. We were waiting by the car when he stepped onto the verandah. He was wearing black cowboy boots, grey jeans, a grey shirt that shone like polished silver, and a jacket made from some soft, black material, stitched with silver thread. He wore a white scarf around his neck, and twirled a white cowboy hat on the end of his cane.

"Uncle Richard! You look like Matt Dillon on television," I said. "He wears fancy boots and a scarf just like yours."

"This here's a bandana." Uncle Richard touched the scarf. "Cowboys wipe the sweat off their foreheads when ridin' the range, or tie it 'round their nose and mouth to keep the dust out. Cattle kick up a powerful lotta dust when they're being rounded up."

"Can I come and help round up the cattle?" I asked.

"You've never even been on a horse," Freddie said.

"I could learn."

"Of course you could, and maybe you can do that sometime, but look at your mother. Doesn't she look fit to be the bride herself?"

"Oh Richard, you sweet-talker!" Mom bent to pick a spec of lint off the long, blue dress she was wearing. "But no time to stand around admiring ourselves. We've got to get to the church."

We got into the Impala with Mom and Uncle Richard. Mom was driving, but that didn't stop her from giving last minute instructions. "You boys just watch the adults and you'll know when to stand and when to sit—and no fidgeting, no talking during the ceremony, not even whispering. We don't want to embarrass your Uncle Richard."

"They'll be just fine." Uncle Richard flipped down the mirror on the passenger side and adjusted his bandana.

When we got to the church the priest was waiting on the step. We talked to him until we saw Dad coming with Aunt Millie in the Cadillac. Then we followed the priest and Uncle Richard up the aisle. Mom smiled and nodded to everyone as though she was still 4-H Queen.

The minister signaled to the organist. She stopped whatever she was playing and started *Here Comes the Bride.* Everyone stood as Dad walked Aunt Millie up the aisle. She looked beautiful to me, like a snow queen in her long, white dress. Dad lifted her veil and kissed her. Uncle Richard took her hand and they turned to face the priest.

He said some prayers and someone sang a song. The priest did some more talking and then asked if there was any reason Aunt Millie and Uncle Richard shouldn't get married. I looked up at Mom. She was crying. I thought she was sad because she knew how disappointed Aunt Millie would be when she learned about Uncle Richard's tattoos. I reached for her hand. "Please Mom, don't say anything," I whispered.

She just put her finger to her lips, gave me a funny look, and reached into her purse for a handkerchief. No one else said anything either, so the priest went on with the wedding. He had Aunt Millie and Uncle Richard promise to be good to each other until they died. They exchanged rings and in no time at all the ceremony ended. Aunt Millie and Uncle Richard walked down the aisle hand-in-hand as Mr. and Mrs. Toombs.

We followed them out of the church and stood watching people taking pictures of them. "Mom, why are you crying?" Freddie reached for her hand.

"I'm crying because…because that's what mothers do at weddings."

"I know why she's crying," I said.

"You do not." Freddie poked me in the stomach.

"Yes I do. It's because she knows what's funny about—"

"Funny about what? About who?"

"I can't tell you. It's a secret. Only Mom and I know. But we can't tell." I tugged at Mom's other hand and looked up at her, winking like Uncle Richard.

"I don't know what you boys are going on about. Now quit your scrapping and come along. We have to get home to help set out the food. You boys can keep those thieving magpies away until people start arriving."

Mom and the ladies who'd come to help had most of the food set out by the time Dad drove the Cadillac onto the yard with Uncle Richard and Aunt Millie sitting in the back. As they got out of the car and walked to the head table everyone clapped and cheered. The priest said another prayer and then everyone started to eat.

I liked the tiny egg salad sandwiches made from rolled up bread, and the pickles and olives. The ice cream and cake were good too, but the reception was pretty boring for me and Freddie. The adults kept making speeches and tapping their spoons on their glasses to make Uncle Richard kiss Aunt Millie. I was glad when Mom finally let us change into our play clothes. We were playing with our cousins in the tree house in the old maple when Dad came looking for us. "Come children. It's time for the gifts."

It was the tradition in our family for wedding gifts to be personally handed to the bride and groom. Mom gave us our packages—carved wooden horse-head book ends—one from me, one from Freddie.

"Make sure you boys speak up when it's your turn." Mom pushed us into the line of people waiting to present their gifts. "And don't turn and run away after handing your gift to Aunt Millie. Listen to what she has to say, and if she thanks you, say, *You're welcome.*"

We watched as the people ahead of us handed over their packages. Aunt Millie and Uncle Richard opened each one, then handed them to Mom who set them on a table. There were three toasters, a couple of radios, six clocks, lots of dishes and bowls and other stuff for the kitchen. I felt badly for Uncle Richard because there was hardly anything for him.

Freddie was ahead of me. He stepped forward with his wrapped horse's head and mumbled something.

"Louder!" I whispered, but Freddie thrust the parcel with its big yellow ribbon into Aunt Millie's hands and stepped aside.

"Thank you, Freddie." Aunt Millie started to remove the bow.

"You might want to wait until Trevor has given you his gift," Mom said. "They're a set and then you can both open one. Trevor, your turn."

I stepped forward, held up my package and in a voice loud enough for the magpies in the top of the evergreens to hear, announced, "Aunt Millie, this is for you, for you and Uncle Richard. And...And someday I'm going to marry a man just like Uncle Richard."

Since Aunt Millie was already holding Freddie's package, I handed mine to Uncle Richard. He was staring at me like he hadn't heard me, so I raised my voice. "Uncle Richard, this is for you. Someday I'm going to—"

"There's no need to give a speech." Mom laughed.

"You fool. You stupid, stupid fool." Freddie pointed a finger at me. Then everyone burst out laughing, the adults as well as Freddie and my cousins. Tears burst from my eyes as I stood at the front of the line, wondering what I'd said that was so wrong, so funny.

"You can't marry a man," Freddie said.

Aunt Millie handed Freddie's package to Uncle Richard, then stood up and drew me into her arms. "I know what you mean, Trevor." She kissed me on both cheeks. "I know exactly what you mean. My Richard is someone very special and I hope one day you'll be as happy as I am today."

Freddie kept on pointing at me and making circles around his ear to show that I was crazy. Mom took my hand and led me aside

so the next person could present their gift. "Don't pay any attention
to your brother. You know how he is sometimes."

"But what did I say? Why is everyone laughing?"

"We all know what you meant. Like all of us, you're happy to
have Uncle Richard in the family."

A few moments after my big announcement, the gift giving was
completed. Aunt Millie and Uncle Richard stood and thanked
everyone for so many fine gifts and for a day they'd remember
forever. Then they went into the house to change their clothes.
Mom and the other ladies packed the gifts into boxes. Freddie and
I helped Dad put them into the Cadillac's trunk and back seat.

When Aunt Millie and Uncle Richard came out of the house
everyone clapped and cheered again. Aunt Millie was wearing one
of the dresses Mom and she had made, and Uncle Richard was
wearing ordinary blue jeans and a cowboy shirt: this one black
with red pockets and red stitching.

While the adults were saying good-bye, Freddie poked me in
the ribs. "Fool! Stupid, dumb fool! You're dumber than the dog,
dumber than the cat, dumber than a cow, dumber than a dumb
cluck chicken."

"Am not."

"Yes, you are, and now you're crying. You're nothing but a
dumb crybaby."

To escape his tormenting, I squeezed between Mom and Dad so
I was standing in front of the adults. Uncle Richard started the
Cadillac and slipped it into Drive. Before releasing the brake he
reached out the window and put his hand on my shoulder. "You
keep on working for your dad like you're doing, young cow poke,
and maybe one summer, when you're a wee bit older, you can
come ride the range with me. How would you like that?"

Tears were blinding my eyes and it felt like a crab apple had got
stuck inside my throat, so all I could do was nod. Then the car was
moving. We all waved as it turned onto the road, and then we
stood watching until it disappeared beyond the trees.

Lying in bed later that evening, I realized Freddie might be right. Maybe I couldn't marry a man, but I knew I wanted to live with someone like Uncle Richard. Though it would be years before I understood the exact nature of my affectional orientation, I hatched a plan that very night. Instead of buying bubble gum and candy with my allowance, I would save it up. As soon as I could, I would buy myself a Cadillac. I'd drive to Alberta, all the way to the Rocky Mountains. I'd buy a ranch and find myself a cowboy. We'd have a thousand, maybe two thousand, head of cattle, and we'd ride the range together.

Visiting Hours

Those walking along the pier on that wintry morning in White Rock said it was exactly eight o'clock when the visitors arrived by boat. Some said it was a trawler: blue hull, white wheelhouse, with *Mary Anne* inscribed on the hull in gold paint. Others swore the name was *Mary Joe*. Everyone agreed several people got off, though the exact number varied. Some said there were a dozen men, others reported three women among them, though in their raingear and knitted caps it was difficult to tell.

Newlyweds Heinrich and Phyllis Trochtlein were on the float at the time, fishing for crab. "We waved them away," Heinrich said. "I told them there was no tying up at the fishing pier, but they didn't listen. The tall fellow in the yellow slicker who seemed in charge said, 'Good morning, Heinrich', like he knew me. Just then Phyl pulled up a trap with five big fellas and I ran to help her. In the excitement we forgot about the fishermen, and when we turned around they were half-way along the pier."

Several women reported passing the group. They thought it odd to see so many fishermen at once, but paid them no heed. A squall was racing across the bay so everyone was pulling up their collars and hunkering down against the freshening wind.

Bill Oakner saw them walking up Oxford Street. "I was letting Beau out for his morning business when I saw them blokes," he said. "Most folk are coughing their lungs out on this hill, but those chaps were swinging their arms and legs like they were on the flats, especially the fellow out front in a bright yellow slicker. I could barely look at him, so bright he was, like he had fire inside him. I figured they must be some fitness group, high on one of them new energy drinks."

The visitors first stopped at Evergreen Baptist Seniors Home at the top of Oxford. Mazie Ritaller, one of the care aides, saw what happened. "Gone eight-thirty it was. I was wheeling Mr. Hutchinson into the dining room. The men came charging through the door, well not charging, more like floating, like their big, black gum boots were barely touching the floor. Looked to be off some fish boat. Before anyone could question them they were moving among the tables, bending down, talking to the residents, hugging them, carrying on as though they knew them.

"I pushed Mr. Hutchinson to his table in the corner. When I turned around there was total chaos. Mrs. Rankin, who hasn't walked in three years, was doing a jig. Mr. and Mrs. Cremshaw were holding each other's hands and waltzing out the door. They had not a single line on their once wrinkled faces. I wouldn't have recognized them except they always wear the same thing: she a faded purple cardigan, he a white shirt and tie as though he's going to some bankers' breakfast meeting.

"Two minutes later we care aides were standing all by ourselves. Everyone, including the strange visitors, had left the dining room. We ran to find Wilma Beenbaas. She's the Director of Care. By the time we told her what had happened, and started going through the building room by room, the visitors had been everywhere. The residents were packing their bags and wondering what they were doing in this *hellhole*. Terrible thing to say, because it's not a hellhole. It's a good place for the elderly and frail, but you see, they weren't elderly and frail anymore. They were folding their clothes, yanking family pictures off the walls, calling cabs and relatives in a rush to get back to their former lives. I even heard Mr. Hutchinson talking about entering some sort of golf tournament.

"I asked Mrs. Beenbaas what was going to become of us. We had no one to care for. She shook her head and scurried into her office. I watched her pick up the phone."

Other care homes along North Bluff Road reported similar visits. Facilities, once groaning with the feeble, were suddenly alive with dancing. In less than an hour the visitors were at Peace Arch Hospital. There the commotion began on the palliative care ward.

"I was completing morning rounds," Jordan Schenck, RN reported. "I had gone over to pull the drapes back from the window in Marilyn Bailey's room. She loves the outdoors. Before the cancer struck she led the White Rock Wanderers on their weekly treks.

"I straightened the drapes and when I turned around, Marilyn, who a moment before had been still as death, barely breathing through an oxygen mask, was standing beside her bed. I rushed over to her. 'No, no, Marilyn,' I said. 'You get back into bed right now. You're going to fall.'

"She told me a man in a yellow coat had ordered her to get up. I'm used to terminal patients suffering delusions. It's the morphine and other drugs. I was trying to get her back into bed when I heard the commotion in the hallway. Patients wearing their street clothes were dashing toward the elevators."

Fraser Health Authority went into high alert. The Board Chair called an emergency meeting. It was getting underway just as the visitors entered the chemo facility at Surrey Memorial Hospital. Those waiting for loved ones to complete their appointments with the life-giving poisons saw the fishermen walk in. Some said they heard the tall fellow give orders, calling out names, telling them which ward to visit.

Jeffrey Klossack had been lying in the recliner since seven that morning, receiving his third dose of chemo for lymphoma. "I was dozing off when this fellow in a yellow slicker gently touched my shoulder. He had the kindest face I've ever seen. He smiled, then called me by name, 'Jeffrey,' he said, 'you don't need to be here. Go home.'

"At the same moment the needle fell out of my arm, not leaving so much as a bruise."

A few minutes later the excitement overtook customers at Mercedes-Benz Surrey on 104th Avenue. Buyers who passed within a shadow's whisper of the visitors before entering the dealership began acting strangely. They tore up contracts for expensive SUV's and SLK-Class convertibles. Margaret Wilson, Branch Manager at the Royal Bank Guildford, said, "I don't know what came over me, but suddenly I tore up the contract for a new E Class Roadster. I demanded to be shown a used model, thinking I'd donate the difference to the food bank."

And so it went all afternoon and into the early evening. In Whalley, former drug addicts and mentally challenged folk observed the world through clear minds while queuing at pay phones to reconnect with loved ones. Bar owners, pimps and other dealers of misery stood on street corners, imploring ex-customers not to abandon them.

By five o'clock the visitors had made their way downtown to the Rogers Centre where the Canucks were playing an exhibition game against the Oilers to raise money for Children's Hospital. The game started as usual with the singing of *O Canada,* followed by a roar of excitement as the puck was dropped, and the players took off: checking and slashing, tripping and sticking, frequent fisticuffs bringing the cheering fans to their feet.

Two minutes into the second period Oilers' Petrell slammed blindly into Canucks' Raymond, sending the smaller man crashing to the ice. Immediately Petrell abandoned the puck, did an about face, skated back and bent over Raymond. In the hush that descended upon the Rogers Centre at the sight of this unusual play, fans as far up as the tenth row heard him say, "Are you all right, Bro? Here, let me give you a hand up," and then he reached for

Raymond, lifted him to his feet and steadied him on the ice before giving him a healing hug.

The fans went ballistic. "Hit him! Smash him! Kill the bastard!" Instead Raymond gave Petrell an appreciative pat on the side of his helmet, which brought a groan of disgust from the fans. After three more similar acts of concerned care for each other by players on both teams, the fans stood up, stamped their feet, shredded their tickets, and elbowed their way out of the arena.

At NHL headquarters in New York City owners and managers met via video conference call to investigate this dangerous development. Reports were sketchy but it seemed that some unauthorized persons had gained access to both dressing rooms during the intermission. What was said or done couldn't be pinned down, but it was clear that players on both teams had been affected. If this caring brand of hockey spread, the sport would be doomed and the owners would soon be lined up with all the other penniless vagrants outside the arena, begging for a handout, not that there'd be anyone coming out to give them a dime.

Other hastily convened meetings were in progress at the highest levels of government. Questions were asked. How will we handle massive unemployment in the health sector? What's to become of the pharmaceutical companies? What if this spreads to other cities, to all of North America, to Europe and Asia? What will happen to the stock markets? What about the world economy? And what will happen if all professional sports teams adopt brotherhood as their *modus operandi*?

The premier of British Columbia declared a state of emergency and called for federal aid. The Canadian prime minister sent in a military SWAT team with orders to hunt down and neutralize the visitors before they destroyed every pillar of Canadian society. At the same time US Homeland Security called in the National Guard to bolster border patrols in case the visitors decided to head south.

The six o'clock news reports caused great excitement in the lower mainland's religious community. Many faith leaders became convinced that the visitors were not aliens from some far-off planet, as radio pundits and learned professors from the universities were speculating, but visitors from the heavenly country. The healings and miraculous changes in people's behavior pointed to only one possibility: Jesus Christ and his disciples had returned.

A delegation of the city's highest church officials, garbed in their costliest and most colourful robes, chartered a limousine and directed the driver to take them to the Master. The driver wasn't sure where to go, but since the aborted hockey game had been the scene of the last sighting, he drove in that direction. When the limo pulled up at the Rogers Centre, the clerics elbowed and shoved their way out, each one determined to be the first to greet the Good Shepherd.

They charged through the doors, only to meet disappointment. There was no sign of the slicker-clad visitors. Only the two hockey teams remained, the players skating amicably around the ice, holding friendly shoot-outs on each other's net.

The clerics, gathering their robes about themselves, turned on each other. "You said he was here."

"I did not."

"I heard you tell the limo driver to come here."

"Like hell I did."

"Are you calling me a liar?"

"I am."

And then fisticuffs, far more deadly than any inspired by professional sport, broke out. Arms were twisted. Legs were broken. Heads were smashed into the concrete floor and foul words, bluer than those of any gum-chewing hockey coach escaped anointed lips. The hockey players, alarmed for their own safety, fled to their dressing rooms while the referees grabbed their cell phones to call for assistance in dealing with the crazed clerics.

Meanwhile, across town men in gum boots and rain gear were seen excusing their way through a gaggle of protesters waving placards protesting same-gender marriage. The fishermen ran up the steps at St. Andrews-Wesley United Church as though they were late for some great event.

Pastor Curt later explained what took place. "I was almost finished the wedding ceremony for Phillip and Allan when about a dozen big fellows, tall and ruddy in the face, came bounding into the chapel. At first I thought they were protesters who had broken into the church, but they sat down peaceably among the invited guests.

"When I pronounced Allan and Phillip husbands for life, the visitors clapped along with everyone else. The fellow who seemed to be the leader actually called out 'Bravo'.

"I was worried when the visitors followed us from the chapel to the room for the wedding supper. Allan and Phillip aren't that well off, so we had arranged a simple meal of sandwiches and salads. We'd set everything up in the church hall before the ceremony—one table for the grooms and their two attendants, another for the eight guests.

"When we entered the hall what a sight met our eyes! There were enough tables to accommodate the extra guests, and off to the side where we'd set out salads and sandwiches was a feast fit for a king: steaming mashed potatoes and gravy, Brussel sprouts glistening with butter, and between them a platter bearing a large salmon garnished with lemon slices. Off to one side were several dessert trays, and on a separate table, a three-tiered wedding cake neither groom could remember ordering.

"Everyone found a place, and as I was about to offer thanks to God, the fellow who seemed to be the leader came forward and put an arm on my shoulder. 'Please, let me,' he said. Then he put one hand on Allan's shoulder, the other on Phillip's and prayed the most wonderful prayer.

"It was like he was talking to someone he knew really well. He offered words of thanks for bringing the couple together. He prayed that they'd have many years of good health and happiness.

"Then we all helped ourselves to the food. It was after I had loaded my plate with a second helping that I looked around and saw that the visitors had disappeared. Someone said when the leader stood up, the others followed him out the door. We all ran out and looked up and down the street, but there was no sign of them. One of the guests said he overheard the leader mention catching a boat. We thought of the ferry and assumed they were going to The Island."

At a quarter to eight that evening Agatha Mobey was walking her Pekinese past the rugby field next to Semiahmoo Secondary School in South Surrey. Pausing to let Snoofie sniff a discarded McDonald's burger wrapper, she noticed a group of men sprawled on the grassy slope ahead of her.

"There's often a rugby practice going on," she said, "so I paid them no mind until I got closer and heard some familiar words. Of course I wouldn't want you to think I'm religious myself, but I did go to Sunday school when I was a wee girl. We all had to memorize The Lord's Prayer. This tall fellow in a yellow slicker, whom I took to be the coach, was standing in front of the others, reciting. He started out the way I remembered: *Our Father who art in heaven, hallowed be Thy name. Thy kingdom come. Thy will be done on Earth as it is in heaven.*

"He paused. I wondered if he'd forgotten the words, but then he raised his head. I saw that he was weeping, great heaving sobs, as though he'd lost his best friend. Three of the others stepped forward and put their arms around him, trying to comfort him. When he regained control he said, 'See, I told you. In two millennia nothing has changed. The inhabitants of this planet don't want things to be as they are in heaven. The majority have no use for love, brotherhood, compassion, and generosity.'

"Then all the men did a curious thing. They bent down, removed their gum boots, and slapped them three times on the ground, knocking big chunks of mud off them. That reminded me of a story from Sunday school, something about shaking dust off your sandals if people don't want you around.

"When they'd got their boots back on, the leader beckoned to them and they set off down 148th Street. I followed them as far as

47

North Bluff Road. There they disappeared over the hill towards the beach."

All was calm down at White Rock's pier. The squalls that had plagued strollers throughout the day had bedded down for the night. Folks who walked the pier again that evening noticed the visitors board their boat, cast off the lines, and disappear into the fog that was rapidly settling over the Lower Mainland.

Helen and Gerry

Kenneth and I were eating dinner when the lawyer called. "This is James Franklin of Franklin and Fernwood law office in White Rock, British Columbia. Are you Michael Baylohr, Helen Baylohr's nephew?"

"I beg your pardon? Whose nephew?"

"Helen Baylohr's."

"Well yes, I suppose I am, but—"

"I'm sorry to inform you that your aunt has died."

"Died?"

"Yes. Helen passed away on Friday night. She designated you as her sole beneficiary."

"I think there must be some mistake. Are you sure you have the right Michael Baylohr?"

"She left me your name, address and telephone number. Do you live at 465 Wellington Crescent in Winnipeg, Manitoba?"

"That's me."

After the call I laid the phone down and said to Kenneth, "I don't understand what this guy's talking about. Dad always said his sister Helen died just before I was born. If this woman really was my Aunt Helen, why did Dad lie about her death? And if she knew I existed, why did she never contact me? If there were hard feelings between her and Dad she could have called me after he died. And how did she get my name and address if she wasn't in touch with the family?"

"I do believe I smell a family mystery, a skeleton in the closet," Kenneth said, rubbing his hands together. "Maybe we've got an Agatha Christie mystery to solve. As for finding your contact information, she probably looked you up using the online White Pages. Our telephone number isn't unlisted, and B-A-Y-L-O-H-R is a rather unique spelling."

Growing up on the family's prairie farm, I rarely heard Dad mention his sister Helen and her husband Gerry. The few references were always derogatory, her wasted life a shadowy example of how I would shame the family if I didn't keep the cow's drinking trough pumped full of water, didn't maintain a knife-edge line around the flower beds facing the road, didn't stop to grease the cultivator every hour when murdering mustard, wild oats and stinkweed on the summer fallow, or shape up in a thousand other ways. The exact nature of Aunt Helen's misdemeanor was never spelled out, though both Grandma Baylohr and Dad hinted at a romance with David Hadden, one of the neighbour boys. Apparently there was an engagement, and a wedding, a wedding from which Aunt Helen fled down the aisle before David could slip the ring onto her finger.

Then she ran off to the coast where she married Gerry, some no-good artist fellow, and then died. The main point of the story was always that Helen's shameful behavior had made it impossible for Grandma Baylohr to hold her head up at meetings of the Women's Institute or United Church Women.

The story hadn't seemed important when I was young. I was more interested in hanging out with Tommy Lawler at his dad's garage in town. There we tinkered with a beat up fifty-five Pontiac, thinking we'd restore it to its former glory. Now I wished I'd listened more carefully, and asked questions about Aunt Helen. But it was too late now: Grandma, Dad, Mom, Uncle Ralph and Aunt Merle, were all lying side-by-side in the graveyard at Twin Meadows.

A week after the telephone call, Kenneth and I flew to Vancouver where the lawyer met us and drove us to White Rock. He told us Aunt Helen had died instantly when she stepped in front of a freight train.

"How did that happen?"

"Wait til you see the rail line in White Rock. There's always someone getting killed or losing a leg or arm to the coal trains. Your aunt was quite agitated the last I talked with her, so she may have been distracted that evening. You see, Gerry had died the previous week, heart failure. They'd been together fifty-three years, which is a long time for any couple, married or not. Missing Gerry so much, she may have forgotten to look both ways before crossing the tracks. I remember both her and Gerry telling me they walked the pier last thing every evening. In fact, both wanted their ashes scattered off the end."

The lawyer pulled up in front of a weed-grown shack on Marine Drive. Before giving me the key, he handed me the death certificate and a copy of the will.

"She left everything to you," he said. "There's not a lot: just the house, its contents, including some paintings that will have some value, and a bank account. Drop into my office tomorrow and we'll run through what needs to be done."

He handed me the key to the house and drove off, leaving us to look the place over. The sidewalk was cracked and riddled with weeds. A push mower, its reel pitted with rust, cowered beneath a shrub gone wild by the front door. I had to pull the doorknob towards me before the key would turn the deadbolt. The hinges squealed as I pushed the door open and stepped directly into the living room.

"They must have been smokers," Kenneth said before running about, throwing up the windows.

The shack was more like a two room cabin than a house. Some amateur carpenter had added two smaller rooms to the sides, and a kitchen lean-to onto the back, none of the floors quite lining up with each other. The two original rooms had tongue and groove

51

paneling painted light blue, the mauve trim around the windows decorated with hand-painted, buttery yellow and dusty red roses. The furniture was mismatched: a lumpy green sofa, a can of stewed tomatoes propping up one corner where the carved lion's foot was missing, two armchairs on either side of the fireplace, their leather covers cracked and torn, a roll-top desk someone had painted canary yellow, and a scuffed coffee table covered with brown MACtac. It was the sort of furniture you'd expect to find in a seasonal beach house.

The smaller add-on room corroborated the artist part of Dad's story. It was set up as a studio with an easel and a table littered with tubes of paint and brushes standing stiffly in jars of turpentine, long since evaporated. On the wainscoted walls hung seascapes: ocean, islands, boats and clouds in an endless variety of interpretations. In a lean-to at the back of the house was a heavily curtained darkroom with a photographic enlarger and trays for developing prints. A high boy had drawers full of black and white and colour photographs: mountain-ringed lakes, sailboats slumbering in quiet coves, wedding groups, and family portraits. Apparently Gerry had been a photographer as well as an artist.

After our long trip, we were hungry and tired, so we locked the door and strolled back towards the business area where we enjoyed a halibut dinner at *The Boathouse Restaurant*. Then, somewhat rejuvenated, we joined scores of other folk walking along the pier, enjoying the cool evening air. When we got back to the house it was well aired out by the sea breeze. We hunted up clean sheets, changed the bedding, and after a quick dip in the claw foot tub, retired for the night, me snugged against Kenneth's furry chest and thighs for warmth, since he insisted the windows needed to be kept open twenty-four seven.

Kenneth is not a morning man, so while he slept on, I tiptoed around the house, making a cursory inventory. The kitchen was a period piece from the fifties—a Frigidaire fridge and Viking electric stove, their corners rounded off in the airstream style so popular in that decade. A rough stone fireplace dominated the living room. A framed photograph of Grandma and Grandpa Baylohr sat on the mantelpiece, along with another, probably Gerry's folks. Bookshelves held coffee-table-sized volumes featuring art and photography.

On the bottom shelf were a number of five-year diaries. I pulled out the first one and flipped it open. *Property of Helen Baylohr*, her name in a school girl's careful hand.

> *January 1, 1959. Momma gave me this diary for Christmas. New Year's dinner at Auntie Merle's. Ate too much.*
> *January 2. Back to school. My last term at Twin Meadows. Davie Hadden all googley eyes again.*
> *January 3. Gymnastics with Miss Boddor, blond ponytail swinging like a horse's tail when she runs and jumps. I help her put equipment away.*

I scanned through her final school days and weekends spent doing homework and helping with chores around the farm. Apparently she had a pony named Emma. She would ride it into Twin Meadows to visit Miss Boddor. I began skipping ahead, searching for the infamous wedding.

> *June 14. Davie asked me to marry him. Everyone very happy for me.*
> *July 15. Momma making wedding dress. Too hot to stand still while she pins the hem—we have a fight—told her I don't want to get married.*
> *August 24. Tomorrow I marry Davie. Momma so giddy and gay. You'd think it's her getting married. Wish it was.*

The entries for 1959 end there, with no explanation of what happened to make her dash down the aisle and out of the church before the minister could tie her to Davie Hadden. In July of the following year she once again began recording her life.

July 12, 1960. Full-time work at last, waiting tables at Hotel Georgia. Sore feet by day's end. Must get new shoes.
July 13. Got new shoes at Eaton's. Signed up for course at Modern Photography on Granville.

I heard Kenneth stirring in the bedroom. A moment later he groped his way into the living room, rubbing his eyes, combing his curly blond hair off his forehead with his fingers. I got up off the floor where I'd been sitting and wrapped my arms around him, kissed him on the ear. I don't know why, but it's when he first gets up in the morning, wandering through the house like a lost child, that I love him the most.

He returned the hug, then asked, "Was your Uncle Gerry a cross-dresser?"

"I don't know anything about him. Why do you ask?"

"I just checked out the closet and chest of drawers in the bedroom. There's nothing but women's clothing."

"Maybe Aunt Helen cleaned out his things after he died."

"Within days of his death? It usually takes widows a year or more before they can throw stuff out."

"That does seem odd. Maybe this will tell us," I said, holding up the diary. "I just read about Aunt Helen's aborted wedding."

"Does she say why she ran out of the church?"

"No. The entries are very matter of fact, just describing what happened in the lead-up to the wedding, not much about how she was feeling, though it appears Grandma was more excited about the marriage than she was. The entries end the day of the wedding and don't resume until months later when she was already in Vancouver. Let's go out for breakfast. I'll bring the diary. Maybe she'll explain what happened."

While waiting for our food to arrive I read some more entries to Kenneth.

July 18. First photography course with Mr. Huey.
Assigned homework— take photos in Stanley Park,
something different.
July 19. To Stanley Park. Met artist. She let me take
photos of her working at easel, different angles.

"Maybe that dark room was Aunt Helen's," I said. "Dad never mentioned what she did. It was always 'Helen and that no-good artist Gerry'."

July 20. To Stanley Park again. Talked with artist,
Geraldine Agnes McComb. Says to call her Gerry.
July 25. Mr. Huey praised two of my photos. Says
Geraldine McComb is a famous artist. I'm
embarrassed the way I chatted with her.

I laid the diary down and looked at Kenneth. "What are you grinning about?"

"I'm thinking that I married into a family with a long history of bent affectional orientations. Geraldine McComb must be the Gerry in Helen and Gerry."

"I guess I come by my affections naturally then. That must have galled Dad when he thought about it, that I inherited the gay gene through him. Remember how he hurled his *Labatt's Blue* at the kitchen wall and called me every filthy name he could think of when I told him you were more than just a roommate?"

"Oh yes. I remember it very well. I was there. I was ready to run for cover and drag you with me if he picked up another bottle."

"No wonder he yelled that I was going to drag the family name through the manure pile just like Aunt Helen. There was obviously a bit of history there."

"Didn't he say your newsflash would kill your grandmother? Except she was already dead?"

"Dad was probably right about that. It would have been a double whammy for Grandma. First her only daughter runs out of the church and away to Vancouver where she hitches herself to someone of the wrong gender, and then me, her first grandson, moves to Winnipeg after grad and falls in love with a man."

"Not much wonder your folks never warmed to us as a couple," Kenneth said.

I scanned ahead in the diary. Helen and Gerry were soon spending their spare time together, walking by the sea, picnicking in Stanley Park, shopping on Georgia Street, then spending nights together. Gerry gave Helen two yellow roses on her twentieth birthday, and just as they were apartment hunting Gerry's mother and father died, leaving her the cabin in White Rock.

> *November 12, 1960. Gerry and I moved into the cabin on Marine Drive. Cold and wet. So tired. Sandwiches by the fire. To bed early.*

Kenneth and I spent the morning renting a car, buying groceries and stopping at the lawyer's to sign the necessary papers. After lunch we got boxes from U-Haul and spent the afternoon cleaning out the closets and drawers. I was cleaning out the bottom drawer in the roll-top desk in the living room when I came upon a stack of envelopes tied together with a yellow ribbon. They were addressed to Helen Baylohr. The return address listed no name, just a box number in Twin Meadows. I pulled out the top one. The postmark read 30 June 1999. It contained a folded up page of foolscap. The writing was in red ink. I scanned it, then called to Kenneth.

"Kenneth, you'd better read this letter. It solves the mystery of how Aunt Helen knew I existed. It's from Davie Hadden."

Dear Helen and Gerry,

Thank you for your letter with the exciting news of your show at the Vancouver Art Gallery. How fitting that after all these years you and Gerry should share the spotlight. I hope it results in renewed interest in Gerry's work as you are both hoping.

I have some news too. After thirty-seven years' teaching I have decided to take my pension. I will certainly miss the students, even the ones who had as much use for Shakespeare as they did for a face full of zits. However, I'll be glad not to have to drive to school every day, especially in the winter. This last one we had so much snow I wouldn't have gotten through without the four-wheel drive.

I'm saving the sad news for the last. Your brother's wife Ermelda passed away from cancer last week. I would have been at the funeral but had to supervise final exams that day. I heard it was a large gathering with pretty well everyone from the district attending. She was buried in Twin Meadows churchyard. I don't know how your brother Frank will manage without her. He's quite a bit older and of course not in the best of health. Without her to care for him he may have to go into Valleyview Lodge.

The next day I happened to be passing through Twin Meadows on the way home from school and saw the new grave, so stopped to pay my respects. While I was there your nephew, Michael, and his friend Kenneth, came along. I introduced myself. They said they were heading back to Winnipeg where they live. Michael is a teacher like me and his friend is something in the social services department at city hall. We didn't chat long, and of course I didn't ask them any personal questions, but I got the impression their relationship is of a special character, just like yours.

I better sign off as I need to get into town for some baling twine. The oats are ready to cut and the weather's looking good so I mustn't dally.
Your friend, David

There were several packets of letters from David. I laid them aside to be perused later. In the back corner was another packet, the envelopes addressed to Grandma Baylohr. Written across the front of each one in Grandmother's beautiful handwriting were the words, *Refused. Return to Sender.* The first was date-stamped *Dec. 20, 1960*, the last *Dec. 14, 1987*, the year grandmother died.

"Should I open these?" I asked Kenneth, feeling there was something sacred about them.

"That's the only way you're going to know what's inside them," he said, sitting down beside me on the lumpy sofa. I slit open the first one, being careful to leave the five cent stamp intact.

Inside were a hand-written letter and three black and white photographs. The first showed a grinning young lady standing in front of the cabin. She had wide-set eyes like Grandma Baylohr's and long blond hair hanging loose over her shoulders. I flipped it over. *Me in front of our new home*, was penciled on the back. Another showed her standing at the railway station. She was wearing a dark, cloth coat and headscarf, a train in the background. The third photograph was labeled, *Me and Gerry on the pier*. The ladies were standing arm-in-arm, both wearing flowered dresses. Helen's long hair blew in the breeze. Gerry was peeking out from beneath dark bangs.

Dearest Mother,

I know you're probably still upset about the wedding last year, but Davie is much better off without me. I hope he's forgiven me and that he'll find himself a wonderful girl who will love him much better than I could. I've written him to say as much.

Enclosed are three snaps to show where I'm living. We're having fun making this little cabin on the beach our own. It belonged to Gerry's mom and dad. They drowned when their sailboat was caught in a horrible storm. I met them only once before the accident. They seemed like nice people.

Since we moved to White Rock I've been working at a sort of boarding house down the road, but one day I hope to make my living with my camera. I've already got one wedding on my calendar for next spring.

Christmas greetings and blessings for the new year to you and all the family. Would love to hear from you. Your loving Helen.

The other letters were similar in content. They reported on trips Helen and Gerry made together—a voyage up the coast following Emily Carr's paddle strokes and hikes into the back country to photograph and paint British Columbia's hidden splendours. There was a tour of European art galleries and month's stay in London. By the time I'd finished reading the letters aloud, both Kenneth and I were wiping tears from our eyes. "I can't believe my grandmother, a lady who went to church every week and who was so loving to everyone, could disown her own daughter."

"People do strange things when they think they're right about something," Kenneth said, kissing the tears from my cheek.

"And how could Dad and Uncle Ralph let her refuse their sister's letters, or did they not know about them? All my life I hated being an only child. I used to wish for a brother or sister so I'd have someone to play with. Didn't they feel anything for their sister?"

"Some people are very stubborn, especially when it comes to sex, and let's face it, that generation sees lives like ours as nothing but sexual indulgence," Kenneth said.

"I know, but just imagine the slap of loneliness Aunt Helen must have felt year after year when her letters were returned unopened. It's a wonder she kept on sending them. I suppose David must have told her about Grandma's death and that's why she finally stopped writing."

"Come with me," Kenneth said, taking me by the hand. "Let's go buy some flowers, two yellow roses."

"And two red ones for Gerry," I said, gently brushing the painted roses on the trim around the window.

Later that evening, as the sun slipped behind the distant islands, we joined the throngs of people walking along the pier. At the far end we stood for a moment, arms around each other's shoulders, then dropped the roses one by one into the sea.

An Evening at the Opera

It's *not* a date. It's an evening out, an excuse to squirm my way out of this tiny apartment. It's a reason to get away from mother for a wee while.

Being her only daughter, I thought it would be a good idea for her to live with me when she came out of the hospital with her new hip. With the extra bedroom, now that my youngest son Brent is gone to Vancouver, and me not earning much as a work-at-home seamstress, I figured she would help with expenses, and get the meals once she got back on her feet. I even thought she might dust the furniture and run the sweeper over the kitchen floor now and again, picking up the toast crumbs she's always scattering off the table with the sleeve of that ratty blue housecoat she insists on wearing night and day. I guess I was wrong about that. Hips must take longer to heal than what I see on them television medical shows.

> *"Melody, I know you need to get those trousers hemmed up for Mr. Barenbottom, but could you make me a cup of tea? Can you spare that much time for your old cripple of a mother?"*

I don't feel guilty about leaving her alone for one evening, really only a couple of hours. I deserve some fun, though like I say, it's not a date, at least not in the sense that Paul asked me out, even though that's what I told mother. I hate lying, but mother's ideas are as brittle as her bones. I figure it's easier for both of us if I don't tell her that I was the one who invited Paul. I asked him if he'd like to go to the Comox Valley Opera Company's production of *Compost in Your Hair*.

Mother would think it was wrong of me to invite Paul, but it wasn't wrong at all. He's new in the valley, a radiologist, retired three months ago from Sick Kids in Toronto. I stand in front of him in the church choir so it's only natural that I should offer to introduce him to some music-loving people. I know quite a few because this spring I began taking singing lessons from Althea Busby. She's our choir director. She teaches piano, organ, voice, and pretty well anything else you'd want to study in the way of music. I know fifty-two's rather late in life to be thinking of a new career, but Althea says I have a good strong voice, so I hope to be good enough to take a leading role in the opera next season.

> *"Melody, my dear, there's no need to shout at me. I can hear you perfectly well if you'd just talk in a normal tone of voice. When you shout across the table like that you frighten me, and I'm liable to choke on this chicken sandwich. You wouldn't want to see your poor old mother do that, would you?"*

I don't expect anything from this evening. I mean, I'm no fool when it comes to men, and I realize that me and Paul are from different worlds, him from Toronto and me from Courtenay. He's probably used to going to the opera or the symphony every night of the week, maybe with women in furs and diamonds, but then you never know. The fact that he came to retire in this little town may mean that he's tired of that life, that he wants a simpler life, and I could certainly give him that, though I'm not expecting anything to happen between us.

My husband Will's been dead going on fourteen years now. Killed at the mill. A Douglas fir, gone berserk, slapped him on the side of the head. It still pains me to think how it smashed in his skull and made it impossible for me to have the casket open.

I've got used to living alone, well at least I was alone until mother came out of the hospital. There are times when I think it would be nice to have a man around the place.

> *"Melody, dearest, I'm not one to interfere, but what would a doctor from Toronto want with a widow lady like you with two grown delinquents; Bobby in jail and Brent nothing but a bar fixture in Vancouver?"*

What shall I wear tonight? It's late June so I won't need a coat. Nothing too formal, but something nice, sort of dress-up, without being too flashy. I don't want Paul to feel ashamed of me, but at the same time I don't want to give the impression that I've gone to too much trouble. I know that would only scare him off, though it's not a real date, just an evening at the opera. Perhaps I'll wear this green blouse along with my yellow slacks. Will used to tell me that green brought out the colour in my eyes.

The night before Will died we went dancing at the Native Sons Hall. He didn't really like going out because he was a very shy man, couldn't get much past the weather when talking to strangers, whereas I could talk to anyone about anything.

Some said it was my fault he didn't dodge that Douglas fir. This town's gossips spread the story that he was exhausted from dancing because I'd kept him out too late. But my Will loved to dance. He was light on his feet, even when doing the gumboot reel on the stroke of midnight, which is the custom in these parts.

> *"Melody, my dear, you're not wearing that blouse, are you? You look sick in green, and surely you're not going to wear pants with it. Your husband may have stranded you in this wretched town with barely*

*enough money to patch your own underwear, but
that's no reason to go to the opera looking like a
mill hand."*

There's the buzzer. I mustn't keep Paul waiting, him in his nice
big car. I don't know much about cars, but I think his is a Cadillac
or a Buick or something fancy like that. He's getting out and
opening the door for me. I like his sandy-coloured suit, the press in
the pants as sharp as the blade on a filleting knife. There's nothing
dull and boring about Paul. I bet he doesn't buy his clothes at
Walmart, but somewhere upscale like Sears or Hudson's Bay. And
look at his haircut, neatly squared off behind. No bowl over the
head and a dull pair of scissors that serve for most of the haircuts
around here. He's wearing some sort of scent, a mixture of
cinnamon and pine trees perhaps, but not strong enough to be
offensive.

The Old Church Theatre is plain, almost embarrassing
compared to the fancy opera houses Paul must be used to, but the
set—a rustic farmhouse in Merville—makes it look elegant. We
take seats on the risers near the back where everyone can see us. I
have to admit that even though it's not a real date I feel proud
sitting beside Paul, and leaning my head towards him to hear what
he's saying above the tuning of the orchestra. I can see Althea in
the front row. Some of her students are performing in the chorus
tonight. I wave to her when she turns around but she doesn't see
me.

Now the lights are being dimmed. Someone's turning them
right down like they sometimes do, so it's completely dark.
Usually this frightens me. What if there was a fire, or an
earthquake, or some madman in the audience had a rifle or a
bomb? Anything could happen, but tonight I feel the warmth from
Paul's arm next to mine so I don't worry like I usually do.

*"Melody, my dear little plum, don't expect anything
from this man. After all, what would a doctor want*

> *with someone who has trouble finding good-fitting*
> *clothes at Pennington's?"*

The first half of the opera zooms by faster than a gull can swallow a crust of bread, and here it is intermission. My evening without mother is already half over. I'm desperate to pee. I join the line of women snaking down the stairs. When are the men who build these things going to install more than a couple stalls for us ladies? I'm anxious to get back upstairs with Paul. I think it's so rude of me to leave him all alone when he doesn't know anyone, but I have to go. If I don't I'll probably start leaking into my panties when I laugh.

Compost in Your Hair is about this big city couple who retire to an old farmhouse in the Merville district which is just north of here. Their neighbours are typical Mervillites: aging hippies who grow their own marijuana and hang out half-naked around their home-built shacks. The story is really comical and Paul seems to be enjoying it, including the nude scenes which I find quite shocking even though the soloists stay behind the rusty old car that sits on centre stage.

When I get into the bathroom stall I rush because I'm desperate to pee and because I want to get back to Paul, and so I've already started peeing when I notice that I'm sitting on the toilet *lid*. Why would someone put the lid down when they know the next person is going to be sitting down before the seat's had time to cool off? Fortunately I've bunched my slacks well out of the way so they hardly get wet, but still it's embarrassing to have to wipe up the mess when so many others are waiting in line.

When I finally get back upstairs, Paul is talking with a man I've seen at Wednesday night's jazz concerts in the Elks Hall. I've never spoken with him and don't know his name. He's always sitting at a table with a bunch of guys, joking and giggling while the musicians are playing. I think that's so rude. One night I saw him and another fellow get up and dance to *Smoke gets in my eyes*. I thought that was pretty weird, but my son Brent, who plays sax in a band in Vancouver, says he sees that all the time, men dancing with men, women with women.

Paul and this guy are so deep in conversation that at first they don't see me standing off to the side. After a minute or so I move into Paul's line of sight and wave and point to where we were sitting. Paul nods. I expect him to call me over, introduce me to the guy, or come and sit with me, but the jazz guy hasn't seen me and he keeps talking, waving his hands about like he's telling some yarn about the fish that got away. Poor Paul. He's probably bored out of his mind. I probably should go right up and interrupt them, help him escape from the chatterer, but I don't want anyone to see the damp stains on my slacks. I go back to our place on the risers and sit down.

When the lights blink, Paul and the other guy shake hands. Paul comes back to me, all smiles. I figure he's glad to see me, but then he starts talking about Jeff Shanks, the guy he was talking with. Until the lights go down it's nothing but Jeff this and Jeff that. I almost wish I hadn't come, but then the second act begins and I feel Paul's arm next to mine and even though it's not a real date, I'm happy to be sitting with a man instead of by myself.

> *"Melody, my dear, I don't want to see you hurt. Any man of retirement age who has never been married must have something wrong with him."*

After a performance I like to stay seated until people have left the theatre. I'm nervous around crowds because you never know when they'll start to stampede like they do in some of them foreign countries, or at football games where they trample all over each other. However, Paul seems to be in a rush and hurries us into the line of people creeping out of the theatre. When we finally get outside this Jeff guy is waiting. Paul introduces me, and he and Jeff exchange business cards, and then we're back in Paul's fancy car. He seems happy with the evening and thanks me for inviting him to the opera.

I decide not to invite him up for a cup of coffee. Mother will probably be in bed, but she might come hobbling out of the bedroom with her housecoat hanging open, or start calling for me to help her to the toilet. Since the evening has gone so well I don't want to risk spoiling it. Perhaps I'll invite him up next time.

It's the last Thursday in August and it looks like I'm going to be late for choir practice. I don't like being late, especially since this will be our first practice after our summer recess. I'm anxious to see Paul, too. I haven't heard from him all summer.

> *Melody, my dear, you seem in an awful rush to get out of the house tonight. I suppose you think you're going to take up with that retired doctor again. I wouldn't count on it if I was you, so just settle down and make me a cup of tea and find my pills before you dash away.*

I don't know how someone who never leaves the apartment can keep on losing her pills. This time I find them in the pocket of her housecoat. I feel like jamming the whole bottle down her throat, but that wouldn't be very Christian of me.

When I walk into the church, our director, Althea, is in the office. She has her head in the filing cabinet, rummaging through the music library. As I pass the door she thrusts a stack of music into my hands. "Melody, could you look through here for *O love, that will not let me go* by Lottenham? I know we sang it last year, but I can't seem to find it."

I want to scream at her. First Mother's pills! Now Althea's disorganized music! This is not what I need right now. I need to get into the church hall and see Paul. I want to be with him, not search for some moldy, dog-eared anthem Althea has misplaced. I throw the stack of music down on the desk and start flipping through it. Five minutes later Althea tells me to forget Lottenham. She's found something she likes better.

I dump the stack of music and hurry into the hall. Paul is not there. Everyone else is standing around like kids on the first day of school, trading stories of *What I did this summer*. Except for running after Mother's every whim and sewing fall wardrobes, I have nothing to report.

>*Melody, why do you work yourself so hard? It's not good for a body to go on like you are, hunched over that sewing machine til all hours of the night. A body needs some other interests besides work. Why don't you sign up for that cooking class? I'm getting fed up with the same old meals.*

It's unusual for Paul to be late. I hope he hasn't had an accident or something. He hasn't been to church all summer, but then a lot of folk have company or go away. Maybe he rented a cottage at Horne Lake, or even a boat to get away from the heat in the valley.

I'm dying to ask about him, whether anyone has seen him, whether he's visiting family back east, but I don't want to appear too eager. In this small town people have nothing to do but talk. If it becomes known that I'm looking for a fellow, the gossip will begin. The last thing I want is to be pitied, to have people shaking their heads and whispering.

>*Melody dearest, I don't know why you're spending so much time in the bathroom putting paint on your face. At your age do you really think anyone's going to notice?*

When Althea finally gets herself into the hall and asks us to take our places, I turn and say to Bill Jakeley who sits behind me, "Are you not leaving a chair for Paul?"

Bill says nothing. He shrugs and moves over. That's a good sign. At least he hasn't heard that Paul's moved away. I briefly thought of marrying Bill after his wife died, but now I'm just as glad I didn't. So long as both of them were in the choir he seemed like an interesting person, but after her death he pretty much disappeared, sort of folded into himself, like a sea anemone when you touch it.

Althea has us warm up by singing through the hymns for Sunday. We're in the middle of the offertory hymn, *Blest be the tie that binds,* when Paul walks into the hall. The yellow shirt he's wearing is a lovely contrast to his dark tan. Over the summer he's grown a mustache and a little beard. I don't care for beards on most men, but on Paul it looks good. It's carefully groomed like the rest of him. He grabs a hymnal off the top of the piano and comes to his place behind me. I turn to show him the page number but Bill beats me to it, so I just give him a little wave of welcome. He nods and smiles.

After the first hour Althea calls a break. I run out to the toilet. When I return there's no sign of Paul. Everyone else is standing around drinking decaf and eating oatmeal cookies—Althea is a great cook as well as a fine musician. They're talking about the fall fair which starts the next day. It seems that a few of them are going together. Evelyn Lawson is the organizer. She probably just wants to drag them through the annex where the prize winning fancy work is laid out, thinking she'll have a blue ribbon to crow about.

"You'll come with us this year, won't you Melody?" she asks.

"I can't really say. If Mother's having one of her spells I'll have to stay home."

That's only partly true. Mainly, I don't think I could spend a whole afternoon with Evelyn, listening to her dine out on how many ribbons she's won for her sewing over the years. She always wins first prize for her hand-sewn aprons, but I've seen her work and my seams are much straighter. One of these years I'll sink her boat by entering an apron of my own, show her how a straight seam is supposed to look. Right now I have no time for anything so frivolous as making aprons someone hasn't paid for.

Melody, when you get a minute would you run down to the drugstore with this prescription? It's for my blood pressure. And you might as well get this one

*for my arthritis while you're at it. I'll pay you back
when I get my cheque at the end of the month,
though there won't be much left over what with
paying for this recliner that nice salesman at Sears
sold me. Maybe you can see your poor old mother
through to the following month.*

After a few minutes Paul comes back into the hall. He must
have been in the men's room. I feel a bit of a shiver when I think
of how we must have been in the toilet together for a time,
separated only by a bit of drywall.

"How was your summer, Paul?" I ask.

Before he can answer Evelyn butts in. "Paul, you'll be joining
us at the fair on Sunday afternoon?"

"The fair?"

"Yes. The Ag Fair is always the last weekend in August. You
must come: see the horse show, the vegetable displays, the
handicrafts and sewing—"

"Oh yes. I did read something about it in the paper," Paul says.
"I didn't realize it was this weekend. What time are you folks
going?"

"We'll meet near the ticket booth at two on Sunday. That
should give us plenty of time to see everything."

Plenty of time for you to blow your own rusty horn, I think, but
of course I don't say anything. With Evelyn it's better to keep my
mouth shut, but I wish I hadn't been quite so quick to turn down
her invitation to join the group. Perhaps I'll nip down to the
fairgrounds for a moment later in the afternoon, while Mother's
down for her nap. I'll just leave a note on the table that I'll be gone
for a couple hours. If I tell her where I'm going ahead of time
she'll somehow wheedle it out of me that I'm going to the fair in
the hopes of seeing Paul.

We practice our anthems for another hour. Althea asks me to
pray when we're done. Mostly people pray that we'll have a safe
trip home and that Sunday morning our singing will be a blessing

to people. I add a request that those who are going to the fair will have a pleasant time.

After everyone says, Amen, I turn around to Paul. I see there are beads of sweat on his tanned brow. He's rolled up the sleeves of his yellow shirt. I don't think I've ever seen his forearms before. They look strong, like he's been chopping wood all summer, and the fine hairs are sun bleached, just like his hair that he always keeps so neat.

"We haven't seen much of you this summer," I say. "Have you been away?"

"I'm afraid I've just been delinquent. Been busy enjoying the delights of your valley."

"Hiking?"

"Some hiking, but mainly kayaking. I've been out to Tree Island and around the Royston Wrecks. How about yourself? Did you get away at all?"

"Oh no. I don't feel the need to go anywhere. Like you said, our valley has so many delights. Summer is one of my busiest times for sewing, what with the graduations and weddings."

"You must not think much of my clothing," he says, pointing to his shirt. "This is one of my old dress shirts, past its best days." He rolls down the sleeves and shows the loose threads where the cuff is worn. "I'd ditch it but it's so hard to find slim fit short sleeve shirts, so I hold onto this one, just roll up the sleeves."

"I could shorten the sleeves for you, cut them off above the elbow and hem a nice new cuff."

"Really?"

"Nothing to it."

"Well, I've got a closet full of them, so if you wouldn't mind, that would be wonderful. In fact, I have a T-shirt in the car I can change into tonight. You can take this one with you, if you like. Of course, I'll pay you."

"No need, Paul. It's just a little job, won't take me more than a few minutes. Bring the others to choir practice next week."

*Now Melody, I hope you're not doing that shirt for
free. Just because a man winks at you is no reason
to let him walk all over you. Besides, the way to a
man's heart is through his stomach, not his shirt
sleeves. You should have signed up for that cooking
class.*

Now that mother's settled for a nap I'll just run out for a few
minutes, buy a few groceries like I told her I would, nip down to
the fairgrounds to see what's going on, take this shirt along in case
I run into Paul.

I haven't been to the fair since Will died. He liked taking part in
the logging sports. Quite often he won the tree climbing contest.

I wonder where Evelyn and the others are? Probably in the
annex. Sure enough. There she is over at the table showing off her
fancy work. I don't see Paul though. Maybe he wasn't able to
come.

"Hi Evelyn."

"Melody, I thought you weren't coming."

"Mother's having one of her better days, and always lies down
for a bit of a nap in the afternoon. I thought I'd nip over and have a
look around."

"Well everyone's scattered. What do you think of my apron?"
She holds it up for me to admire. The material is a deep purple
with big yellow sunflowers appliquéd on the front, tiny ones on the
shoulder straps and ties. From a distance it looks good, but close
up I can see that the stitches are crooked.

"It's quite an apron all right. It must have taken you a long time,
adding all those flowers, especially the small ones, but I must run
if I'm to see anything before I have to get back to Mother. Isn't
that Paul over by the art display?"

I used to paint a bit when I was younger, before the boys came
along. Will thought I did well. Still life was my specialty: plates of
fresh-baked buns, a salmon laid out on a platter, that sort of thing,
not that I ever won a ribbon. The judges they hauled in from
Vancouver had no use for anything that looked real.

71

*Melody, my dear one, when are you going to get rid
of this box of old paints and brushes? It's been
gathering dust on the floor of my closet for long
enough. You might as well toss it in the garbage.
It's not like you ever had any artistic talent.*

As I approach Paul I see that he's studying a landscape. It's three horses in a hayfield. Their heads are too big and there's something not right about their front legs, almost stick-like, as though a child had drawn them. I'm about to call out to Paul when he speaks to someone on the other side of the display board and slips around the corner.

I don't want it to look like I'm pursuing him, which I'm not, so I pause to look at the horses more closely. Besides having swollen heads, they aren't the proper shape. They look more like cows, cows with horses' bodies, manes and tails.

When I step around the corner of the display board I see that Paul is standing with another fellow. They are looking at a huge canvass showing Courtenay's Two Spot steam engine pulling a train of cars loaded with logs. At first I don't recognize the stranger, but then he turns his head sideways and I see that it's the jazz guy. Like every other time I've seen him, he's giggling like a two year old, making fun of something in the painting. I watch as he bends over laughing, pointing.

Then he grabs Paul's hand to pull him over to the next canvas. Instead of shaking off his hand, Paul keeps hold of the guy's hand. They bump shoulders. The jazz guy nuzzles Paul's neck, then giggles some more. They look like high school sweethearts. They must sense me standing there because they both turn around at the same time, still holding hands.

"Hi Melody," Paul says. "You remember Jeff from our night at the opera?"

"Yes, I do," I feel myself blushing though neither one of them seems the least bit upset. I hand Paul his shirt.

"You've shortened the sleeves already?"

"Only took a few minutes," I say. "Snip. Snip. Sew. Sew." I wish I'd never shortened his sleeves. I wish I'd never come to the fair. I wish I could turn and run.

"Do you have anything entered in the fair?" Paul asks.

"No. I used to paint water colours. I never won a prize."

"Jeff's an artist," Paul says, smiling proudly, releasing his hand to pat him on the shoulder. He beckons for me to follow them around the display board. "This one's Jeff's." He points to the cow-like horses in the field.

"I was just looking at it," I say. "I don't see a ribbon on it."

"I didn't expect to win," Jeff says. "It's my first year painting. I took a class in oils last year. I really didn't feel ready to enter anything, but Paul thought I should. You can see that I had trouble with the horses. I should have left the field empty, but I thought since it's an agricultural fair I'd better have some horses. Aren't they the funniest beasts you ever did see?" He giggles and reaches for Paul's hand.

"Well I'd best take a quick look at the other exhibits and then get back home," I say. "Mother will be waking from her nap. She always worries if I'm not home when she wakes up."

"Okay. See you at choir practice next Thursday," Paul says, "and thanks for shortening my sleeves. You needn't have rushed. I'll bring my other shirts to choir on Thursday."

Thursday evening I decide not to go to choir practice. Althea will be disappointed because I do have one of the stronger voices. The other sopranos depend upon me to keep them in tune, but I have a lot of work on my sewing table. There are a number of costumes to sew for the high school drama club, dresses for three fall weddings, and a few requests for Hallowe'en costumes have trickled in already. With all this work I'm afraid I won't have time to take on anything extra, like shortening sleeves on Paul's moldy old dress shirts.

And then there's the new neighbour, Colin Baily. He just moved into the suite at the end of the hallway. He's about my age, a widower from Victoria, says he grew up here though I don't recall any Bailys in these parts. He asked if I could make curtains for his bedroom. I'll call him later this evening, see if I can go and measure.

> *Melody, I hope you're not staying home from choir practice because of that little coughing fit I had earlier. It was really nothing. Just some crumbs from the toast. When you burn it like that I find the taste very irritating, but I'm perfectly all right now. You really should go to practice. It does you good to get out. Won't that doctor who sings in the choir miss you? The one who invited you to the opera?*

Grand Gracious Lady

Coleen O'Brien looked in the mirror one last time before leaving for the Miss Railway Daze Beauty Pageant. She picked up the tweezers and leaned in close to the glass. She mustn't have lopsided eyebrows. While she plucked she muttered, "This year the crown is mine... mine…mine."

Last year Rosalyn Muncie had stolen it from her by filching her shoes before the final event. She'd had to borrow her mother's— two sizes too large—and hobble onto the stage in her bathing suit looking like a baby playing dress-up. Of course Rosalyn hadn't confessed to it, claimed she never touched the shoes, but Coleen knew better.

The little witch had been on her case ever since tenth grade when Brent Brunswick, Semiahmoo High's star basketball player, and Rosalyn's supposed steady, had asked Coleen to that year's prom. Rosalyn, so as not to be left dancing by herself, had been forced to accept a last minute invitation from pimple-faced Bobby Lockette. Not that Brent had been a prize. Coleen had sent him packing that very night after he got wasted and demanded more than a dance from her.

This year was payback time. Coleen would place first in the pageant. She would be White Rock's Grand Gracious Lady, Queen of the Rails, no matter what she had to do to win the crown of golden spikes. She'd show that pock-faced Rosalyn some real talent.

"Hurry up in there," Coleen's mother called. "Must I remind you that a real lady is always on time?"

"On time. On time," Coleen aped her mother's tone. "Quit trying to make me into you, Mother. I'm not going to spend my life volunteering at a moldy old museum or answering phones for the Semiahmoo Arts Council. I'm going to become someone important: a world class model, maybe even an actress."

"I hope you *will* become someone important," her mother said, "but it's unkind of you to belittle my accomplishments. Remember, I didn't have the opportunities you have. When your grandmother died, I had to stay home and help with the little ones."

Coleen rolled her eyes as she came out of the bathroom. She'd heard it all before. Becoming Railway Queen would get her picture on television, and ensure she'd never become a fat old matron in a boring tidewater village like White Rock.

As they drove to the Centennial Arena she closed her eyes and imagined riding with the mayor in the royal blue landau down Marine Drive. She could hear the clip-clop of the four prancing horses, escorted by six RCMP outriders in red serge. At Bay Street she'd step out of the carriage, smile, wave, and walk the few steps to the railway crossing. Her ladies-in-waiting would help her mount the steps onto the flatcar, specially decorated to resemble a royal coach.

What sweet revenge it would be to have Rosalyn bending to lift and arrange her blue satin train. Then pointing her silver spiked scepter forward, she would wave to the crowds as the hunky gandy dancers towed her along the tracks to the pedestrian crossing at East Beach. There she'd alight, blow a kiss to the crowd, and walk across the street to the Sand Piper Pub where she'd ascend her throne. After the city clerk had crowned her, and pronounced her Grand Gracious Lady, Railway Queen, she would read the speech the mayor had prepared for her.

"*And now, I am happy to declare the White Rock Railway Daze open*," she imagined herself saying in accents borrowed from the late Princess Diana. "*May everyone have a simply marvelous time.*"

Poor Rosalyn. During the festivities she would be standing below, pretending she was happy to be a lowly lady-in-waiting instead of Railway Queen.

A crowd already filled the arena when Coleen and her mother arrived. The setup was makeshift. The dressing rooms were tents set up beside the stage at the far end of the arena. One could hear what was being said in the next tent, and wouldn't you know it, Rosalyn's tent was snug against Coleen's. Like the previous year, she'd have to listen to Rosalyn's mother and aunt cooing over their beautiful little pigeon. That's what Aunt Birdie called her niece, "Rosalyn, my little pigeon." In Coleen's mind, pigeons were flying rats, strutting about and leaving their filth for others to trample through.

At the sound of the festival's theme music, *Always a Train in My Dreams*, the five contestants walked onto the stage. Coleen was proud of her gown that highlighted her slim figure and auburn hair—a sleeveless, green silk, cinched in at the waist with a cloth belt her mother had made by stitching together little black steam engines. Rosalyn was wearing a long-sleeved purple rag of some crushed material. Some of the seams were crooked. Probably homemade, Coleen thought.

The first event was public speaking. Each contestant had to speak for ten minutes on the topic supplied by the city council: *Could White Rock survive without the railway?* The other three contestants were novices, so the real competition was between Rosalyn and Coleen. Rosalyn spoke first. She had to glance at her cheat cards three times—not good! Coleen was last, so by the time she gave her talk the other girls had used many of her points, but she wasn't too worried. Her dad was a supervisor at CN's Port Mann shops. Using his input, she spoke convincingly of how the railway benefited the local economy.

She ended with a tear-jerking description of all the little boys and girls who would be disappointed if they couldn't come to see the trains in White Rock. They'd have to go all the way to Fort

Langley or Port Moody, burning fossil fuels to get there, and destroying the environment. "Long live the railway! Long live White Rock!" she concluded, then bowed as the crowd roared its approval.

Contestants next sang their own lyrics to the tune *Working on the Railroad*. Coleen's father had helped her write an awesome ballad about locomotive engineers, but Coleen felt a fool singing it. Her voice wasn't strong, and she felt like a wooden marionette as she made hand gestures illustrating her words. She'd have to concede that round to Rosalyn who was a natural with gestures. She belted out *Railway Momma* like an experienced Broadway diva.

There was a half hour break before they changed into their bathing suits and pranced back onto the stage to recite a railway poem of their own composition. That was the event Rosalyn had sabotaged for Coleen the previous year. It wouldn't happen this time. She'd skew that raven-haired witch with her own broom.

"How'd I do with my speech and song?" Coleen asked as her mother helped her out of her gown.

"I'm pretty sure you came first in the speech. I was watching the judges' faces and they lit up every time you made a point. If you do well in poetry, I'm sure you'll win. You do have your poem memorized, don't you?"

"Of course I do. Must you treat me like a child?"

Her mother just shook her head, then waited until Coleen got back from the washroom. "Sit down and let me touch up your makeup. You've smudged the side of your nose." While making repairs, they heard footsteps and voices in Rosalyn's tent.

"Do they show?" Rosalyn asked.

"Stop worrying, my little pigeon." That was Rosalyn's Aunt Birdie. "I'll touch them up with makeup and no one will notice. Donna, I don't know why you didn't leave Frank years ago."

"Hush. Keep your voices down," Rosalyn hissed.

"I thought I should stick with Frank until Rosalyn graduated," her mother said, "but maybe I was wrong."

"Just look at the size of this one. What did your father do to you, my little pigeon? He must have practically broken your arm."

"It's nothing."

"Please, Birdie, just cover them up. Make sure the judges can't see those ugly bruises," Rosalyn's mother said.

"You need a swimsuit with long sleeves," Aunt Birdie said.

"What Rosalyn needs is to win this beauty contest. Without the prize money she won't be able to afford university. Even with her working evenings after school and weekends it's been difficult saving for tuition."

"Poor little pigeon."

"How sad," Coleen's mother whispered as she adjusted the straps on Coleen's swimsuit. "Your dad told me Frank Muncie can't keep a job because he drinks, and gets violent. That poor woman and girl. Sounds like he abuses them."

"That's no reason for her to steal my shoes and make me lose the crown."

"You don't know for a fact that *she* took them. It could have been— Oh dear! There's the buzzer. Stand up. Let's take a look at you. You look lovely, dear. Put your shoes on and away you go."

"Where are my shoes?" Coleen clawed through her backpack.

"Aren't they there?"

"No. That little witch! She must have filched them again while I was in the washroom. I tell you, I'm going over there right now to—"

"Hush, Coleen. Don't get so excited. They must be here somewhere. Look! There they are, under your chair where you tossed your robe. Now calm down. You don't want to go out all red in the face, looking like you're having one of my hot flashes."

As the contestants stood in the wings, awaiting the theme music, Coleen couldn't take her eyes off Rosalyn's arms. The bruises were barely camouflaged. The judges might not see them, but under the makeup the welts were large and painful looking. To inflict such wounds her dad must have grabbed her forearms with both hands and wrung them as if they were wet towels.

Rosalyn's poem was entitled *Daddy Train*. It told the story of days gone by when White Rock was a cottage community. After working all week in the city, fathers rode the Friday evening train to join their families at the cottage for the weekend.

Considering Rosalyn's abusive father, it seemed an odd subject for her to write about, but even Coleen had to admit it was well done. The last verse, telling how everyone would come down to the station Sunday evening to bid their fathers good-bye, had many of the audience in tears. Rosalyn got a standing ovation.

Coleen's English teachers had always praised her poems, so she thought she stood a pretty good chance of derailing Rosalyn's queenly aspirations, providing she didn't make a train wreck of her own performance.

A Hobo's Ballad told the story of a man leaving his family to find work in White Rock. She cleared her throat, looked the judges in the eye, and began to recite.

I'm headin' Wes' / On the midnight express— / Headin' out to White Rock / Lookin' for work on the dock. Refrain: *But oh, I'm a cryin' / I'm a bawlin' an'a wailin' / For my missus I'm missin' / And my wee ones are starvin'.*

The refrain had been a last minute addition. She was sure the judges would be impressed by her creativity. The next verse told how the hobo missed his daughter. When Coleen began the refrain her voice faltered. She didn't want to, but she kept thinking about Rosalyn. She couldn't imagine living in a home where there was never enough money, or where her dad would beat her up. What a great actress Rosalyn was, coming to school every day, beaten and bruised, but never breathing a word of complaint.

Coleen steadied her voice, then paused before beginning the third verse. If Rosalyn could be an actress all these years, she could be one too, if only for the next minute.

My dearest little—

She looked at the ceiling, pretending she'd forgotten the line.

My dearest little…son / You're…You're…You're the…the…only—

She stopped cold, covered her face with both hands and sat down. After a moment of stunned silence, the audience groaned sympathetically, then applauded as the theme music started, and the contestants paraded off stage to await the judges' decision.

At the bottom of the steps Rosalyn turned and reached a hand toward Coleen. "I'm so sorry you forgot your lines, Coleen."

Coleen smiled and glanced at the bruises on Rosalyn's arms. She wasn't sure whether her tears were for losing the crown, or for Rosalyn.

A Lenient Sentence

Alexandra looked around the community hall and shook her head. It was her fourth Wednesday at the soup kitchen. Mopping spilled soup and rolling up smelly oilcloth table coverings had never been on her bucket list for a happy life. Casting a glance over the masticating crowd, she swallowed her nausea: sixteen more Wednesdays until she completed her sentence.

"You're welcome to circulate and speak to our guests if they want to talk," said Wilmot, the kitchen's supervisor, as he passed by with a freshly-delivered tote of stale bread.

Guests indeed! Welfare bums, that's what they were, and Alexandra didn't want to circulate. The sight of so many grinding jaws and slurping tongues turned her stomach. The scraping of metal chairs on the hardwood floor, the raucous laughter, the stink of unwashed bodies, the greasy hair and vacant stares: everything about the place screamed underclass—pigs happy as could be in their own...in their own filth. Alexandra chuckled at her inability to utter the S-H word. Considering her current position, how stupid was it that she couldn't shake off her upbringing in Ocean Bluffs?

"Remember who you are," had been her mother's admonition every time Alexandra left the house.

"And just who am I?" she used to shout back.

Now, seventeen years later, the question nagged at her as she rinsed the dishrag in the solution of bleach and water mandated for wiping down the tablecloths.

Despite feeble attempts at teenage rebellion, she had followed her mother's recipe for a happy life by marrying James Maitland, the city's best defense lawyer. They had built a monster house overlooking the ocean. She had been elected chairperson of Ocean Bluffs' amateur theatre board. She had borne a child, dear little Jimmy.

How she missed him. It was the loss of Jimmy that had triggered her downward slide. Following his death, her perfectly unfolding life had quickly dissolved in shot glasses of 80 proof vodka. Her husband, weary of her drinking and refusal to seek help, had filed for divorce. She had hit rock bottom one night when driving from the bar to her parents' house, where she was now living. Swerving to narrowly miss a cyclist wearing dark clothing and no lights, she had driven onto the sidewalk and sheared off a hydrant. The judge, claiming to be lenient, had sentenced her to *only* twenty-five hours of public service. Obviously, he had never set foot inside this reeking pit of despair—if he had, he wouldn't have called the sentence *lenient*.

"Look awake, Alexandra! Wanda's baby just spilled a bowl of soup," Wilmot called from the corner where he was laying the days-old bread on a table for the guests to take home. "The bucket and mop are in the closet."

Alexandra despised the sloppy-chested Wanda. She always made a big show of breast feeding her squalling spawn, much to the joy of her half-witted cheering section who crowded around her, bowing and scraping as though she was of royal birth. Wilmot, who seemed to know everything about everybody, confided that the big fellow with the one-eyed leer was the father of her child.

On the fifth Wednesday Alexandra noticed the man with the stroller. He came in late, barely fifteen minutes before Wilmot started snatching up empty soup bowls and coffee cups with a view to chasing everyone out so he could get to the golf course. Little

Daddy—that's how Alexandra thought of the new man, for he was barely her height; five-five, and slight of build—settled at an empty table in the far corner of the room.

She expected Wilmot to be annoyed to see someone come in so late in the lunch hour. Instead he ran to get the high chair for the child, then brought two bowls of soup, a couple of sandwiches and an Arrowroot biscuit, a treat he reserved for the wee ones. Little Daddy's boy looked to be about two years old—the age Jimmy had been when he drank the cleaning fluid Alexandra had forgotten to lock up—and had the most perfect rosy cheeks, curly black hair, and aquamarine eyes, just like his daddy's.

The way the wee fellow grinned and reached so eagerly for everything reminded Alexandra of Jimmy. Within moments he had his sandwich torn to bits, then began throwing the chunks of buttery white bread smeared with jam and peanut butter all over the table and onto the floor. He giggled when a big piece splashed into his daddy's bowl of soup.

Another ineffectual parent, Alexandra thought as she watched the man inhale the soup as though he hadn't eaten for a month. Where did these trashy people get the idea they should have children, she wondered? The child, angelic at this age, would probably grow up to be a delinquent. And where was the mother? Sprawled in front of some soap opera at home? Hatching another drag on society?

Wilmot signaled to Alexandra from across the room that it was time to start stripping down the tables. She yanked her rubber gloves on more tightly, rinsed the rag in the bleach-water solution, and set to work. She forgot about Little Daddy until she saw him pushing the stroller towards the back door.

Oh great, she thought, make a mess and swagger out of here, leaving me to clean up. She finished the row of tables she was working on, then stepped over to where Little Daddy had been sitting. The table and floor were spotless, well, as spotless as anything in a grimy old community hall could be.

"Did you clean up after that dad and his kid?" she asked Wilmot who was moving the high chair back into its corner.

"You mean Jackson, the fellow with the toddler?"

"Yes. The kid was tossing bits of bread all over the place."

"Jackson always cleans up after himself. He was working in the oil patch until the downturn. He came home to a bit of a surprise. I'll tell you the story when I have more time. I gotta run. My tee time is one-thirty."

Alexandra watched each Wednesday as Jackson and his child chose a table off by themselves. Their clothes looked freshly laundered, their T-shirts ironed. The toddler always tore his food apart and flung it about like an out of control lawn sprinkler. Once Jackson finished his soup and sandwich, he took the wee fellow in his muscular arms, settled him on his lap, and fed him. As she watched the two of them she had to suppress the urge to pull out her phone and take a photograph.

Once finished feeding the little one, Jackson removed a damp facecloth from a Ziploc bag, wiped down his son's face, then got the broom, dustpan and a rag for cleaning up. He never talked to the other guests. In fact, Jackson barely noticed anyone, including her, which irked Alexandra more than she cared to admit.

She had to wait until the next month's Welfare Wednesday— the day the guests who received government welfare cheques didn't bother coming to the kitchen—before Wilmot had a free moment to tell her Jackson's story.

"Jackson's a journeyman pipefitter," he said as they stood surveying the half-empty room. "Like I told you the other day, he was laid off from the oil patch. He flew in late one night and discovered his child alone in the house: wet, hungry and wailing."

"Poor little fellow."

"Jackson searched the house and yard for his wife. He phoned family and friends, the hospital and police station, in case she'd slipped out for something and been involved in an accident. No one knew anything.

"He cleaned the little fellow up, fed him, stretched out on the couch with the baby in his arms, and exhausted from his long flight, fell asleep. Three in the morning the wife came home."

"Where had she been?"

"Jackson said she staggered into the house like a drunken monkey, some guy ripping her clothes off. They headed straight to the bedroom, didn't even see Jackson and the baby on the couch."

"That's terrible."

"I guess this had been going on for quite some time—her leaving the child at home alone, going out on the town, dragging fellows home."

"Poor little thing." Alexandra realized she meant Jackson as much as his son. "And now?"

"The wife's taken off with one of those jerks and left Jackson with the child. Jackson could be back to work now, but he's staying home with the child as long as he can. He comes here to help stretch his savings."

The next Wednesday Alexandra watched the child rip apart and throw away two donuts, which was really the best use for them. The volunteers always ate at 11:30 and one bite of her donut had told her they were well past their *Best Before* date. She watched as Jackson finished his bowl of soup and sandwich, then cuddled and fed his son. When Jackson stood up and turned to walk over to the closet to get the broom and dustpan, Alexandra scooted over and began wiping down the table and then the high chair.

"You are the handsomest little man," she said to the child. "You've got your daddy's beautiful eyes, do you know that, little man? My name's Alexandra and I used to have a dear little boy just like you. Can you tell me your name?"

He looked up at her with his big aquamarine eyes, grinned, but said nothing.

"Are you shy? Well I don't blame you. I was shy when I was your age too, but—"

"N-N-No. L-L-Let me. I c-c-can do it." Jackson had come up behind her to begin the cleanup.

"I know you can. You're really good about cleaning up," Alexandra said, "but I couldn't resist chatting with your little boy.

My name's Alexandra. Wilmot tells me your name is Jackson. What's your son's name?"

"B-B-Bradley."

She turned back to the child. "Bradley is a very nice name for a fine looking little boy like you. How old are you, Bradley?"

"H-H-He doesn't talk much," Jackson said. "H-H-He's t-t-two next m-m-month."

"Ah, the terrible twos. He must be keeping you busy," she said. "My Jimmy was two when he—" She was about to say *when he died*, but realized that wouldn't be very encouraging. "Jimmy was two when he started getting into everything."

"I b-b-better get him home for his afternoon n-n-nap," Jackson said. "Thanks for helping cl-cl-clean up."

Alexandra waved good-bye as they slipped out the back door and descended the ramp to the alley. Poor man. She wondered if the stress he'd been through was responsible for his stutter.

She began looking forward to her weekly appointments at the kitchen. Neither Jackson nor Bradley talked much, but gradually she began to have short conversations with them. She learned that they lived on The Flats, a development of cheap townhouses tucked between the railway tracks and the big box stores. On fine days she started riding her bike through the area—she'd lost her driver's license for a year. She didn't know which house was Jackson's, but she hoped she might find him out mowing the lawn one day, or the two of them playing on the jungle gym in the park.

As her sentence reached its final days, things had progressed to a point where Jackson now smiled and said hello when he came in. Bradley held out his arms to her even though she hadn't yet picked him up or given him a hug. She realized that she would miss them desperately. Bradley's smiling face and sandwich-throwing antics appealed to her mothering instinct, but she had come to admire Jackson too: his obvious affection and care for his son, and his willingness to eat with the rabble so that he could stay home and be a loving father.

The evening before her last day at the kitchen, she made the mistake of telling her parents, from whom she'd had to beg temporary accommodation, about Jackson and Bradley. "Now that my sentence is finished, I think I'll volunteer to work there so I can keep in touch with them," she said.

"Exactly what a recovering alcoholic needs," her father said, "an unemployed blighter to hang out with."

"Layoffs are common in the oil industry, so it's not like he was fired or anything," she said. "Besides, I think what he's doing is admirable. By extending his time off work, he's being a good father to Bradley. You should see that little fellow."

"Admirable or not, you know better than to sentence yourself to a life with a tradesman from The Flats," her mother said.

Alexandra didn't argue, but thought, That's just it. I *do* know better.

She knew that Jackson was more functional than many people living in the chipboard and stucco mansions atop the bluffs. There was no reason she couldn't continue volunteering at the kitchen, and some Sunday she could invite Jackson and Bradley to picnic with her in Oceanside Park.

What harm could that do?

Sweet Georgia Brown

Grant went to the gym bright and early every day, well, maybe not always so bright, but early. He enjoyed the morning crowd of guys—he knew their names, they knew his. If he didn't feel energetic he could yak with someone.

He had adopted the gym habit after Fiona died, his wife of thirty-seven years. He had retired from a long and distinguished career in the air force to care for her. Seven months later, the double hit of no job and no wife had left him searching for social contacts. He considered joining a bowling league, or a camera club, but one morning, whilst cleaning out Fiona's chest of drawers, he'd happened upon a newspaper from 1965. He sat down on the bed to glance through it and came upon one of Ann Landers' advice columns. In response to a question from a lonely widowed man, she suggested, among other things, that he join a gym.

Grant had stood up and looked at himself in the full-length mirror on the back of the bedroom door. Turning sideways, he could see that over the last few months he'd gained more than one or two pounds. He'd never get into his air force uniform. And that very day he'd purchased a year's membership at the gym.

Ann's suggestion had been good advice, for not only did he make friends, he shed pounds. Lying in bed at night he enjoyed feeling the new tightness around his middle, tracing the re-emergence of a muscular chest and stomach. At his last weigh-in he'd tipped the scales at two-ten, only twenty pounds away from his goal of one-ninety. Already he'd noticed the ladies were starting to glance his way, especially the new trainer.

Georgia was one of those girls who lit up the room when she walked onto the exercise floor: early thirties, slim, a wide smile to greet the clients each morning. Occasionally she paid Grant personal attention, pausing to point out another way to tighten his middle than the hundred sit-ups he struggled to do. One day she touched the small of his back, encouraging him to keep his core rigid while doing squats.

When he had mentioned Georgia—such an attractive name—to his sister, she had frowned and wagged a finger at him. "Be careful, Grant. It's her job to be pleasant and perhaps even to touch you in a professional way. Men your age sometimes get queer notions about women. Be on your guard."

Grant had laughed off his sister's warning, though at night, lying in the bed he had shared with Fiona for so many years, he dreamed of Georgia lying beside him, touching him, running her carefully manicured fingers over his muscular chest. Then he imagined burying his face in her luscious red hair and kissing her lightly freckled forehead.

When not at the gym, he hung out at the library where he read *The New York Times*. On the Vows page, he noticed that couples often differed in age: the groom ten, even twenty years older than the bride. Women valued more than just physical attributes. They looked for financial security, responsibility, and wisdom. He was sure this was why Georgia was so friendly towards him. Hadn't she said as much one morning when she'd commented, "Grant, you are so dedicated! You're here, no matter the rain pelting down."

She didn't wear a wedding ring, probably because she didn't want to settle for one of the huscular guys preening in front of the mirrors. She must want a mate with character. He could be her mate. *Georgia and Grant, Grant and Georgia, G&G*—their names fit well together. Grant was content to let the relationship build slowly, just like his muscles.

Grant had learned patience while caring for Fiona during her final months, and he exercised the same patience getting to know Georgia. He greeted her each morning on his way into the gym. If he noticed her doing something especially well, like leading a group of seniors in low impact exercises, he complimented her on her professionalism. While he was on the treadmill he kept an eye on her, ready to run to her assistance should someone speak rudely to her.

He often paused in his workout to show her some little attention. "Thank you for telling that bozo to re-rack the dumbbells," he might say, or "Good to see you lubricating the pulleys on the exercise machines," or "Any plans for the weekend?" She sometimes skied with friends at Whistler or motored to Seattle for concerts.

After three months of these attentions, Grant wondered if Georgia was slipping away from him. She wasn't always in her office at six in the morning, awaiting his cheerful greeting. It had been weeks since she'd touched him, and she had stopped giving him exercise tips.

Perhaps he hadn't been demonstrative enough. If he wanted to win her heart he'd better ramp up his little attentions before one of the young sweat hogs muscled his way in. Grant began touching her whenever he had the opportunity: a brush with his elbow when he walked past her, a hand on her arm when he paused to say good-bye, one time a friendly body check when she was passing by with another client. She sometimes shrunk away from him, or snapped, "Hands off the merchandise, Mister," but he knew she was just joking, teasing him by playing hard to get.

February's wind and rain kept Grant indoors. He wished he could pass the evenings cuddling with Georgia on the fake fur rug he'd bought specially with her in mind. He'd spread it on the floor in front of his fireplace.

He would use Valentine's Day to tell her that his intentions were honourable, that he respected her and hoped for a long relationship. On February 13th Grant spent half an hour in Purdy's Chocolates searching out the perfect token to celebrate their budding affection for each other. He chuckled when he discovered a heart-shaped box of Sweet Georgia Browns for seventeen dollars. Not being a chocolate fancier himself, he had no idea what Sweet Georgia Browns were, but he was sure the combination of the red, heart-shaped box and the name *Sweet Georgia* would please her and let her know that he loved her.

From Purdy's he walked to the drug store and chose a greeting card to accompany the chocolates. It took him almost an hour to find the perfect card, one that showed him to be a mature man of quality, rather than a shallow, young buck. Back home he composed a personal message in which he listed Georgia's positive characteristics: a winning smile, cheery words, encouraging touches—and then rather than sign his name, he penned, *A not so secret admirer.*

He hoped to hand the heart-shaped box to Georgia personally, but on Valentine's Day morning she was not in her office when he arrived. The door was ajar and her green jacket was draped over the back of her chair but there was no sign of her. Disappointed, but not wanting to stash the Sweet Georgia Browns inside his locker where they might absorb the odour of sour towels and sweaty runners, he set the box on her desk, the envelope containing the card on top. He then chose a treadmill with a clear view of her office so that he could witness the look of joy when she discovered his gift.

An hour passed and she had still not appeared. What could be wrong? He always enjoyed watching her walk into the gym, making an entrance with her head held high, like a queen entering her domain.

Grant was pretty much finished his workout when Georgia finally came into the gym. She was accompanied by a fellow Grant didn't like. He was thirty-something, tall, flat-bellied, buzzed head, with a sneering curl to his lip. He always wore a white shirt and tie like he thought himself Mr. Big. Grant had noticed him hanging around Georgia's office the past week, using her computer while she was out on the exercise floor, though he seemed to spend a lot of time scanning him and the other guys. Maybe he got his jollies looking at sweaty men.

Grant watched as they went into Georgia's office and closed the door. He saw Georgia pick up the heart-shaped box and card, then lay them aside. She and Mr. Buzz Cut stood gazing at the computer screen. Then they sat down and appeared to be deep in conversation.

Grant did a few more minutes on the treadmill, then mounted a bike that still gave him a view of the office. He was as exhausted as a marathoner on an August afternoon, but was determined to see Georgia's reaction when she read the message on the card and opened the box of Sweet Georgia Browns. He was pretty sure she'd guess he was the *not so secret admirer,* and would come over to thank him for being so thoughtful.

Why didn't Mr. Buzz Cut get out of there? he wondered. What could be so important that he had to take up Georgia's time? Didn't he know she had a job to do: clients to supervise, machines to lubricate, spray bottles to fill with disinfectant?

Finally Grant gave up. He'd put in almost three hours. He stumbled over to the bench beside the lockers and sat down. He closed his eyes and mopped the perspiration from his forehead with his towel. When he looked up Georgia was coming his way. He grinned and stood up, ready to receive her words of appreciation. She said, "Grant, could you come into my office for a moment?"

"Sure thing. My muscles are at your command." He chuckled and touched her shoulder.

Georgia didn't say anything, just hurried into her office where Mr. Buzz Cut was sitting in the chair beside her desk. She motioned for Grant to take the other chair and then sat down herself. "Grant, this is Tim Ives. He's the manager here. I've asked him to sit in while I…while I say a few…a few words to you."

"Pleased to meet you," Grant lied, thrusting forward a sweaty palm for Tim to shake.

Then he turned to Georgia, one eye on the box of Sweet Georgia Browns that lay unopened on her desk. "What can I do for you, Georgia?" He expected she was about to ask him to coach some of the younger clients. If they weren't shown proper form they might injure their backs for life.

He was imagining what a joy it would be working with Georgia when she said, "Grant, I need to tell you that you've been making me very uncomfortable these past few weeks."

"What?"

"I know you're a friendly person and probably mean no harm by it, but the way you touch me isn't…isn't normal, isn't comfortable for me."

"But surely you can't think—"

"I know that I have sometimes touched you when modeling a new exercise, but that's been strictly on a professional basis."

"What kind of monster do you think I am?"

"Grant, judging by some of the things you say, and how you always have your eye on me, I feel that you've somehow misunderstood…you've misunderstood the nature of our relationship."

"Really, Georgia, I never thought one or two friendly touches—"

"There have been *more* than one or two." Tim spoke in a scratchy falsetto, like a fingernail on a chalkboard. He pointed to the computer screen. "Over the last week I've been watching you. I've documented the inappropriate touches, the unwelcome words. Look here."

Grant looked at the screen. He saw a list of dates and times followed by short phrases. He felt his face flush red as he scanned what Tim had recorded.

"I'm sorry if you think I stepped over the line, Georgia," Grant said. "I never meant to make you uncomfortable. I thought I'd found a friendly face…after my…after my Fiona died...you know."

"We think it will be best if you patronize another gym," Tim said.

"I'm sorry. I'm so very sorry," Grant said, standing up. As he turned to leave, he glanced at the unopened, heart-shaped box of Sweet Georgia Browns on the desk. He was glad he hadn't signed his name. Perhaps she wouldn't guess it was from him, and clearly, that was for the best. He opened his locker and removed his gym bag. He pulled off his workout gloves and stuffed them along with his towel and water bottle into the bag. Then he walked out of the gym, feeling very old and very foolish.

Bird Without Wings

Mike paused to read the sign at the jewelry counter. *60% off diamonds*. He bent over the glass case, surprised to see that engagement rings came in so many different designs.

"May I help you?" The saleslady had appeared unexpectedly.

"I wish you *could* help, but no, not today, probably never."

Mike shoved his hands into his pockets and walked briskly away from temptation. Before Sunday he would have taken the sale as a signal that God was smiling upon his plan to ask Jackie to marry him. Now everything was different. To even think of proposing marriage would be stepping right into the devil's snare of doubt.

"Oh God, why? Why are you demanding this sacrifice of me?" he mumbled as he returned to the bank where he worked as a financial planner. What was the use of anything anymore? What was the point of his job? There was no use planning a financial future if the world was going to end in seven years.

Why counsel clients to save or invest their money if God was going to crack open the bubble surrounding Earth and clear away all the greed, all the me-first thought patterns? Mike might as well advise everyone to withdraw their savings now, blow it on that new house they've always dreamed of, or take that cruise around the globe before the planet was repurposed.

When he got home from work that evening he called Jackie to see if she wanted to walk down to the pier. They'd been walking together twice a week since they'd first met at church six months previously. Mike had never considered himself a churchy person, and wouldn't have stepped inside The Glory Tabernacle if the singing hadn't attracted him.

On that warm, spring morning the windows in The Glory Tabernacle had been open as Mike passed by on his way to the beach. He had paused on the sidewalk to listen as the congregation sang a barbershop favourite: *When the Roll is Called Up Yonder I'll Be There*. It was unusual to hear a congregation singing in four-part harmony, and so Mike had stepped inside and sat down in the back pew.

While living in Kamloops he'd enjoyed the camaraderie of singing with a barbershop quartet. Since the bank had transferred him to its White Rock office, he'd been unable to find a suitable group to join. It was a treat to hear the familiar harmonies once again.

When the Roll was followed by *When the Saints Come Marching In*, another favourite. The sermon hadn't made much sense to Mike that day: readings from *The True Path to World Harmony*, written by some prophet who claimed to have had visions of end-time events. Still, Mike had stuck around for the final song—*Life is Like a Mountain Railway*—and afterwards, over juice and muffins, he'd met Jackie. She was about his age—late twenties—and pretty in an understated way, though like him, she needed to lose a few pounds. She'd walked partway home with him that Sunday, and next week he had gone back to enjoy the singing. He was surprised at how soon he was tithing his income to the tabernacle, and reading and quoting The Prophet.

Over the months his relationship with Jackie had progressed through friendship to what Mike now thought of as companionship. Not only did they walk off pounds during the week, but weekends they occasionally attended concerts—those approved by the local bishop—and sometimes they went camping—in separate tents of course, for they believed in following The Prophet's order to be chaste until marriage.

"What did you think of The Prophet's message yesterday?" Mike asked as they set off down Johnston Road to the pier.

"Which part?"

"His prediction that God is finally fed up with this ugly disaster of a planet mired in selfishness and plans to break into our history in seven years' time?"

"Well, things are getting pretty bad," Jackie said. "Look at our own country. We've got a government willing to rape the planet, fracking all over the place, never mind that ground water is being polluted. I'm sure God must be fed up."

"True enough, and I see greed first hand at the bank, families scrapping over money, rushing in to clean out bank accounts before the undertaker has had a chance to embalm their loved ones, but what about The Prophet's order not to marry?"

"That does seem harsh, but if life's going to get as bad as he predicts, perhaps we're better off without families to worry about."

"But doesn't God want us to love one another? Isn't he pleased when people get together to create families? Didn't he say it wasn't good for Adam to be alone, even though he must have known how his creation was going to be hijacked by The Destroyer?"

"I hear what you're saying, and I admit I was disappointed when Bishop Redmond read The Prophet's' edict. Still, I suppose we must obey."

"You just said *we must obey*. Oh Jackie my dear, dear friend." Mike reached for her hand. "Does that mean you've been thinking the same as me, that *we* should get married?"

"You're making me blush, Mike."

"So you *have* been thinking about me in that way. Does that mean you would marry me if I asked you?"

"Oh Mike, yes. Yes, I would marry you, but it's pointless to even think about such a thing now."

"The Prophet could be wrong. Others have predicted the end of the world, but life staggers onward."

"I know, but this is *our* prophet. His predictions always come true."

"Like what?"

"Like 9-11."

"He predicted those planes would fly into the Twin Towers?" Mike asked.

"Yes, though not exactly how it would happen. He warned that the Western World could expect something like that."

"But he didn't predict the exact day or how it would happen?"

"No, but now he's given us a timeline. *Seven years and all life will cease as we know it.* Isn't that what Bishop Redmond read yesterday?"

"But life of what? Maybe he's talking about global warming, or some species of whale that will become extinct. That statement could be interpreted a lot of different ways."

"Mike, I'm as disappointed as you, but you know The Prophet warns us about questioning his predictions."

"I know, but I'm new to The Glory Tabernacle. Have you ever seen this prophet guy?"

"Prophet Maximillian Murphy lives in California. I've never seen him but our bishop had an audience with him."

"And what did he report?"

"The Prophet gave him a special blessing and a signed copy of *The True Path to World Harmony.*"

"But what are his circumstances? Is the prophet married? Does he have children?"

"Oh yes. I've heard he has a large family—nine children I think—and lives in a beautiful home overlooking the Pacific Ocean."

"So it's okay for him to be married?"

"Really Mike, we've got to stop talking about this. You know The Prophet's warning."

"I know. *The Prophet hath spoken: with gladness we will obey.* Still, I think—"

"Please, Mike."

"Okay. I'll change the subject. How would you like to go to a concert Saturday night?"

"Who's giving a concert?"

"Celtic Thunder is coming to the Rogers Centre. I've got all their CD's and would love to see them live."

"Will Bishop Redmond approve?"

"Approve or not, I'm going, and I'd like you to come with me. They sing traditional Celtic songs like *Amazing Grace*, and some of their own compositions. It's all good."

Mike knew that Jackie was nervous about buying tickets without consulting Bishop Redmond, but he wasn't going to miss this concert. He had to pay almost a week's salary for good seats, but it would be worth it.

As they joined the lineup outside the Rogers Centre to collect the tickets on Saturday night, he noticed Jackie nervously scanning the crowd. "What's wrong?"

Jackie giggled. "Just looking to see if Bishop Redmond or anyone else from the tabernacle is here."

"So what if they are?"

"You haven't been coming to The Glory Tabernacle very long. You probably don't know that Bishop Redmond sometimes comes to events like this—not to attend them, but to see if any of the congregation are trying to sneak in. He once turned some folks back from a Paul McCartney concert—after they'd paid for their tickets and everything. He escorted them straight home."

"That is so sick."

"He was just protecting them from the devil. I think that's rather noble of him."

"Well you won't find the devil here. You'll love Celtic Thunder."

"Still, don't you feel a bit wicked," Jackie whispered, "coming here without permission? Celtic Thunder sounds ominous, like druids dancing around a bonfire or something."

"Now stop it," Mike said. "Relax and enjoy the evening. You won't hear or see anything evil here." He squeezed her hand.

Celtic Thunder began their program with *My Land*, a ballad about Ireland's green hills and shining waters. As the six men sang, Mike sensed Jackie relaxing. She hummed along with *Amazing Grace* and *Song of the Myra,* though she frowned at *Whiskey in the Jar*. The last song before intermission was *A Bird Without Wings*, a solo by the group's youngest singer, the baby-faced Damian McGinty.

As the arena's lights came up for intermission, Mike let go of Jackie's hand to wipe the tears from his eyes. "You're weeping too," he said as Jackie fished a tissue from her purse.

"Who wouldn't be moved by all those images of loneliness: a bird without wings, a motherless child."

Mike took Jackie's hand again. "You realize that is what The Prophet is asking of us, to go through life like a bird without wings, like a song without words. He demands that we live alone in a black and white world while he splashes about in the ocean with his wife and dozen kids."

"*Nine* children."

"Nine or a dozen, it's a family, something he doesn't want us to enjoy. I think we should ignore his advice, but come along now. Let's find something to drink."

They had difficulty finding something suitable because Jackie would not let him buy a soft drink from any place selling alcohol. The Prophet forbade encouraging the liquor trade, which they would have been doing, even if it were only a Ginger Ale they purchased. Finally they found a stand selling only chips, candy bars and soft drinks. Jackie offered to pay for the drinks, though she flinched when Mike chose a diet Coke. The Prophet frowned upon Coke, labeling it the main street to cocaine.

Celtic Thunder sang more of Mike's favourites during the second half: *Home from the Sea, Caledonia* and *Heartland*, then ended with *Take Me Home*. As they stood to applaud Mike said, "I don't have a drop of Irish blood in my veins, but that song always tears my heart out."

"It should be sung in the tabernacle," Jackie said, wiping her eyes. "It really is a hymn, if you think of it as all of us wanting to go home to heaven where we'll meet those we love."

"You're right," Mike said. "It would make a great gospel song, but you realize The Prophet is asking us to remain single and lonely. He doesn't want us to establish a home where there is love to come home to."

"Oh Mike, please. I don't want to think about it."

"We *should* think about it. In fact, right now I'm going to—" Mike dropped to one knee and took her hand.

"Mike! Not here!"

"Why not? We've heard so much about love tonight. Jackie, will you marry me?"

"But The Prophet—"

"Don't think about him. He's obviously a man without a heart. Think about God. God is love. Isn't that what we've been taught?"

"Well, yes, but—"

"Jackie, you know God said it wasn't good for humans to be alone, so let's obey Him. Meet me at the mall tomorrow. You can choose an engagement ring."

"Oh Mike, do we dare?" Jackie reached for Mike's hand. She loved the feel of strength in his fingers as they entwined hers. She wanted to wear his ring. She wanted to be his wife.

As they walked away from the Rogers Centre she smiled at the thought of defying The Prophet. It was something she'd often thought of doing, but had been afraid to do on her own.

Robert Ramsay

The Night Uncle Rolly Beached the Caddie

I was ten years old the Christmas Uncle Rolly beached the Caddie. That was the year Dad started calling me Bob, instead of Bobby, the year I grew tall enough to reach the clutch and brake pedals on the John Deere tractor. Finally, I could help Dad with the chores instead of just getting in his way. I could drive the tractor while baling hay, dumping feed for the Herefords and spreading manure on the summer fallow after cleaning out the stock pens.

That year was also memorable because Mom discovered Jesus, though to be fair to the meek and lowly Savior, Mom's Jesus was a harsher version than the one described in the Good Book. Her Jesus was a lusty warrior who bellowed *Onward Christian Soldiers* while brandishing a flame thrower to persuade folks to join his kingdom of love.

It wasn't like we were infidels before that summer. Sundays we attended Twin Meadows Community Church. We always sat in the front pew because Mom, a former Fall Fair 4-H Queen, felt it her duty to set a good example.

Ailene Bell, the new bank manager's wife, was to blame for Mom's sudden conversion to an edgier version of Christianity. Ailene had grown up in Saskatoon, an advantage she reminded the other ladies of whenever she detected a lapse in their country-poor sense of style.

"Saskatoon women are streaking their hair," she might say, resulting in a lineup at Twin Meadows's only beauty salon.

"Saskatoon ladies wear their skirts just below the knee," forced Mom to spend several evenings hunched over her sewing machine, updating her wardrobe.

"Thoughtful people are abandoning mainline churches." This pronouncement sent Mom scurrying to Ailene's church, the Tabernacle of Believers' Assembly, beyond the fairgrounds. Dad and I accompanied her the first Sunday. A five-person band of wailing guitars and pounding drums led the singing, and there was a lot of holy hollering and tossing of hands into the air. Accustomed to raised hands in school, I whispered to Dad, "When will the preacher let them go to the bathroom?"

After that first Sunday, Dad and I returned to the community church, while Mom worked hard to endear herself to Ailene and the Tabbers. She gave up her volunteer work at the Red Cross so she could sew banners for the sanctuary, clean up after their weekly potlucks, and knock on doors handing out booklets promoting the Tabbers' fiery view of end time events.

"Don't you think you were more useful at the Red Cross?" Dad asked after enduring a month of her new enthusiasms. "Seems to me the Tabbers are using you to promote themselves. Didn't Jesus serve others—feed the hungry, heal the sick, even wash dirty feet—instead of jumping every time the temple authorities made a suggestion?"

Mom just shook her head and went on fetching and running for her new-found friends.

That Christmas, Ailene and her family went to California for the holiday. Mom decided we should go somewhere exotic too. "Let's take a week and drive out west, visit my baby brother, Rolly. He's alone on the coast. It's not right that we never visit him."

"I thought you didn't care for your brother's lifestyle," Dad said.

"It's time we patched things up."

"We can't leave a thousand head of cattle to starve while we go gadding about the country like your friend Ailene," Dad said.

Uncle Rolly was a mystery to me. Our only connection was an annual exchange of Christmas cards. He usually sent along a photograph. In the last one he'd been standing beside a white Cadillac, a big grin splashed across his freckled face. I thought he was the handsomest man I'd ever seen, though I didn't dare say that to Mom or Dad. From the little I'd heard, a few years before I was born there'd been some trouble with him and Joey Simms, one of the neighbour boys. I figured they'd fought over some girl. Without finishing high school, Rolly had taken off for the coast where he did construction work.

That year we ate Christmas dinner with Dad's family in Saskatoon as we always did. While driving back to the farm Dad must have been feeling good with his belly full of his mother's roast turkey, because when Mom started fussing, he agreed to make a quick trip to the coast. "We'll only be able to stay a couple of days," he warned. "I'll ask Jack Henderson to look in on the cattle, but can't leave them for long at a time like this."

The evening before we were to leave I lay in bed dreaming of the fun I'd have. I'd get to see the Rocky Mountains, and walk beside the ocean. I might see whales and seals. I was dozing off when I overheard Dad mention my name.

"I'm surprised you're willing to expose Bob to your brother."

"He's not likely to do anything funny with us there," Mom said.

What was funny about Uncle Rolly? I wondered. Did he do tricks, or tell jokes? If so, what was wrong with that, unless they were dirty jokes?

It took two long days to drive from Manitoba to White Rock on British Columbia's coast. As we got closer Dad said, "Audrey, shouldn't you let Rolly know we're coming?"

"I want to surprise him. Bob, please hand me that cloth bag with my Bible and the booklets I brought for Rolly."

"Will Rolly want your booklets?" Dad asked.

"Don't try to discourage me, Earl. You don't want Rolly to burn in hell, do you?"

"Maybe he's already a Christian."

"A Christian? Living that lifestyle?" Mom shook her head and clucked her tongue.

"Mom, what's a lifestyle?"

"It's...It's how you live."

"Do you think Uncle Rolly will take us for a ride in his Caddie?"

"How do you know he's got a Cadillac?" Mom asked.

"He was standing beside one in the picture he sent this year," I said.

"It was probably someone else's," Mom said. "Your uncle always liked fancy cars and fancy people, but I doubt he can afford a Cadillac on the pittance he earns pounding nails for a living."

After two long days on the road we left the mountains with their snowy summits behind us. As the Trans Canada Highway descended into the lower Fraser Valley, the snow-laden rocks and forests were replaced with green fields. Holsteins grazed beside tall silos, crows picked at scraps beside the road, and Mom asked Dad to turn the heat off in the van.

It was almost four o'clock when we got to White Rock. Dad had a bit of trouble finding Uncle Rolly's place. Mom was holding the map up-side-down, but after Dad yelled at her, grabbed it out of her hands, and twisted it around, and she whimpered that she'd never been good with maps, and it didn't help to have him shouting at her, she directed Dad to Oxford Street, the steepest road I'd ever seen.

"There's the ocean!" I cried. "Can we go swimming?"

"Hush. Don't shout. You'll upset your father," Mom said as Dad braked and maneuvered around a brick median. "Besides, I'm sure the water will be too cold for swimming at this time of year."

When we got to the bottom of the hill we turned right and drove along the beach, then turned up another steep street.

"Are you sure this is Rolly's house?" Dad asked, looking at the giant shoebox tucked into the hillside. "I thought you said he lived in a little shack on the beach." This house looked expensive. It had cedar walls along the sides and green-tintcd glass acruss the front.

"Maybe he's been out of work and he's renting a room from these folks," Mom said.

I wanted to jump right out and run down to the ocean, but Mom had to powder her face and tidy her hair. Then she led the way up the ten steps—I counted them—to the front door. There was a palm tree and a bush with bright red flowers in a planter beside the door.

"Flowers at Christmas time! Imagine that," Mom said as she pushed the doorbell. A tall man opened the door. He was wearing a white shirt, grey pants and a blue tie that he was loosening from around his neck.

"Oh, I'm sorry," Mom said. "Maybe we've got the wrong house. You're not Rolly Selbie. Is there another entrance, a basement suite perhaps?"

"I'm George Kirkland, Rolly's partner." The man ran his fingers through his thick, black hair which showed a touch of grey at the sides. "And you are?"

"I'm Audrey, Rolly's sister from Twin Meadows in Manitoba. We've come to visit."

"Rolly didn't say anything."

"I wanted to surprise him."

"I'm sure he *will* be surprised." The man opened the door and stood aside. "You'd better come in. Rolly's not home yet. He's working in Fort Langley these days."

"I didn't know he had … had anyone living with him, but I guess it's pretty expensive here. Rolly probably needs help with the rent."

"Rolly built this house. We own it, mortgage free. I'm a physician."

"A physician?"

"I head up the surgical team at Peace Arch Hospital. Won't you come into the living room and sit down? I just got home. Would you like something to drink?" George asked.

"Oh no, we don't touch alcohol" Mom said.

"I was thinking of hot chocolate," George said. "Let me turn the fire on in the living room. You can sit down and rest after your long trip."

The living room was cool and bright: snowy white rug, white walls, a long white sofa and two loveseats, arranged in a U-shape facing the glass wall. There were real paintings on the wall, and in a mirrored corner, lit by a tiny spotlight, a white marble statue of a naked man, a string of Christmas lights strung around his head like a crown. The mirrors made it so you could see him front and back at the same time.

"Dad, can we walk down to the ocean?" I pointed to the beach where I could see people strolling along a walkway.

"There'll be time for that later," Dad said.

"I didn't know he had a live-in partner," Mom whispered to Dad. "Why didn't he tell me?"

"He probably knew how you'd react."

"Maybe we should go to a hotel," Mom said, nodding in my direction. "We don't want you-know-who to see this, to think we condone this…this lifestyle."

"We can hardly do that now that we're here," Dad said.

"Then maybe I can kill two birds with one stone." Mom grinned and patted the cloth bag holding her Bible and the religious booklets she'd brought.

"Now don't you go forcing—"

George came back into the room carrying a tray with three mugs and a silver pot filled with steaming hot chocolate. "I gave Rolly a call. He's on his way home. Now if you'll excuse me, I'll go and change out of these work clothes."

I was standing at the window, sipping my second mug of hot chocolate and watching the lights come on along the walkway that bordered the ocean when headlights came up the hill and a black pickup rumbled to a stop behind our van. *Rolly's Contracting* was printed on the side. "Does Uncle Rolly drive a black pickup?" I asked.

"I don't know what he drives," Mom said. She and Dad joined me at the window. A man wearing a black and red plaid jacket, paint-stained blue jeans and a baseball cap flipped backwards, jumped out. He grabbed a metal lunch box and disappeared around the side of the house.

"Is that Uncle Rolly?"

"I haven't seen him for over ten years, but from the pictures he sends us, I'd say that's him, that's my baby brother. He used to have blond hair that curled down over his ears, but I see he's cut it short." We heard a door open and close somewhere down below.

"I'm home, Love," called a deep voice. Work boots thudded on a hard floor. Feet pounded up steps. A door opened, there were whispered words, and then Uncle Rolly ran into the living room.

"My big sis Audrey! Is it really you?"

Mom stood up, clutching the cloth bag. Uncle Rolly threw his arms around her and gave her a tight squeeze. "Excuse the sweat. If I'd known you were coming I'd have got home early. And Earl, how are you doing? How's the cattle business? Steaks cost an arm and a leg, so you must be doing well."

He shook Dad's hand, then turned to me. "You must be Bob. Just look at you, half way to being a man already. Seems you wrote me only yesterday, Sis, saying you had a little one on the way." Uncle Rolly shook my hand. His was rough like sandpaper.

George, dressed in tan slacks and a blue golf shirt, came back into the room. "Shall I start dinner, Love?"

"No one will cook tonight!" Uncle Rolly said. "This calls for a celebration. Let's go to *The Boathouse*. Why don't you phone and reserve a window table while I shower and change?"

Our table was on the second floor, overlooking the ocean and the railway track that ran along the beach. I could watch people walking on the boardwalk, and just as we were giving the waiter our order an Amtrak passenger train came by, the engineer blowing the whistle again and again to warn people to stay off the track.

The tables had white tablecloths and fancy glasses on tall stems. While we ate, the men talked about cars, the townhouses Uncle Rolly was building, and operations George had done to help sick people. Mom talked about the Tabernacle, how refreshing it was to hear Bible-based sermons, how Apostle Hewbell was brave enough to call sin, *sin.*

While waiting for our dessert to come—ice cream and strawberries—I dropped my napkin. I had to get off my chair and bend under the table to reach it. As I grabbed it I noticed Uncle Rolly and George had their knees snugged together and were holding hands. I thought that was kind of funny, but kind of cool too. It made me think of how in Sunday School we sometimes stood in a circle and held hands while our teacher prayed. Some of the boys screwed up their faces at having to touch each other, but I kind of liked holding hands, especially with Billy Henderson. He was my best friend.

It was late by the time we got home. Uncle Rolly helped us carry our suitcases inside, and then showed us to the basement. It was nothing like our basement on the farm with its cracked concrete walls, spider webs and a big furnace taking up most of the space. Uncle Rolly's basement had a living room, white like the one upstairs, a bathroom, and two bedrooms. I wanted to stay up so I could look out the window at the beach. The trees along the boardwalk were sparkling with lights, but Mom said I'd had a long day, and if I didn't go to bed right away I'd wake up cranky.

Next morning I was awakened by what sounded like cats fighting outside my bedroom. I ran to the window. Two seagulls were sitting on the roof of the next-door house. Their mouths were wide open and they were screaming at each other.

I watched as two people launched kayaks. Then I ran to the bathroom, washed my face, and got dressed. Mom and Dad were already upstairs, sitting in the kitchen while Uncle Rolly prepared breakfast. George had already gone to the hospital.

As soon as breakfast was over I asked Uncle Rolly if we could go kayaking like the people I'd seen. "I'm afraid I don't have a kayak," he said, "but maybe I've got something better."

"What? What have you got, Uncle Rolly?"

"It's a surprise. You'll need to dress warmly and follow me. Then you'll find out."

Dad and I got our winter coats and tuques out of the van and Uncle Rolly gave me a scarf to wear because I'd forgotten mine at home. Mom said it was too windy for her—she'd just stay home and read her Bible and enjoy the view from the living room. Uncle Rolly showed her how to turn on the gas fireplace. Then he led us outside and down the hillside to the beach.

As we walked along the boardwalk the sun popped out of the clouds. Gulls were flying overhead while crows and robins hopped on the grass bordering the walkway. "Look up," Uncle Rolly said as we walked past some tall trees. "Look way up."

"Why? What am I supposed to see?" I asked.

"On the branch of that tallest tree, something big and brown with a white head."

"An eagle? Is that an eagle, Uncle Rolly?" At that moment it leaped into the air and flew out over the ocean where it dived almost straight down at the water, then skimmed over the waves before flapping its wings back into the air.

"It's got something in its claws," I yelled.

"Looks like it's going to have a fish for breakfast," Uncle Rolly said.

"I wish Billy was here," I said. "He loves birds. He's always drawing them."

"Who's Billy?"

"Billy Henderson. He lives down the road from me. He's in my grade at school, and in my Sunday School class too. He's my best friend in the whole world. Sometimes we ride our bikes to the railway tracks. While waiting for a train to come we lie on our backs in the grass alongside the tracks. We watch the hawks circling. Last summer we saw one dive down just like that eagle—it grabbed a baby bunny in its claws and flew away with it."

"Sounds like you've got a good friend there. Come along. We have to walk out on the pier now."

The pier stretched way out into the ocean. At the end Uncle Rolly unlocked a gate and led us down to where a bunch of boats were tied up. "We *are* going kayaking," I said, skipping ahead to where some kayaks were stacked on metal racks.

"Not kayaking," Uncle Rolly said. "Something better," and then he stopped beside a humungous white motorboat with the name *Mates Forever* painted on the side. It was so big it had a smaller boat hanging out the back, just like a lifeboat on the *Titanic*.

"We didn't know your uncle had a boat, did we, Bob?" Dad said.

Uncle Rolly reached for my hand to help me onto the boat, then showed us all over it. There was a little cabin down below with bunk beds, a tiny kitchen and even a bathroom with a shower. Up top were all the controls and a steering wheel with spokes, just like on the *Titanic*, only a lot smaller. Uncle Rolly started the motor, let it warm up awhile, then showed me how to untie the ropes holding us to the pier. Then we all sat up top—Uncle Rolly said it was called the wheelhouse—and he guided *Mates Forever* past the other boats and out beyond a tall rock wall—Uncle Rolly called it a breakwater.

He pushed a lever forward. The engine roared and the big boat speeded up. It ploughed into the waves, sending silvery spray over us.

"I can taste salt," I yelled, licking my lips. "The ocean really is salty. I wish Billy could be here."

Dad looked at his watch. "It'll be one o'clock in Manitoba. Billy's probably tying on his skates and heading out to play hockey. You can tell him all about this when you get home."

"Would you like to take the helm?" Uncle Rolly asked.

"The helm?"

"The steering wheel. Would you like to steer for awhile? Your dad can take a picture so you can show Billy when you get home. Come here. I'll show you what to do."

I stood up but the boat was rocking so hard that I staggered back down onto my seat.

"Pretty heavy swell," Uncle Rolly said, standing up and extending his arm. "Here, take my hand."

Holding onto him I managed to walk the few steps to where he was sitting. He sat down, and putting his arm around my waist, snugged me onto the edge of the seat between his legs. "Now, take the wheel with both hands." He took my hands in his and positioned them on the wheel. "The trick is to keep the bow headed into the waves."

"It keeps wanting to turn," I yelled.

"You'll get the hang of it. A little to port—that means left—now starboard, which means to the right. That's the way. You'll learn fast." As he leaned forward, steadying me within his arms, Uncle Rolly's breath was warm on my neck, smelling faintly of onions from the omelet he'd fed us for breakfast.

"You're a fine sailor," Uncle Rolly said after about fifteen minutes. "You keep on steering while I get out of the way so your dad can take a picture. Then we'd better head back to the marina—don't want your mother to think we've gone to China."

Back at the house Uncle Rolly and Mom prepared salmon sandwiches and a big salad for lunch. We ate on the deck where the sun made the air warm, and then Uncle Rolly asked if we'd like to see the townhouses he was building. We went downstairs to the garage. "See Mom," I said, "Uncle Rolly really does have a Cadillac."

It was the most beautiful car I had ever seen, nothing like our rusty Dodge van. The Caddie was white with red leather seats. Uncle Rolly let me sit in the front with him. He showed me how to enter an address into the GPS. It was fun to hear the voice telling him how far to drive and where to turn. On the way home the wipers came on automatically when it started to rain.

George was already home from the hospital. He took Dad and me downstairs where he had a room full of model trains. There were passenger trains, freight trains, steam and diesel locomotives, high wooden trestles and tunnels, just like the real ones we'd seen while driving through the mountains. George handed me a controller and showed me how to operate it.

We could hear Mom and Uncle Rolly talking upstairs. When it sounded like they were arguing, George closed the door. It was almost suppertime when his phone buzzed. Two transit buses had collided and he was needed at the hospital. Dad and I went upstairs. Mom and Uncle Rolly were sitting across from each other on the white love seats. Mom was holding her Bible. The booklets she'd brought were scattered across the glass coffee table.

"Earl, I think you should have a word with your brother-in-law," Mom said.

"What about?" Dad pulled at his mustache like he always did when he was nervous.

"About his lifestyle."

"Do you think this is the time and place for that?" Dad nodded in my direction.

"Bob might as well hear the truth about his uncle."

Dad sat down beside Mom. "I'm not sure I have anything to say. Rolly's an adult. He's old enough to decide how to live his own life."

"Oh Earl, you're no help." Mom snapped her Bible shut, gathered up the booklets, and stuffed them back into the cloth bag.

"I bet someone's hungry," Uncle Rolly said, getting up. "Playing with trains always makes young men hungry."

"Can we eat at *The Boathouse* again?"

"Don't be rude," Mom said. "Uncle Rolly treated us last night. He won't be wanting to take us out again. We can eat at home."

"No, I've got another place in mind," Uncle Rolly said.

"We don't have to go out to eat all the time," Mom said. "I can help you make supper if you show me where things are."

"I think I'd rather go out," Uncle Rolly said. "It's been a tiring afternoon. You'll like *The Roadhouse Grille*. It has lots of cool stuff."

We got into the Caddie again and Uncle Rolly gave me the address to enter into the GPS. *The Roadhouse Grille* was up the hill, and Uncle Rolly was right about it being a cool place. One room was full of chrome kitchen tables and chairs, just like my grandma had in her kitchen, and there were pictures of old cars and movie stars on the walls. I ordered chicken fingers.

While we ate Mom hardly said anything at all. Uncle Rolly asked Dad about some of his old school chums. Dad told him Geordie Tibbs had lost a leg when he tripped over the dog, lost his balance, and got tangled in the grain auger. Maureen Ralston was killed right in front of her husband when the tractor flipped while she was trying to pull the grain truck out of the swamp. Sammy Rockerbie lost three of his best milk cows when they went belly-up in a drainage ditch.

"What about Joey Simms? How is he getting along?" Uncle Rolly asked.

"Last we heard he was in Toronto," Dad said. "I don't think he comes home to the farm very often."

While waiting for our dessert, apple pie and ice cream, Mom reached into her purse and pulled out one of her booklets. She handed it to Uncle Rolly. "I know we don't agree on everything," she said, "and that you don't want to hear my views, but for my sake, for your own soul's sake, please read this one."

Uncle Rolly read out the title. "*Going Straight: Healing the Homosexual.*" He swallowed, cleared his throat, handed the booklet back to Mom. "I know you mean well, Sis, but haven't you heard that sexual orientation can't be changed? Those programs that claim to change gay people are all going belly-up in the ditch, just like Sammy Rockerbie's milk cows."

"Jesus can change anything."

"True, but guys like me and George don't seem to be on his radar screen."

"Apostle Hewbell says—"

"Sis, it doesn't matter what anyone says. Just like you, I went to Sunday School—"

"Exactly," Mom said, "so why are you living this evil lifestyle? Is it George's fault? Has that wicked man got an evil hold on you?"

"George is not wicked, and he has nothing to do with it. I was this way long before I met George. Don't you remember that last summer at home, the summer you caught Joey Simms and me—"

"Of course I remember. Do you think I can ever erase the image of that…that filthy thing you and Joey were doing when I walked into the henhouse to collect the eggs? But you were kids then, teenagers. We do foolish things at that age, but we grow up. We remember what we learned in Sunday School and we—"

"And that's what I was trying to say when you interrupted me," Uncle Rolly said. "I remember those Sunday School stories. What I don't remember is Jesus getting his shorts in a knot over sex. Selfishness, pride, and especially those who set themselves up to judge others were his targets."

"Are you accusing me of judging you?"

"Not accusing. Just stating a fact."

"Better that I judge you now, than have God judge you and fling you into hellfire. Do you think I can ever be happy in heaven knowing my little brother is roasting in the fiery pit?" Mom reached into her purse for a paper tissue.

"That whole hellfire thing is pagan mythology," Uncle Rolly said. "I may be a lowly carpenter who doesn't go to church every week, like you do, but I read. I know a fistful of lies have been taught in the name of religion."

The waitress came with the bill. While Dad and Uncle Rolly wrestled over who would pay it, Mom, her lips pressed tightly together, dabbed at her eyes and tucked the booklet back into her purse.

When we got outside raindrops as big as marbles were bouncing off the Caddie's roof. Uncle Rolly had to drive slowly through the big puddles.

"Rolly, I apologize for getting angry when you won't listen to reason," Mom said, "but you do understand, don't you?"

"I understand that you're worried about my soul, but I don't see things quite the same as you. Can't we agree to disagree?"

"How can I agree to disagree when my baby brother is going to roast in hell?" Mom wiped her eyes and blew her nose. "You've got to give up that wicked man. Just kick George out of your life. Tell him to go away."

"I'm not going to split with George. We designed and built our house together, but more than that, what you don't seem to understand Audrey, is that we love each other. We love each other

116

just as much as you and Earl love each other. We're not going to trash eleven happy years together."

"Hellfire will last a lot longer than eleven years." Mom had to shout to be heard above the pounding of the rain on the Caddie's roof, and the wop-wop-wop of the wipers.

"Watch the red light!" Dad shouted from the back seat. The Caddie's hood dived towards the street as Uncle Rolly stamped on the brake pedal. "Audrey, you'd better drop it. You'll distract Rolly and get us all killed. Besides, can't you see that Rolly and George love each other?"

"It's not love. It's lust, sinful lust." Mom began to sniffle. The traffic light turned green. Uncle Rolly started down Oxford Street. The water was cascading down the road like we were on a water slide. Uncle Rolly was leaning forward, trying to see where he was going.

Mom started in again. "Don't try to shut me up, Earl. It's my Christian duty to speak plainly to my little brother. He's got to realize—"

There was a loud crash. Mom screamed as the Caddie swung sideways. The front end bounced up, then crashed down hard. The engine revved but we weren't moving.

Uncle Rolly lowered his window and stuck his head out, trying to see what he'd hit. Dad jumped out and ran around to the front. "You've beached the car," he shouted. "It's hung up on the median. The drive wheels are off the ground. Put it out of gear."

"Look what you've done now," Mom said. "We'll all be killed if this car tips over and rolls down the hill."

"Then you'd better get out," Uncle Rolly said.

"Oh Rolly, my dear baby brother, if this isn't a warning from God, I don't know what is."

Uncle Rolly pulled his phone from his pocket and called for a tow truck, while Dad stood in the rain, waving other cars by. Mom and I got out. There was no sidewalk. We stumbled into someone's flowerbed. Mom lost her balance and fell forward, plunging her hands into the muck. I helped her up and onto someone's driveway.

A man wearing only a pair of red boxer shorts ran out of the house. After finding out what had happened, he gave Dad a flashlight and a yellow raincoat, and invited Mom and me to take shelter in his garage while we waited for the tow truck to arrive. He grabbed a rag out of a box and handed it to Mom to wipe off her hands. While we were standing there another man, wearing a blue bathrobe and flip-flops, and drying his hair with a towel, came out. "What's going on?" he asked, putting a hand on the other man's shoulder.

"Fellow got hung up on the median. These folks are from the car. I guess we should introduce ourselves. I'm Ivan and this is my husband Jeff."

Mom took a step back. "I'm...I'm Audrey. This is my son Bob. That's *my husband* Earl. He's directing traffic, and my brother Rolly's in the car."

"How did it happen?"

"I don't know. We were going along perfectly fine and suddenly there was a bang."

"Almost impossible to see in a storm like this," Jeff said. "Ah, there's the tow truck."

Uncle Rolly got out of the Caddie and talked to the truck driver. When he stepped onto the driveway to let the tow truck winch the Caddie off the median Ivan called him into the garage. "You're not gonna drive that car home tonight," he said. "You may have ripped the oil plug out. Where do you live?"

"West Beach Avenue."

"Not far. Let me drive you folks home."

By the time Ivan had driven us home and we'd all had hot showers and dried off, it was past my bedtime, but Uncle Rolly said we had to unwind after such an exciting evening. He turned on the gas fireplace and told us to sit down while he prepared Ovaltine. He said it would help us sleep. He was bringing in the mugs filled with the steaming, milky mixture when George arrived home from the hospital. He sat down on the loveseat beside Uncle Rolly.

"I've never performed so many surgeries in one evening," he said. "Broken arms, legs, fractured skulls— you name it, we had it."

"You must be tired," Uncle Rolly said, patting George's knee.

"More like terminally exhausted." George stretched and rubbed the back of his neck.

"You need a massage, Love." Uncle Rolly got up, walked around behind the loveseat, and began massaging George's neck and shoulders. I'd never had a massage, but seeing the way George closed his eyes, and smiled, and went all loose like my dog Rover does when I scratch his belly, I wanted to ask Uncle Rolly to give me a massage. I didn't dare ask though. I saw Mom giving Dad a sour look. As soon as we'd finished our mugs of Ovaltine we all went to bed. Before falling asleep I heard Mom and Dad talking in the next room.

"We've wasted our time," Mom said. "The town's full of them. That Ivan is living with a man, both of them standing out there half naked, touching each other, and calling each other *husband*. This place is worse than Sodom."

"How can you say that when the man was good enough to give you shelter, lend me his flashlight and raincoat, and then drive the whole lot of us home?"

"That doesn't make things right. And you saw the way Rolly was stroking George just now, right in front of us, in front of Bob. He's completely besotted with the man, ready to be burned in hellfire with the rest of the perverts."

"Audrey, whatever happened to the Jesus who said he didn't come to condemn the world? Have you forgotten about him?"

The next day George didn't have to work until the afternoon, so we all had breakfast together. George made pancakes and Uncle Rolly fried eggs and hash browns. Then we went downstairs to pack our suitcases. When we came back upstairs George was standing by the front door.

"Any word on the car?" Dad asked.

"I called the garage a few minutes ago. There's a dent in the oil pan, and they're doing a front end alignment. It'll be ready by ten o'clock."

"Where are my shoes?" Mom asked. "Didn't I leave them by the door last night?"

"Rolly's giving them a wipe-down in the bathtub."

"He's doing what?" Mom ran down the hallway. I followed her. "Rolly, you're not cleaning my shoes, are you?" Uncle Rolly was down on his knees, sponging off Mom's white sneakers. Mine were already cleaned and sitting on the edge of the tub.

"I'm afraid they'll never be completely white again," he said, holding them up for Mom's inspection, "but they look a lot better than they did a few minutes ago."

"Rolly! I can't let you do this."

"Why not?"

Mom's voice went all funny and she started to blub like the Kindergarten kids do when they get hit by the dodge ball. "My baby brother, how can you wash *my* filthy shoes after I've treated you so...so wickedly?" She knelt down and put both arms around Uncle Rolly. "Can you forgive me? Can you ever forgive your big, wicked sister?"

A few minutes later, when we had our shoes on and we'd said good-bye, and there didn't seem to be anything more to say, everybody hugged everyone else. Mom even hugged and kissed George on the cheek. As we walked down the steps she was crying so hard Dad had to take her by the hand so she wouldn't stumble and fall. By the time we were driving up the steep hill where Uncle Rolly had beached the car, she had dried her eyes enough to ask Dad to drive real slow past Ivan and Jeff's place.

"What now?" Dad asked. "You're not going to drop those Tabber booklets in their mailbox, are you?"

"I'm going to write down their address, and then you're going to stop at a florist's shop. I'm going to buy two bouquets of red roses, one for Ivan and Jeff, the other for Rolly and George."

"Is that necessary?"

"Didn't you hear what Rolly did?" Mom blubbed. "He washed my shoes. If you could have seen him down on his knees in that bathroom you'd know how I feel. He was washing my muddy shoes, just like Jesus washed the disciples' feet. I feel so ashamed of myself."

Back home I couldn't wait to show Billy the picture of me piloting the boat. He thought it was cool, and then I told him about the tiny cabin on *Forever Mates*, the Caddie with GPS, and how Uncle Rolly and George lived in a house with a room full of electric trains. I told him if we worked hard in school and graduated we could maybe move to the coast and live in a big house overlooking the ocean. We might even have a boat and a Caddie. He said that'd be real cool.

On Sunday morning as we drove to church in Twin Meadows, Mom said, "Earl, don't bother dropping me off at the Tabernacle. I'll come to church with you today. I don't think that loud music is healthy. Sometimes the drums hurt my ears and I can feel their pounding inside my chest. I'm afraid all that noise may damage my heart."

Therapissed

Never had one of these recordin' machines shoved in my face before, but 'parently I gotta record my thoughts. Therapissed says it's part of the therapee, though I don't know whose gonna listen to this cruddy crap. I was never good at fancy things in high school like poetry and public speakin'. No matter. My little faggot bro challenged me to this 'speriment, so here goes. If you got nothin' better to do, go ahead, give this a listen.

My name's Richard Mercury but youse can call me Dick. And quit yer laughin' cause my name's got no double meanin', though if you was to ask my Georgina 'bout that, she'd say she got no complaints in that department, if you knows what I'm meanin'.

First off, I want youse all to know I'm totally male, elfa male I think its called, and I'm straight, like totally one hundred percent straight, just to get that off my chest, like up front. For every single one of my thirty-one years it's been women for me all the way, and I mean *all* the way. I think youse got the picture, though if not, I'm not sayin' nothin' more 'cause I ain't one of 'em exhibitors like to walk around naked or spell everythin' out. I'm totally for women, and hope youse got that straight.

Like I already mentioned, Georgina's my principal one and only squeeze, and I'm tellin' you from the first word get-go, I ain't tradin' her in on any guy, no matter how this crazy 'speriment goes. I'm a man's man, into huntin' and fishin', watchin' real sports like hockey, and baseball, and football, though I got my questions 'bout that there last one—not sure I'm into men crouchin' in a tight huddle with their arms 'round other sweaty guys whose moldy socks stink so's to scare a skunk—and all that butt pattin'. Somethin' a bit queer 'bout that I'd say.

So to cut the crap, my little faggot bro, four years younger 'n me, flunked outa this program my old man forced him to attend when he come blazin' outa the closet last year. Little Bro says there's no therapissed can change him inta a lady-chasin' normal dude. I say he just didn't try hard enough, put enough sweat into it, like I do when huntin' them bears and moose up in the northern bush country. If Little Bro had put out like I do up there in them woods he'd be married to some hot chick by now, with half a dozen young'uns crawlin' over his feet.

We was sittin' round the Xmas dinner, demolishin' Mommsie's turkey and fixins. We was tellin' Little Bro he was a wimp and a lazy bones quitter for failin' the therapee. He batted his big eyelashes across the table at me and said, "Kay Big Bro, if changin' yer sexyule nature is so easy, let's see you do it."

I said, "You got yerself a deal, little faggot bro."

Big Daddy almost choked on the turkey leg he was strippin' the meat offa. "No way I'm losin' both my sons to fairydom," he said. But after us three argued like drunken football fanatics, Big Daddy agreed to fork over another five thousan' big ones for six months' therapee for me. Don't that just prove, that like me, he's willin' to step over the line, outa his comfort zone so to speak, to save my little bro from all that rainbow flag wavin' and pansy-assed stuff?

If this therapee thing works, and I knows it will, then Little Bro will have to give it another try. I'm gonna prove changin' my sexyule nature is easy as changin' oil in one of them big rigs I maintain down at the shop.

So, here goes. Fasten yer seatbelts if yer listenin' to this crud.

January, 2015: Georgina cryin' when I went to the therapissed this evenin' after wrenchin' all day. She hugged me tight, not wantin' her man to change, and she can hug real good, bein' the spittin' image of Dolly Parton, if you get my meanin' and I knows I don't need to 'splain nothin' 'bout that.

I told her not to worry. If I can change into a Nancy boy I can change back, and anyways, the risk is worth it if I can show my little bro repair-type therapee works. Whole family keen to see Little Bro walkin' down the aisle with a fine chick on his arm, not some precious dude with blush on his cheeks, gelled hair and his dainty feets skippin' along in Brockenstocks. 'Sides, my three young-uns need some cousins to play with before they's all growed up.

Got to therapissed at seven. He's a runt of a man with wee hairy hands like a squirrel. Gives me the creeps. Wouldn't be able to defend his own nuts on a football field, never mind grab the pigskin. Has me lie down on this couch that squeaks and stinks like rats is nestin' inside it. We got them filthy vermin in the shop, always tryin' to sneak into them big rigs. You see, they've got a taste for the nuts, chips and burger crumbs the drivers drop when chawin' on the road. I says nothin' to the wee therapissed 'bout the stench. Don't want to get off on the wrong foot, so to speak.

Wee fella starts askin' me 'bout when I was a kid—like how'd I get along with my old man and Mommsie. What bloody nonsense! At the end of two hours he's dancin' up and down, says he's figured out I'm straight coz my old man was 'round too much, always showin' me how to repack bearin's on the truck, how to manhandle a chainsaw, stuff like that. He says, "Easy. I can turn you into a flaming, limp-wristed Nancy boy in six months flat, carbon copy of your little bro."

I think we're done for the night when he hands me a black dress and high heeled shoes and tells me to smuggle these into the house when my Georgina ain't lookin'. Two, three times on the weekend, when she's at work slingin' hash down at the café, he wants me to sneak into our bedroom and try them on, stand in front of the mirror and get off on myself. Sounds crazy to me. Never saw little bro dressin' up in Mommsie's things, but therapissed says it'll bring out the fem in me. Still think it's stupid, but anythin' to prove to my little bro this stuff works.

February, 2015: New month so therapissed has me change into a red blouse and black skirt when I get to his office. Wants to help me pull the silk stockings up, but I tells him to keep his distance. Couldn't stand to have his hairy wee paws approachin' anywheres near the family jewels, if you get my meanin'. Silk feels kinda good on my legs, though I'm not tellin' Georgina that.

Second week added string of pearls and diamond earrin's while I lie on his ratty couch. The earrin's are the clip-on type—they hurt my ears—relief like takin' off skates when I'm allowed to remove them. Don't mind the lip gloss and blush so much. Washes off easier'n truck grease.

Growin' my hair longer now—fussed with it this week, but still too short—says I gotta get it long enough to wear in a pompadoor. Didn't have a clue what he meant until I got home, checked it out on the 'puter. Looks like a big pile of hair likely to get caught in the fanbelt when I'm under the hood revvin' one of them diesels in the shop.

Practiced walkin' in high heels 'round therapissed's office. I tells him I'm fed up prancin' 'round like a princess, 'specially since Little Bro and his fancy-assed boyfriend are now into army boots. Therapissed says heels'll help me develop poise and glamour. Tells me to say, "I'm a pretty boy. I'm a pretty boy," every time I look in the mirror. Like I needs to be a pretty boy when wrenchin' one of them Peterbilts that's clocked over a million miles.

Spent time in therapissed's kitchen, learnin' to cook gormay. Waste of time, so far as I can see. What's the point of spendin' six hours preparin' a meal that wouldn't keep a sparrow alive for more'n half a day. I'm no good around knives and bowls and mixers. Slicin' them veg into tiny pieces ain't for me—bloody cut myself six times. Torkin' lug nuts on a Mack truck is easier than makin' ant-sized food. How do gay dudes survive if this is how they have to live?

March, 2015: My hair long enough for pig tails. Georgina's jealous of such luckshureus hair—that's what she calls it, luckshureus. Feels good when she brushes it every night. Love the way it shines reddish in the light.

Therapissed took me shoppin'. Says I can't be a fancy boy without knowing how to shop. Spent all evening in the mall. Looked at Spode, Wedgewood and Royal Albert. Don't like flowery things but pretended I did. Bought porcelain figurine: lady in a pink dress, like the one therapissed has me wearin' on the couch this month.

Shopped for clothes after studyin' GQ magazine. Bought three shirts—pastel pink, buttercup and lime—and two pair them skinny Chinos: olive and vibrant red. Prefer myself in buttercup shirt and red pants. Georgina's gonna get matchin' colours so we look like a couple when we go out.

April, 2015: This month the wee therapissed started showin' me pictures of furniture and fancy-assed rooms. He's teachin' me to speak Victorian, Edwardian and Chippendale.

Teachin' me 'bout them long-haired, fancy-assed musicians too. Sent me home with a CD I'm 'sposed to listen to an hour a day—them big name, dead composers like Bach and Mozart. With hockey playoffs on the tube every night not much time, so turn down the TV's sound and listen to fairy music durin' game—Bach works best with the back and forth of the skatin'. Beethoven terrible: too slow and mournful—won't listen to him no more, least not durin' hockey season.

Learnin' to sew. By end of month therapissed says my apron is best he's seen, even though I had to rip it apart six times. Says I got the lingo down pat too: yard goods, bastin', seam, bobbin. Makin' a lavender shirt to go with my vibrant red chinos.

May, 2015: Called Georgina *George* this mornin' when kissin' her good-bye as I left for the shop. She cried. Told her the 'speriment will be over soon as I prove I've changed. I'm still me inside even if I like wearin' buttercup and lime shirts. Picked up dye at Wal-Mart after work—dyin' white coveralls buttercup. Looks good with a pink baseball cap.

Therapissed wants me to carry my tools in a purse. Not sure 'bout that, though guys at shop pleased I'm tryin' to save Little Bro. Bought a red, leather purse—will be easy to find on the workbench.

Worked on baseball this month—learnin' to throw and bat like a wimp. Therapissed says to think of swattin' a fly when battin', and tossin' a weddin' bouquet when throwin'. Hard to do, but I'm gettin' hang of it. Little Bro coaches me weekends. Teachin' me how to cover my head with my glove and run away screamin' my brains out when he hits a fly ball. Used to play center field in high school. Loved snatchin' them flies outa the sky, so not easy retraining.

June, 2015: Therapith teachin' me to lithp—not ath eethy ath I thought but I'm gettin' the hang of it. Today I yelled at apprentith to hand me tranthmithon fluid—he laughed, everyone at thop lithpin' now. Big joke.

Lyin' on the couch. Therapith showin' me pictures of naked men while listenin' to fancy ath music. The sight of naked men makes me thick, so focuth on faythes. Some pretty boithes, but feel nothin'. Pretend to be excited by thinkin' 'bout Georgina. Therapith imprethed with my progreth. Theth he'll make a pretty boy outa me yet.

June 30, 2015: Last night of therapee. Went on field trip to gay leather bar with therapissed. Must have slaughtered a feedlot of bulls to clothe the pack of men inside that sweatshop.

Only couple women in the whole place. I caught sight of a nice lookin' number in the far corner—big, shiny blond wearin' blood-red dress with sequins. I knows women and can tell when they're givin' me the eye. The moment that bombshell waved her elbow-length, white gloves at me I forgot all about my therapee. I pushed my way through the crowd of sweatin' guys, tryin' to get to her.

Youse might be thinkin' I was cheatin' on my Georgina, but no way. Would never do that. Just thought talkin' to some dame would be better'n yakkin' at a buzz-headed guy who's all trussed up like a turkey ready for the oven.

Only one problem: when I got close enough to focus through the beer fumes I noticed somethin' queer 'bout that blond bombshell. She was a he, old as my daddy, five o'clock shadow though he'd tried to cover it up with makeup, thick like drywall mud.

I turned away, pretended I was goin' to the head, and when I come outa there I made sure I kept my back to her, started yakkin' to a young buck wearin' enough leather harness to pull a stagecoach—gave me his phone number, wants me to call—told him I would, but won't. Told therapissed I was plum done in, exhausted from all that therapee and just wanted to get home. All I could think of was how I was wantin' to shower the stink of leather off me, then get naked with Georgina.

Guess that means the therapissed has failed to change me, just like he failed with my little bro. Only one thing to do—me and everyone else in the family gotta cut Little Bro some slack, let him have his fancy shirts, his loddy-daw music, his dainty food, and his pretty-faced boyfriend. Won't be easy, Mommsie bawlin' her eyes out every night for more grandkids, and me wantin' cousins for my wee ones to play with.

Still, may all work out. Little Bro says when he and pretty-boy get married they'll have kids. Can't think how they'll manage that but 'parrently there's ways, though it's not somethin' I'm hankerin' to think about anytime soon.

Even though the 'speriment failed I learnt a thing or two. Georgina wants the rec room spruced up. I suggested buttercup and lime walls with pastel pink drapes. Sears is havin' a sale on yard goods so I can save a bundle by runnin' up my own curtains. Think Hudson's Bay has a sale on Spode china—saw a tea set that'll match the curtains.

As for me, I'm lookin' forward to watchin' golf on The Sports Channel without them fairy tunes tinklin' in my ears. I'll probably keep my pastel shirts and Chinos—Georgina says I look hot with a bit of style. Now that I'm puttin' on a few pounds, that can't be a bad thing. Gonna keep my buttercup coveralls for work too. That way my lazy-assed 'prentice won't be grabbin' mine instead of his own all the time.

One of the Men

Sunday, February 3, 2008 will be forever engraved in sweat on the pages of my journal, for that was the day I became a real man. It was the day I watched the Super Bowl with the guys. It took me several decades to morph into a real guy, but I can honestly state that it was worth the wait.

My only regret was that Dad couldn't have been there to see me attain manhood. He would have been so pleased. He might even have stepped forward and proudly owned up to being my father, though the queer thing is that he was the one who inoculated me against sports.

On Saturday nights when my two brothers wanted to watch Hockey Night in Canada, Dad gave in grudgingly. Throughout his life he worked hard, clawing a living for his family out of the prairie dust, and so he found the sight of grown men being paid to chase a rubber disk around an ice rink an insult to those who knew what real work was. He heaped his greatest scorn upon the sportscasters who sat behind their mahogany desks and dissected the game as though it really mattered. I absorbed a good bit of his disdain.

It didn't help that during my school years I was small for my age, skinny as a scrub oak, not likely to stand tall in a prairie windstorm or on a football line of scrimmage. Throughout my school years the faintest whiff of testosterone-tainted sports intimidated me. It wasn't that I didn't like to play games. In grade school I was popular with the girls who played dodge ball. They liked me because I didn't fling the ball hard enough to make them cry. When indoor recess was the rule during the frigid prairie winters, I did pretty well at ping pong.

High school catapulted me, still an elfin-like skeleton, into a physical education class of fleshy football jocks bearing stout names like Lavallee and Thorleifson. Even Coach Harris was unsure what to do with me. Often he assigned me to swabbing down mats in a far corner of the gym while the rest of the guys played with their balls.

My one moment of glory during those four hellish years of high school was the night I played second violin in the school orchestra. I had been fighting a head cold and Dad thought I should stay home, but I was determined to display my musical talent. (Today I wonder if the real reason Dad wanted me to stay home was so that he wouldn't have to be seen with such a lame excuse for a son.) All went well until the middle of Offenbach's *Gaite Parisienne* when my tender nose began to bleed. I dashed off stage, great red blots of blood fouling my white shirt. My only comfort was that Lavallee and Thorleifson were not there to witness my humiliation.

Once living on my own, I confined my leisure-time activities to admiring art and playing the pipe organ. Those pursuits kept me out of trouble so long as I lived in the city, but upon moving to the Comox Valley on Vancouver Island, where the arts community was slenderer than I was used to, it was only natural that I would adopt more manly pastimes.

The truth was that I had always wanted to be one of the boys. I secretly wished that I could be a star on the football field or the basketball court, feted by the cheerleaders and called up on the stage on graduation day to thunderous applause. I admired, dare I say worshiped, the rough men-in-the-making who swaggered about the locker room, chewing gum like their lives depended upon it, and leaving their smelly underwear in a heap on the floor for the janitor to pick up. My admiration was carried out on the sly and after my high school failures, I was afraid to enter the arena of manly sports, even as a spectator.

Upon moving to the valley, I struck up an acquaintance with a guy who had played football in high school. Rodrick proudly wore a long white scar down his left shin, evidence of where the broken bone stuck out after he was tackled. For some unknown reason I didn't find his sports talk threatening, and he didn't find my lack of knowledge disgusting. Rodrick and I swam, cycled and hiked together.

Then the momentous day of the Super Bowl approached. I knew some great event was imminent because for weeks Rodrick was inseparable from his New York Giants baseball cap, even during our most intimate moments. He constantly studied the newspapers to determine yards ran and touchdowns touched. A week before the big game he prepared me for mingling with the football fellows by having me repeat seasonal standings and names of football greats like Tom Baker, or was it Brady? I know it was something that started with a "B" because it reminded me of my first violin teacher, Frank Bader. Another player was Manning. I think both he and Baker were quarterbacks, or running backs, guys who manhandled the football when they got hold of it, the sort of guys I had envied in high school: extremely macho in their grass-stained jerseys and foul-smelling shoes.

I was nervous when the big day arrived. Rodrick had decided that we would make my initiation a celebration. He asked where I wanted to go to watch the game, but I wasn't much help because since moving to the valley the only place I had been was the Sid Williams Theatre to watch Sarah Hagen, a classical pianist, weave together a few of Bach's *Three Part Inventions*. Rodrick finally gave me a choice between the Whistle Stop Pub and the Elks Hall, where a Super Bowl party was advertised. Since as a righteous little Christian boy I had signed the temperance pledge at age nine to never touch or taste alcohol, I opted for the Elks Hall.

Rodrick was disappointed when he saw the sign on the door reading, *Absolutely no hats*, and he would have headed to the pub, except I told him it was almost three o'clock, time for the face off. He yanked off his hat and shoved it into his rear pocket.

I had never been inside an Elk's hall before so I was disappointed not to see the walls decorated with rifles, stuffed elk heads and racks of polished antlers. We had to sign our names in a large book on a table beside a notice board listing titles like Grand Exalted Ruler and Supreme Honoured Royal Lady. I wondered whether I should rush home and exchange my torn jeans and red flannel shirt for my blue and white regalia from the Royal Canadian College of Organists, but I saw that no one else was wearing ceremonial robes.

The room was gloomy—six rows of black-topped arborite tables were lit by three-globe chandeliers, some of the bulbs burned out. The brightest spot was a bar at the back. Apparently it was a sin for the Elks to wear hats, but they could drink until they didn't know which end of the gun to load. Perhaps that explained the lack of stuffed trophies on the walls. Rodrick led me to the bar where he ordered a Coke, me a diet Pepsi, which I realized, too late, wasn't very macho, but I'm sensitive to sugar—the sight of an *After Eight* mint gives me mouth ulcers.

I'd expected a colossal crowd of thick-necked men, but there were only a few milling about, all rather run-down and tired looking, like cattle after a long, cold winter. Rodrick didn't know any of them, which was a relief, because if he'd introduced me to someone who expected me to say something meaningful about the game, I'd probably have embarrassed him by blurting out, "Rocket Richard's been having a pretty good season, eh!" The Rocket's name is one of the few I remember my brothers getting excited about, though I think he was a hockey player, and he may even be dead by now, so mentioning his name would have interfered with my acceptance as one of the good old boys.

As we sat down, the pre-game show was on. It was mostly advertising with a few minutes allotted to two guys talking about Baker's ankle injury. Apparently he had twisted it, and even though it had looked pretty good during practice, they wanted to create a bit of tension by speculating on whether or not it would hold up throughout the game. I noticed that both commentators had almost too-perfect make-up jobs, like they'd stuck their faces in a spray booth operated by robots. I didn't say anything to Rodrick, of course, but I thought they looked like a couple of sissies who were probably wearing pink pantyhose beneath their carefully pressed grey slacks. I had expected them to be retired jocks, hunched over from old injuries, their tongues sticky with phlegm. But as these sleek excuses for men tossed glib words back and forth and ran this way and that with their senseless ideas, I thought I could hear Dad guffawing from inside his coffin.

At the table across from us sat a rather distinguished-looking older couple, she with clacking knitting needles, her blue rinse hair all screwed up on the back of her head like Queen Mary wore when launching her namesake ship in 1934. I wondered if she might be the Supreme Honoured Royal Lady and got ready to curtsy should she nod in my direction.

The man, whom I assumed was her husband, wore a lightly checked sports jacket, grey flannel trousers and what looked like a private school tie. Perhaps he had once played some wildly competitive game for Princeton or Harvard. With this couple was a rather loud woman, perhaps their wayward daughter, with mouse brown hair that stuck out as though she'd come to the party fresh from her electro-shock therapy.

The game started and all went well until the second quarter when a large, sloppily constructed man came bumbling our way and plopped into a chair behind me. I could smell his mouthwash as he leaned forward and inquired about the score. Afraid that I would say the wrong thing and reveal that I was an imposter at the afternoon's festivities, I kept my mouth shut and my eyes on the screen. Fortunately Rodrick knew what he was talking about and replied with some information about the score, or touchdowns, or field goals, or maybe all three. After a few more comments the rumpled fellow lumbered back to the bar and I could breathe easier again.

At half time the bartender announced that hot dogs, chips and pretzels were available, so we got up and ambled over to the counter with everyone else. Beside a stack of shiny brown buns sat a tin bucket half filled with steaming water. In it a dozen scorched wieners, looking like ancient carp, swam around lethargically. Being a vegan, I left those for Rodrick and the other carnivores, and settled for a few corn chips, a couple of pretzels and a regular ginger ale so the bartender would know I was a regular guy.

Rodrick was getting pretty antsy towards the end of the game, hootin' and hollerin' at his beloved New York Giants who didn't seem to hear a word he said. I tried to calm him down by pointing out that there were still ten minutes left in the game, and things could change rapidly. I was surprised when he agreed with me and sat back down.

His agreement brought on the same feeling I experienced one hot summer afternoon when I was a teen. My cousin and I were performing pirouettes with his '52 Chevrolet out in the middle of the south quarter, when the engine died. I told him it was probably vapour lock, and to my own amazement, I was right. I still don't know what vapour lock is, but it was one of those moments that builds camaraderie among men, and I'd just experienced another one with Rodrick by advising him that the score could change in favour of the Giants. Was it really that easy to be one of the men?

And wouldn't you know it, the game did turn around, though I missed it because about five minutes before the end I had to make an emergency trip to the Men's Room. I was standing at the urinal when the door burst open and a little stud in a yellow jacket came bounding in. He undid his zipper and roared, "Big bruisin' bastard."

I couldn't think what to say. Whom or what was he talking about? New England, New York, or a part of his own body? Or was he referring to me? Had something tipped him off that I wasn't a true sports fiend? Had he followed me into the restroom to give me a bruisin' for pretending to be one of the men? I was saved by the door opening, His buddy rolled up to the next urinal and unzipped his fly. From their muttered grunts and groans I gathered that the New England quarter round had bungled in some unforgivable way.

When I exited the restroom Rodrick and the electro lady were jumping up and down and pounding the table. Rodrick hugged me, slapped me on the back, then grabbed his lucky cap and threw it in the air. If we'd been at a Sarah Hagen concert I'd have tried to shut him up, but since I was with the guys I let it pass, though I felt rather awkward because I had missed the final goal. I'd paused in the hallway to study the list of titles on the bulletin board, wondering whether a Supreme Honoured Royal Lady would be demoted to a Supreme Dishonoured Royal Lady if she burned the coffee or something.

I thought we'd all mingle after the game, regurgitating it play by agonizing play, but no, everyone grabbed their caps and melted away into the evening gloom. The real thrill came the next day when the guys in the locker room at the gym where I do lite aerobics started yakking about the game. For the first time in my life I was able to chime in with an intelligent comment.

"Yeah, that was some game, eh? So close right up to the end. I thought for sure New England was going to wallop New Brunswick. One more home run and they'd have carried off the trophy."

Something

Things are tidy by the time Rodger arrives at the Greenfield airport. His sister, Margie, is there to meet him. On the way to the hospital she describes their father's collapse at her Thanksgiving table.

"He was just handing me his plate, asking for a second slice of roast turkey," Margie says, "when he got this funny look in his eyes, like he was worried about something. He fumbled his plate and grabbed onto his head with both hands."

"What did you do?"

"We dropped everything and raced to Emergency. He was still coherent when we got there. The doctor tried to dissolve the blood clot but it backfired, caused a bleed."

"But he's still alive?"

"Yes, though I don't know if he's conscious."

The walls in the palliative care unit are painted in soothing earth tones. Their father is lying beneath a white sheet stamped *Property of Greenfield Hospital*.

Rodger thinks his father looks smaller than the last time he saw him, his body barely a whisper beneath the sheet, except for his head, which appears unnaturally large. Has his father always had a large head or has the bleed caused swelling? With the big head and thin body, Rodger thinks his father looks like a ventriloquist's dummy. This one is lying helpless on its side, as though flung onto a shelf and half covered with a dust sheet to await its next performance. A bristly, white stubble covers the chin and cheeks. The right eye is closed while the left is half open as though observing them on the sly.

Margie steps over to the bed, bends down and kisses the dummy's forehead. "Rodger's here," she says. She steps back and moves around to the far side of the bed. "I think he can hear us," she says, "and maybe even see us out of that left eye, though the doctor said the bleed was so massive that the brain may hardly be functioning."

Rodger stands with his hands in the pockets of his black, leather jacket, his mind replaying snippets from *Hallmark* television movies. In those stories the sons always run to their fathers' sickbeds, enfold them in their arms and cry out that they love them.

"You can take his hand," Margie says. "He may know it's you."

Rodger nods his head but keeps his hands in his pockets. He doesn't know how to take his father's hand, or what to say. He's grateful when Margie doesn't insist, and after standing for a moment, they sit down on opposite sides of the bed.

> *Rodger is four years old, mooning about the house by himself because Margie has started school. He hears the truck keys rattling as his father grabs them from the hook just inside the kitchen door. "Are you going out, Daddy?"*
>
> *"Off to town for the mail and to pick up some chicken feed."*
>
> *"Can I come with you, Daddy? Can I come?"*
>
> *"I don't care." His father hurries out the door and before Rodger can search out his rubber boots from the back of the closet, he hears the pickup's engine start. A moment later he stumbles out the door, his boots only half on and flapping about like chickens with their heads cut off. A dust cloud is all*

that's left as the truck rockets down the gravel driveway.

"His face is getting stubbly," Margie says, running her fingers down their father's cheek. "I brought his electric razor from the house. Would you like to shave him?"

Rodger shakes his head. "No. No, you'd better do it. You're probably gentler than me, having had experience with your own boys, and the children at school."

Margie takes the razor from her purse. "Well, so far none of my kindergarten students have needed shaving," she laughs, "and our twins are old enough to shave themselves. In fact, we got electric razors for them for Christmas last year. I don't think Brent has used his yet. Did you never want children of your own, Rodger?"

"Shawn never wanted them," he says. "He's got jet fuel for blood, his father being a test pilot. He's a captain now, flying routes to Asia. Children would just get in his way."

"But what about you, Rodger?"

"With my long hours at the restaurant I'd be a pretty poor excuse for a father. Besides, I'd be afraid to even try."

"Afraid?"

"Afraid I might be just like him." Rodger nods towards the dummy under the sheet.

"He wasn't that bad, was he?"

"You have to remember, Margie, we had two different fathers. You could do no wrong, whereas I don't think I ever pleased him. Even when I graduated from culinary school and won that scholarship to study in Paris for a year, he wasn't pleased. I was an embarrassment to him. I'm sure he never bragged about me to his cronies, at least not like he did when you were crowned Prom Queen."

"I guess we're all made differently," Margie says, running her fingers gently over their father's face.

"You and me should have been switched around," Rodger says. "If you'd been the son, Dad would have been thrilled. You still help with farm chores?"

"The twins do most of that now, but afternoons when I'm not teaching I sometimes give a hand." Margie snaps the plastic cover over the razor and slips it into the drawer of the metal table beside the bed. "There, Dad, does that feel better?" Margie lifts their father's right hand, the one missing two fingers, and holds it against his cheek. "Can you feel your face, Dad? Can you feel how nice and smooth it is? You're all ready to go to town now."

The dummy makes no response. Roger wonders whether he's aware of Margie's companionable chatter. Can he feel his own face? Does he care that his two children are putting aside their own lives to sit at his bedside?

Rodger is nine years old. He's helping his mother chop green onions, peppers and tomatoes for an omelet. When finished, he arranges the diced vegetables in a swirl of colour on the cutting board.

"Look Mom," he says. "I've made a rainbow. See Mom? Can I keep it like this until Dad gets home?"

"It looks lovely, Rodger, but your father will probably be too tired to look at it. He's been working on the north quarter all day, didn't even come in for lunch, so he'll want supper on the table the moment he gets home. Is that the tractor I hear now?"

Rodger runs to the living room window. "Yes, it's him. Margie's opening the gate for him and he's driving into the yard. He'll be here in a minute, so can I keep my rainbow for him to see? Please, Mom. Can I?"

"Where's that bicycle your grandmother gave you for your birthday?" his mother asks. "You haven't left it lying on the yard somewhere, have you? You know how upset your father gets when he has to stop and move it out of the way."

140

*Tossing the knife into the kitchen sink, Rodger
dashes outside, banging the screen door behind
him. He races across the yard to the machine shed.
"Dad, stop! Please stop!"*

*His father stares straight ahead as he drives the
big John Deere tractor over Rodger's bike,
flattening the wheels and frame.*

Rodger shakes his head to clear the sense of betrayal he felt that long ago afternoon. Of course, it had been his fault. He had been told not to leave his bike lying around the yard where it could get in the way of farm machinery. He should have parked it safely in the lean-to behind the garage, but couldn't his father have punished him in some other way? Couldn't he have sent him to bed without dessert, without any supper at all? Couldn't he have locked the bike up for a week, or given him a paddling? Why couldn't his father have been more like Uncle Frank?

Rodger remembers being at Uncle Frank's for a sleepover with his cousin Jerry. They were about seven years old, building roads in the sandbox out behind the house when Uncle Frank came striding up from the barnyard.

"Jerry, did you carry water for the calves this afternoon?"

Rodger watched in fear as the colour drained out of Jerry's face. "No, Dad. I forgot."

"Well, you'll not forget again. Come here," and right there in front of Rodger, Uncle Frank had yanked Jerry's pants down and given him three hard smacks on his bare bottom. "Now, off with you to the well and fill the calves' trough."

Rodger had helped Jerry pump and carry pails of water to fill the calves' drinking trough, and when they'd gone into the house after dark Uncle Frank had asked, "Jerry, did you take water to the calves?"

"Yes, Dad."

"And did you wait until they'd finished drinking and then make sure their trough was filled for the night?"

"Yes, Dad. It was almost overflowing. Rodger helped me."

"Good boys." Uncle Frank stretched out his arms and hugged them both. "From now on you make sure to keep water in that trough. These hot summer days those calves could die of thirst if they run out of water. You need to top up their water several times a day."

The memory of Uncle Frank's hug brings tears to Rodger's eyes. What prevented his own father from touching him, hugging him, patting him on the head, like Uncle Frank was always doing?

Rodger is twelve years old. It's a warm spring evening. He's sitting on the verandah swing flipping through a new cookbook he has pestered the school librarian to add to the collection. Margie flounces out of the house to show him her new hairdo. She and Mom have been trying out new styles in preparation for Margie's first formal dance. "What do you think of my new hairstyle, Rodger? Think it will impress the guys?"

"It looks like a pile of horse shit," he says, not because he wants to hurt his sister, but because it really does look like a mound of thick brown rolls piled on top of her head.

"What's this about horse shit?" his father asks, coming around the corner of the house with a milk pail in each hand. He sets them down on the sidewalk, steps onto the verandah and clamps a rough leather glove around Rodger's skinny neck. "If it's horse shit you want, then come with me." He drags Rodger off the porch, around the corner of the house and down to the barnyard.

Margie runs after them. "Dad, he didn't mean it in a bad way. It's a really dumb looking hairstyle."

"If this boy wants horse shit, then it's horse shit he'll have." His father shoves Rodger to his knees and grinds his face into a pile of still steaming

*manure. "Maybe that will teach you to use filthy
language around your sister."*

The evening of the third day at the hospital, Cousin Jerry brings
his dad to visit. Pushing a walker, Uncle Frank shuffles into the
room. Rodger jumps up to offer his chair. Uncle Frank parks the
walker out of the way, then raises trembling arms for a hug.
"Rodger, my boy, haven't seen you since your mother's funeral.
How are you?"

"I'm okay, Uncle Frank. I'm okay," Rodger murmurs. "Thank
you for coming. Here, you can have my chair." He watches his
uncle fall silent as his watery blue eyes rest on his brother beneath
the sheet. He leans forward, lays one blue-veined hand over his
brother's hand, then takes it in both of his, turns it over like he's
examining a mango for ripeness in the supermarket. He runs a
finger over the scar where the fingers are missing.

"Lost those fingers in the new combine," he says, "the Massey
Harris. We hadn't used it a day when the feeder chain broke. Had
to run to town for repairs. When we got it mended I ran to the other
side and started the motor. I thought Jack was standing clear, but
he wasn't. He got this hand caught between the chain and the
sprocket. I feel guilty every time I look at these missing fingers,
how it put an end to your father's musical career."

"Musical career?" exclaims Rodger. "I knew Dad once played
the violin—it was up in the attic in a trunk with a bunch of old
newspapers—but I never heard that he had a musical career."

"Used to play at dances. That's where he met your mother. It
was at a dance in the Farmer's Institute Hall in Greenfield. He
called his band *The Rural Rhythm Pals*. One night your mother
came from the city to visit her cousin. Your dad couldn't take his
eyes off her."

"I remember Mother telling me that story," Margie says, "but
why would missing a couple of fingers have made Dad give up the
violin? It wasn't his left hand, the one he'd use for picking out the
notes."

"When we asked him about the violin he would just snort and say he couldn't spare the time, not with two children to feed and clothe," Rodger says.

Uncle Frank pats his brother's hand. "Your dad had a thing about deformities, about anything he thought weak or unnatural. It maybe had something to do with our sister, Bessie. You've both seen the little lamb tombstone in the cemetery?"

Margie and Rodger nod.

"Wee Bessie was born with what we called water on the brain. I suppose there's a better name for it nowadays. She only lived a few days after Mother and Father brought her home from the hospital. We boys were already in school, maybe first and second grade, and we were so excited about having a baby sister.

"What a shock we got when we saw her. She had a high, thin wail, like some frightened animal, and terrible convulsions. It was awful to see. When she had one of her spells, your father, just a tiny lad himself, would run out of the room.

"'Do something! Do something!' I can still hear him screaming those words from the next room, but there was nothing anyone could do. It was a blessing when the poor little thing died. Your dad never got over the loss of his sister, and he developed a phobia about anything that was deformed." Uncle Frank squeezes his brother's hand. The dummy makes no response.

"After the loss of his fingers, he seemed afraid that people would judge him, that they'd label him some sort of freak."

"But we see people with artificial limbs all the time today," Margie says, "and we think nothing of it. They just go on with life as best they can, some even running races in the Olympic Games and playing hockey."

"Which is what your father should have done," Uncle Frank says.

Rodger is fourteen years old, heading out to the barn to help his father with the morning milking. Opening the barn door he finds his father bent over a tin bucket. There are scratching, splashing

144

sounds, as though something is struggling to free itself.

"What are you doing, Dad?"

"Don't come near, Rodger. Just get on with your milking."

"No Dad. What are you doing?" A fear grows in Rodger's belly. Ignoring his father's order, he approaches, frightened to know what's happening, yet needing to see for himself. He can hear the little toenails scratching the bottom of the pail. He sees the furry, black bundle his father is holding under the water.

"Don't Dad. Please don't. I'll look after him."

"On with your milking, boy."

"But Dad, I'll look after him. I really will."

The previous day Rodger had arrived home from school to find Goldie, his golden retriever, nursing five pups. Four of them were perfectly formed, carbon copies of their mother. Rodger had been drawn to the fifth one, the runt of the litter, coal black with a white patch on its chest but only a paddle-like stump for its left hind leg.

"Please, Dad, don't drown him." Tears are flowing down Rodger's cheeks.

"It's for the best, boy. The others will pick on him. Get on with your milking so you're not late for the school bus."

"No! You can milk your own damn cows." Rodger dashes from the barn, holes up in his room for the rest of the day, refusing to go to school or come out for meals.

The days feel like an eternity as Rodger and Margie keep their vigil on either side of the hospital bed. They watch the ever darker trickle of urine seeping into the clear plastic bag hanging at the foot of the bed frame. They marvel that someone without nourishment can live so long.

Margie keeps on talking as though their father is conscious. Every couple of hours she takes the special pads the nurses have provided and moistens his lips and the inside of his mouth, then rubs lotion on his face and hands. Every second day she shaves off his whiskers while Rodger watches and listens to Margie's cheerful chatter, to the hushed voices of the nurses in the station across the hallway, and to the clanking roll of the meal carts as they pass by without stopping.

The dummy's left eye sometimes opens wide. It seems to Rodger that his father is staring accusingly at him. When that happens Rodger turns away. He studies the pictures hanging on the wall, looks out the window where the maple leaves are turning crimson, or heads to the lounge for a coffee.

> *Rodger is eighteen years old, graduated from high school, his last summer on the farm before going to college. His father pries him out of the kitchen to help him change one of the travelling chains inside the combine. He has removed the safety panel beside the straw walkers and is reaching deep inside the machine, rattling and banging on parts that are totally foreign to Rodger. "Hand me a Phillips screwdriver," his father shouts.*
>
> *Rodger panics as he looks over the tools in the red steel box at his feet. Phillips screwdriver? None of them are labeled Phillips. Which one is Phillip's? He grabs the one with the red handle, prays that it's the right one, and puts it in his father's outstretched hand. The hand goes back inside the combine. Loud rattling sounds, a curse, a chain falling. Like a mad bull his father yanks his head out of the combine and turns toward Rodger. His eyes are blazing with anger as he brandishes the screwdriver. "I said a*

Phillips screwdriver, not a Robertson. What's
wrong with you?"
Rodger takes a step back as his father strides
over to the tool box, hurls down the red-handled
driver and grabs the yellow one. "Now I've let go of
the chain, and all because you can't tell one blasted
screwdriver from another. I don't know what I did
to deserve a son like you."

Rodger is sleeping when the telephone wakens him just after four in the morning. He listens as Margie answers, then hears her pad up the stairs to knock on his bedroom door. "The hospital just called to say that Dad has passed away. They need to know whether we want to spend some time with him before they call the undertaker. Dave and I are going up to see him."

"I don't think there'd be much point in me going," Rodger says. "I'll stay here with the twins, see that they get their breakfast, make their school lunches."

Neighbours crowd the country church for the funeral. Rodger hasn't seen most of these people for decades, yet their sympathetic smiles, now framed by graying hair and wrinkling skin, are kindly familiar. He is so busy noticing them while following the minister up the aisle that he doesn't see the open casket until he sits down in the front pew between Margie and Uncle Frank.

He doesn't want to look at the casket, but cannot help himself. His dad, dressed in his black suit, a white shirt and blue tie, is barely recognizable. The last time Rodger saw his father in a suit was at his mother's funeral. Now, he thinks it would have been more appropriate to clothe him in his dusty denim coveralls, the old straw hat crammed onto his head, a toothpick in the corner of his mouth, grease-stained leather gloves on his hands. Those hands are now folded, the scar on the right hand clearly visible.

As everyone stands to sing the first hymn, Rodger fights to stifle the panic of grief welling up inside him. This flood of emotion takes him by surprise. He had expected to feel nothing but a numb *let's get this over with as soon as we can.* Instead, the words of the hymn, familiar from Sunday School, break some dam within him.

What a friend we have in Jesus,
All our sins and griefs to bear!

Tears blur the words on the program and cascade down Rodger's cheeks. A great lump of loneliness and regret for what might have been explodes in his belly. He doubles over, covering his face with his hands. Margie reaches an arm around his shoulder but he sinks down to the pew, where Uncle Frank, too weak to stand, is seated. He puts both arms around Rodger and rocks him. "I know. I know, my boy. I know what it must have been like for you, but it wasn't your fault."

Rodger clings to the old man, hangs onto those words as Uncle Frank repeats them over and over: *not your fault, not your fault.* Rodger is both surprised and comforted to know that Uncle Frank was aware of the dysfunctional relationship he had with his father. Though he doesn't know exactly what the old man means, he realizes that many things were not his fault.

It wasn't his fault that he couldn't drive the tractor and cultivator in a straight line when doing the summer fallow. It wasn't his fault that he sometimes took out a fence post when turning at the far end of the field. It wasn't his fault that he was more at home in the kitchen than in the farm repair shop.

The rest of the funeral service is a blur. There are prayers thanking God for his father's life. There are more hymns—Rodger stays seated, his shoulder snugged against Uncle Frank's. Neighbours praise his father's virtues: a hard worker, a successful farmer, a faithful member on both the school and grain boards.

At the reception, neighbours offer their sympathy. "Your father was so careful about everything. No one could plow a straight furrow like him," says one.

"Your dad helped us out in '64 when hail destroyed our crop," one of the neighbour ladies tells him, laying a black-gloved hand on his arm. "He knew we didn't have crop insurance so he went to the bank and made a deposit to our account. He wouldn't hear of us paying him back."

An old gentleman pushes his walker across the hall to where Rodger is sitting with the rest of the family. "I used to play with your dad in *The Rural Rhythm Pals*," he says. "We enjoyed going around the country playing for dances. Your dad was a lot of fun."

On the way out of the hall, Rodger accompanies his uncle to the car. "Uncle Frank, what did you mean when you said it wasn't my fault?"

Uncle Frank pauses, then carefully eases down so he's seated on his walker. "Rodger, it's not something I like to talk about, or even think about. I probably should have said something to your father long ago, but you know how stubborn he was. He'd fly into a rage if anyone crossed him.

"When I said it wasn't your fault, I meant we all could see how your father resented you."

"Resented me?"

"Yes, I think that's the best word for it. You see, just after your birth he received a contract offer from some talent scout in Nashville. As I recall, the offer was to record a couple of songs for a 45 record like they did in those days: one song on each side. It would be sent out to radio stations and if it was popular, he'd be on his way to a musical career."

"Dad never said anything about that."

"No, I don't suppose he wanted to talk about it. He'd have had to pay his own way down there and find a place to stay. With another mouth to feed, your dad felt he couldn't risk it, so he never took them up on the offer."

"Are you saying Dad blamed me for destroying his musical career?"

"It's not something we talked about, but I suspect that may have been why he abused you the way he did."

"Why didn't someone tell me this years ago?"

"Abuse wasn't something we talked about in those days. We just pretended it wasn't there."

"But I always blamed myself. I thought it was something I'd done. I thought it was because I didn't measure up to his idea of a son."

Uncle Frank struggled to his feet, took his hands off the walker and reached to hug Rodger. "I'm sorry, my boy. I'm sorry I didn't say something sooner. I should have tried to talk sense to your dad. Least of all, I should have made sure you knew it wasn't your fault."

The next morning Margie and Rodger leave early for the airport so they can drop by their father's cottage in town. Rodger feels uneasy being in the house. Looking through the closets and examining cupboards and drawers to determine what can be kept and what should be tossed, seems an invasion of his father's private life. He keeps looking over his shoulder, fearing that his father will walk out of the bedroom at any moment and bawl, "What the hell's going on here? Is a body not to have any privacy?" But of course he doesn't come out of the bedroom, or out of any other room, which is just as bad as if he did.

Rodger glances through the kitchen cupboards. He sees a few things he'd like to have.

"What about mother's Mixmaster?" he calls to Margie who's looking at the china in the dining room. "I wouldn't mind having it, and look at this—her old hand-cranked food chopper, still in its original box."

"You're welcome to them," Margie says. "I don't have room on my counter for another appliance."

Rodger carries the food chopper out to the car, wraps a shirt around the box and snugs it between the clothing in his suitcase. He remembers how he loved cranking it at Christmas time, making mincemeat for pies. What fun he and his mother had preparing shortbread cookies, plum pudding, and on the big day itself, roasting the turkey his father had slaughtered. Rodger smiles as he remembers how he'd pretend he was the head chef at an exclusive restaurant, preparing a banquet for the Prime Minister or the Queen.

Back inside the house he finds Margie sitting in the living room, the family photograph album open on her lap. The album has a soft deerskin cover. The velvety black pages smell of damp basement, the black and white photographs secured with gold-embossed corners.

"Here's Mom and Dad's wedding picture," Margie says. "They were a smart looking couple. Dad looks a lot like you in that photograph."

Rodger agrees that they were a smart looking couple, but the thought that he might look like his father makes him uneasy. "Is this you in the baby carriage?" he asks, pointing to the next photograph.

"Yes, that was taken on the verandah when the house was new. You can see that the railing hasn't been installed yet. I wonder where Dad found the time to work on the house while putting in the crop and looking after the livestock? It must have taken him an ice age to get all that fancy scrollwork completed. I guess he and Mom had lots of energy in those days. They must have had dreams like all of us have." Margie sniffs and brushes a tear from her cheek before turning the page.

"And here you are," she says, pointing to a photograph of a toddler sitting on their father's lap.

"That can't be me," Rodger says.

"Who else would it be? There are only the two of us."

"Maybe it's one of the cousins."

"No, that's you. I know it's you because one of my earliest memories is of mom making that little blue and white sailor suit for you. She was using the old treadle sewing machine and I was down on the floor, fascinated by the mechanism until I stuck my finger between the belt and the wheel. Almost took my finger off."

Rodger draws the album along the table so that he can get a better look. In the photograph his father is wearing a pair of blue jeans, a cowboy shirt and boots. Rodger thinks he can remember the shirt, a red plaid with black pockets on which horses' heads were embroidered with silver thread.

Rodger tries to conjure some memory of that little boy staring out at the world, safe and snug in the shelter of his daddy's arms. Then he flips through the pages, looking for more photographs of his father holding him. There are none. He turns back to the first page, runs his finger over the black and white image.

"Would you mind if I take this one?" he asks. "I could get it copied and send the original back to you."

"Go ahead," says Margie. "You could get it enlarged, framed, even coloured. It's wonderful what they can do with photographs these days." She glances at her watch. "We'd better be getting to the airport."

As the aircraft climbs, Rodger slumps down in his seat so he can look out the window. As Greenfield falls away he watches the familiar landmarks slipping beneath the wing: the junior college where he first enrolled in culinary arts, the small town where he attended high school and the two-room country school where he started his education. Across the road is the church with its red, tin roof. The plane is still low enough that he can make out the dark rectangle marking the freshly filled in grave. He cranes his neck to watch until a low bank of clouds cuts off the view.

He reaches into his shirt pocket and pulls out the photograph. It isn't much, and it doesn't explain anything, but at least it's something.

The Comfort of a Faithful Cook

"What will you do today?" Carol asks David as they linger over breakfast.

"I'll work on my model trains and on that story I started yesterday."

"The one about the evil banker?"

"No, Carol. It's a fantasy. It's about a generous banker. Won't it be a hoot if it wins first place in the library's story contest?"

"While you're doing that, I'd better invent something for lunch. Is there anything special you'd like?"

David lays aside *Forbes Magazine*. "I'll leave the food to you, Dear."

"I thought you might like something special on your seventieth birthday."

"It's my sixty-seventh birthday, Dear. A chocolate cake would be a treat."

"That's a lot of work."

"I'll help you." David closes the magazine. "If you tell me what to do, I can take care of the hard work. Let's get started." David gathers the breakfast dishes and carries them to the sink.

Carol's deteriorating health has forced David to retire from a senior position at the bank. He'd enjoyed giving customers financial advice. He would have continued, but Carol was having some minor heart problems. She wanted them to travel while she was still able.

She had booked a coach tour of Britain. Unfortunately, her heart began performing somersaults while they were in Glasgow, forcing them to abort the tour.

Now, instead of showing clients how to grow their assets, David is running and fetching for Carol. He reminds himself that he married her for better or worse. They enjoyed many better years so he shouldn't complain about the worse ones, though he wishes Carol were capable of doing more than reading novels and watching television.

Downton Abbey is her favourite series. Every week he strolls to the library to check out another season. She watches them non-stop, then starts over again. Sometimes he fears the drama is feeding the dementia that her physician says is caused by impaired circulation to the brain.

Occasionally, when David hands her a book or a cup of tea, she says, "Thank you, Barrow."

"I'm not the footman," David says, who sometimes watches *Downton Abbey* with her. "We're just ordinary people living on Blackwood Street in White Rock. You're not a duchess and I'm not a lord."

"Of course, Dear. I was only joking." Carol blushes, still aware enough to be embarrassed by her little collapses in mental acuity.

"You'd best wear my apron if you're going to mix the cake," Carol prompts from her chair in the breakfast nook. "You'll not be wanting flour all over that nice football jersey you bought in London."

"I bought it in Glasgow, Dear." David reaches for the apron hanging on the pantry door, shakes it out, turns it around.

"Come here. I'll help you on with it," Carol says. "It's a full bib apron. Remember, I got it at the gift shop in Highclere Castle. Hold out your arms."

She slips it over his arms, fastens the tie, then turns him around and smoothes the ruffles over his chest. She takes a step back and giggles.

"What's so funny?"

"Even though you're turning grey, your hair still has some reddish tints. Put a white dust cap on your head and you'd be a dead ringer for Mrs. Patmore, Downton's cook."

"Are you going to make sport of me, or do you want me to help with the cake?" David looks at himself in the hallway mirror. He's shocked to see that Carol is right. Excepting the flat chest and mustache, he could pass for the cook.

Carol chuckles again, hugs him, then sits down at the breakfast table, the cookbook open in front of her. "I do love Mrs. Patmore. Wouldn't it be a comfort to have a good cook like her seeing to things?"

The cake turns out a tad dry, but quite edible, and David is pleased to see that he's managed the whole operation without soiling his jersey. After washing up, he helps Carol into the bedroom for her nap. He hurries downstairs to work on his model train layout. While mixing a tub of plaster of Paris to build up his mountains, a few drops spatter the front of his jersey. He wipes them off, then tiptoes upstairs to get the apron.

An hour later, leaving his mountains to dry, he goes to the den to work on his story. He's deep into it when there's a knock at the door. Glancing through the window, he sees the UPS lady with a package for him—probably the model steam locomotive he ordered.

"Well, hello there. Aren't we looking special today!" She grins, pointing at his chest.

David looks down, sees the white ruffles, and blushes. "Was helping the wife with baking," he says.

"Yes, sure you were." She holds out the electronic clipboard for him to sign, an impish smirk on her face.

What does the woman think he's up to, David wonders as he closes the door. Is it so unusual for a man to wear an apron? As for the ruffles, what about those pictures showing Louis XIV in wig, ruffled lace, tights and high heels? There's no telling when such dress might return. Still, it's rather embarrassing to be caught in such a getup.

As the weeks pass Carol's mental health continues to decline. She gives up reading, spends the day in front of the television. Hoping to wean her off the *Downton* obsession, David brings home some gardening DVD's from the library—she always took pride in her flower garden.

She abides them only a few minutes. "Where's Barrow?" she hollers. "What has that footman done with my *Downton* dramas?"

"All the *Downton*s were checked out," David lies.

"Barrow, you lazy bones. Get me Mrs. Patmore. She'll sort things out."

"Mrs. Patmore isn't here, Carol. And neither is Barrow. It's me, David, your husband."

"I demand to see Mrs. Patmore. She's the only one does any work around here. Summon her to the morning room immediately."

Eventually David stops trying to sort Carol out. It's easier to play along with her imaginary life. Every morning he lays the breakfast table. Then he helps Carol wash and dress. After assisting her to her chair he reaches for the apron and puts it on— he's figured out how to do it himself.

Carol's agitation dissolves at the sight of her faithful cook. "Finally you've come, Mrs. Patmore. Shall we go over the meals for today?"

David reaches for the notepad on the windowsill. At first he only pretends to write, but Carol soon catches on to that and now demands to see what he has written. "Will that be all, Your Ladyship?" he asks, when her interest wanders.

"Yes, Mrs. Patmore. That will do for now, but I see you've forgotten to cover your hair. We don't want hair getting into the aspic, do we?"

David goes into the living room, takes one of the crocheted doilies off the piano, and lays it on his head.

"That's much better, Mrs. Patmore," Carol says. "I think it's best for the servants to be properly attired, don't you agree?"

"Yes, Your Ladyship. Shall I do your toast now?"

Carol enjoys mealtime—it gives her something to focus on—but suddenly she has difficulty swallowing. Her weight, never robust, drops alarmingly. After a battery of exhausting tests the doctor diagnoses cancer of the esophagus. She is too weak to survive the required surgery so a stent is inserted which permits her to swallow once again. She is partial to omelets so David fills them with the things she likes: green onions, red and green peppers, but no feta cheese.

"Feta cheese smells like baby puke," Carol says. After a life of reticence about expressing her own opinions, the brakes on her grey cells have all but given out.

"I hate all banks and bankers," she announces one evening, watching a commercial for a local bank.

"But you married a banker," David says. "Don't you remember?"

"I would never marry a banker or anyone associated with a bank." She pouts like a scolded puppy.

"Surely you remember working at the bank," David says. "You started as a teller and in no time you were secretary to the financial planner—and then you married him."

"Phooey! Such nonsense. Where is Mrs. Patmore? Isn't it time for my cup of tea? What can be keeping that woman?"

David sets the kettle to boil, arranges a cup and saucer and a plate of biscuits on a tray. When all is ready, he reaches for the apron and the doily. Properly attired, he carries the tray into the living room.

"About time you got here, Mrs. Patmore. I'll have to let you go without a reference if you're constantly late with my tea. And don't give me some excuse about that naughty Barrow messing things up. You're in charge in the kitchen…"

David hands her an arrowroot baby biscuit, the only kind she'll eat these days.

Weekends David takes Carol to church. She especially enjoys the singing. "Oh goody, they're singing my favourite today," she says about every hymn. The music seems to renew her energy, and though she cannot stand on her own, she sings heartily. She likes to hold his hand, and looking down at her, he can think, for a few precious moments, that all is well.

She nods and smiles at everything the priest says, but on the way home asks, "Who was that young man in the frock who stood up front and screamed at us? Can't he get a real job?"

Eventually, David calls in reinforcements to care for Carol. Even though she weighs no more than a child, the constant lifting, especially when he has to bend over when helping her in and out of the tub or onto the toilet, has resurrected a high school football injury. The first day the agency sends a young man.

"What are you doing?" Carol shrieks when he tries to prepare her for her bath. "Away with you, Barrow. Why are you touching me? Are you trying to rape me?" She will have nothing to do with him.

The succession of young ladies is more successful. David coaches them to address Carol as *Your Ladyship*. By this stage though, Carol's interest in *Downton*, along with everything else in life, is giving way to the pain that is overtaking her frail form. She spends all of her time in bed, running her fingers over the chenille spread as though searching for something.

"Where am I? Am I in the hospital? Are you my doctor?" she asks David each time he comes into the bedroom.

"I'm your husband."

"I don't have a husband. You must be Barrow. Where is Mrs. Patmore? Tell her I'm hurting. Ask her to brew a potion, something to relieve the pain."

David puts on the apron and wearing the doily on his head brings her a cup of tea. He has to hold the cup for her. After a couple of sips she touches his cheek. "Thank you, Mrs. Patmore. You are such a comfort. What would I do without you?"

As the cancer spreads, the morphine patches lose their effectiveness. Stronger dosages are prescribed. Still, Carol cries out for Mrs. Patmore. Several times during the day and night, David crawls under the blankets, cuddles her, tries to warm her Tinkertoy-like bones, but she won't settle. She calls for Mrs. Patmore with greater frequency. Each time he gets up, slips on the apron and doily, and brings what comfort he can.

Late one night he wakes to find her barely breathing, but agitated. "Where is Mrs. Patmore? I need Mrs. Patmore."

David sits up, reaches for the apron and doily on the bedside table, puts them on, sits down on the bed beside Carol. He smoothes the hair from her brow.

A smile flickers across her thin, blue lips. "Mrs. Patmore, it's time," she whispers, her voice thin and hoarse. "Take me back to Downton, Mrs. Patmore. Take me away from all this pain."

His tears falling onto the bedclothes, David reaches for his pillow, and like a faithful cook, obeys Her Ladyship's order.

See, the Conquering Hero Comes

Ryan McDonald was upstairs in his bedroom, studying for his math final. It was a hopeless endeavour. Even though he was a musician and music was supposed to be the spawn of mathematics, he'd never been good with numbers.

He read the problem again.

> *Two cars approach each other from opposite ends*
> *of a road 10 miles long. The blue car is moving at*
> *70 miles an hour. The red car is moving at 60 miles*
> *an hour. How many minutes will it take for them to*
> *meet? Where on the road will they meet, assuming*
> *the blue car started at mile 0 and the red car at mile*
> *10?*

Ryan grabbed his ruler, pencil and a sheet of paper. He traced out the road, ten inches long, each inch marked off with a tick. He tore scraps of paper and labeled them *Red* and *Blue*. He placed them at either end of the road, settled back in his chair and stared at them.

After a few attempts at inching the cars forward, he crumpled the paper and hurled it into the wastebasket. He'd never pass math. He'd never complete Grade Twelve. He wouldn't be able to enroll in political science at university. He wouldn't be able to get a job in the city. He'd have to be a farmer like his dad, sweating a meager living from the prairie dirt. He'd spend his whole life playing butler to cows and calves. Faced with such a miserable future, he might as well end his life now—drown himself in the cow's drinking trough, feed himself into the grain auger, step in front of Canadian National's *Super Continental* as it thundered across the trestle spanning Cottonwood Creek.

He reached for Sprucegrove High's yearbook, still smelling of printer's ink and glue in its glossy blue and white binding. He flipped it open to the seniors' section, looked at his own photo. His face was a little too narrow to be labeled handsome, but he wasn't ugly either—kind of nerdy looking with his mouse-brown hair parted on the left side and flipped into a cowlick. Once he was away to college he'd grow his hair longer, like the Beatles were making popular. He'd tell his folks he was saving them money by getting a trim every eight weeks instead of monthly.

> *Ryan MacDonald has been our dependable accompanist for school assemblies*, read the write-up beside his photograph. *He wants to work in government but don't be surprised if one day you find him playing the piano with the Winnipeg Symphony Orchestra—or even in New York's Carnegie Hall.*

What a pile of horse manure! He'd never be good enough to play with an orchestra. Like everything else he put his hand to, piano playing was a struggle that ended up being more enthusiasm and wishful thinking than skill. Most people didn't know that much about music, so it was easy to fool them into thinking he was a budding talent. Too bad there wasn't a way to fool the mathematical examiners.

He flipped the yearbook's page and scanned some of his classmates' write-ups. Shirley Morguard, his second-best friend, said she planned to be a Kindergarten teacher. She'd make a good one, Ryan thought. He could remember her helping with the little ones when they were both in grade school.

Next on the page was Bill Oakner. He was a shy little fellow who sat behind Ryan in homeroom. He wrote that he wanted to join the American air force. He hoped to fly spy planes over the Soviet Union.

Ryan turned the page and stopped at Geoff Stephens' photo. Now there was an excruciatingly handsome, make-you-faint-in-your-tracks, young man—a broad forehead, blue eyes, a wide, roguish smile, a mass of blond curls that refused to be parted.

> *Geoff Stephens, star football quarterback and whiz*
> *kid with the slide rule. Geoff plans an engineering*
> *career. We look forward to driving over the roads*
> *and bridges he will design.*

Ryan laid the yearbook open on his desk. He tiptoed over to his bedroom door and pushed it closed, being careful not to let the latch snap. Then he reached onto the shelf for a Kleenex tissue.

He was cleaning up when he heard the throb of eight cylinders funneled through two Hollywood Mufflers. A moment later Ryan's mother called from the bottom of the stairs, "Ryan, are you up there?"

Ryan yanked up his underwear and jeans and cracked the door. "Yes, Mom."

"Geoff's here. He wants to see you."

"Send him up." Ryan wadded the soggy Kleenex into a ball and stuffed it between the box spring and mattress. He fastened his belt and snapped the yearbook shut.

Geoff had been Ryan's best friend as long as he could remember. The two boys were born within days of each other, lived on neighbouring farms, and neither had brothers or sisters. If those facts didn't create enough of a bond, both families belonged to fringe religious groups. Ryan's parents were fourth generation Seventh-day Adventists—Gladventists or Sadventists, depending upon who was talking.

Geoff's family were members of the Tabernacle of Believers Assembly, or the good old TBA as they liked to call it. Others referred to them as Blabbers, due to their habit of leaping about and uttering unintelligible sounds when they got into the spirit of worship.

Both families were deadly serious about their religions, maybe even a wee touch proud of being *peculiar* people. For several years both resisted purchasing idiot boxes. They knew God hadn't designed human beings to be couch slouches, staring at flickering black and white images of actors shooting each other up. However, eventually both families succumbed to the common culture, and shiny aluminum aerials appeared on their rooftops. Ryan's family confined its viewing to the news, weather and the farm report. On rare occasions, when Ryan's mother was ironing shirts in the basement and his father had his head buried in *The Country Guide*, Ryan might sneak a peek at *The Beverly Hillbillies*.

Geoff's family got the box so they could keep abreast of end-time events—the wars and rumours of wars Jesus spoke about. Occasionally they bent their viewing rules a tiny bit by watching baseball and football games—educational exercises for Geoff who excelled at athletics.

Both sets of parents shunned movies. Hollywood productions were part of Satan's plot to destroy morals. The fictional stories showcased dancing, drinking and other lewd activities. Both families wanted their boys to develop into morally upright men. Social interaction should take place in a religious environment, where, when the time was right, both boys would meet respectable girls—Christian girls who enjoyed Sabbath or Sunday services, Wednesday night prayer meetings and summer picnics.

Until the previous January, neither of the boys had shown much interest in girls. The few times Geoff and Ryan had discussed the topic, they'd agreed that the girls who showed up at church and tabernacle were too dim to be of any interest. Marriage would have to wait until they had escaped to the city, perhaps Winnipeg, where both denominations had large congregations of believers.

That June evening Geoff came bounding up the stairs into Ryan's room. He glanced at the books spread out on Ryan's desk. "Cramming for math, I see." He cuffed Ryan playfully on the ear, then sat down on his bed, leaning back on his hands. He was wearing blue jean cutoffs and a yellow tank top, a costume that showed off his sunburned shoulders and solid quarterback thighs to good advantage.

"How's it going, Ryan? Gonna score high enough in the math final to win a scholarship to university?"

Ryan snorted. "Not likely. I barely passed my mid-term. I'll be satisfied if I can squeak through with a fifty-one percent."

He tried to keep his eyes off Geoff's legs. Ryan was on the slight side himself, always trying to gain weight, so he envied his best friend's physique. He glanced down and saw that Geoff was wearing sandals. His stomach gave a sickening lurch. Wearing sandals in the country, on the farm with its dusty fields and cow manure, was a pretty stupid thing to do. Ryan didn't want to consider who had prompted Geoff to wear such impractical footwear.

"I don't have to write the math exam," Geoff said.

"Don't rub it in." Ryan leaned forward, poked Geoff in the chest. "Mr. Wizard got exempted from everything, didn't you."

"Except French. I'm the pits in French, especially the oral part."

"Think you'll pass it?"

"Probably skim through, especially now that Coralinda's helping me."

"I thought she spoke German. Wasn't her dad some big shot with the RCAF in West Germany?"

"Yup, a wing commander, but while her dad was posted there, Coralinda went to France a lot. She learned to speak French—real Parisian French."

"Bully for her."

Geoff ignored Ryan's tone of voice, leaned back, scratched his crotch, and said. "She's been coaching me three nights a week. I'm pretty sure I'll be able to pass the exam. But never mind that, there's something I need to ask you."

"What's that?"

"Coralinda and I have decided to get married right after grad."

"You've got to be kidding."

"No kidding, Ryan."

"But you can't marry Coralinda."

"Why not?"

"You and I have plans to room together at university." Ryan wondered if the old farmhouse was really swaying beneath his chair or if he was just imagining it.

"College may have to wait a few years."

"Wait for what?"

"Wait until me and Coralinda get established. You know why Coralinda's dad bought the Skarnilatti place, don't you?"

"Not really."

"He's gonna take early retirement from the air force in a couple of years, try his hand at farming."

"What does he know about farming?" Ryan rocked back on his chair.

"That's just it. He doesn't know a pitch fork from a toothpick. I figure I can help him get that old farm whipped into shape."

"But what about your plans to be an engineer—to design bridges and factories and all that stuff we talked about last year when we were camping down at the swimming hole?"

"No rush. I'll eventually get to that. Two years or so and I'll have some money saved and can head to university. But hey, the reason I came by is to ask if you'll play the piano at our wedding. It'll be the third Saturday in July. I know Saturday is your Sabbath, but it'll be okay for you to play for the wedding, won't it? It'll be in the tabernacle in Twin Meadows."

"You're getting married in the tabernacle?"

"Of course."

"But aren't you forgetting that Coralinda isn't a TBA? Your folks won't be pleased to see you marry a non-Tabber. And your Apostle Lawrence won't marry you to a non-believer, will he?"

"Coralinda's a Catholic, but she's been coming to meetings with me. She wants to be baptized properly the Sunday before our wedding."

"Oh Geoff, I can't get my head around this. I knew you liked Coralinda, but I had no idea you'd be getting married so suddenly. Are you sure about this?"

"Don't worry about me, pal." Geoff leaned forward and cuffed Ryan on the ear. "A guy's got to get married sometime, right? And why not now? I'm taking Coralinda to Banff for our honeymoon. We'll stop in Beeverville where the TBA started. She wants to see the Mother Tabernacle and the grove of trees where Brother Tingley was praying when he was taken up to heaven. But enough about that. You *will* play for our wedding, won't you?"

"I guess I'll have to, but I think you're making a huge mistake."

"Excellent. Coralinda doesn't know spit about music, so I told her to leave it up to my best friend, Ryan. Let her know what you're going to play and she'll make sure it gets printed in the program. I better get over to the Ronsons' now. Time for my French lesson."

Geoff stood up, gave Ryan another cuff on the ear and turned to go. "Hey, what's this?" He picked up the framed photograph from the top of Ryan's chest of drawers. "That a real photograph of President Kennedy?"

"Yes. It's real."

"How'd you get it?"

"I wrote to Mrs. Kennedy after the President's funeral last November. She sent me the photograph and the mass card on the back. It was given out at his funeral. Shirley Morguard got one and said I should write too. Might be worth a lot someday."

"Neato man. You do the boldest things. And what's this little box with the stag's head carved on top? You make that?"

"Aunt Vivian gave it to me for Christmas last year. She got it in Europe." Ryan went over to stand beside Geoff. "It's made of wood from the Black Forest in Germany. Open it."

Geoff lifted the lid. "Hey Buddy, you still got that?" He lifted out a silver ring.

"Haven't you got the one I gave you?" asked Ryan.

"Fraid not. Mom tossed it when she was cleaning out my room. She takes these fits, blazes through the house, throwing out everything that isn't nailed down."

The idea to exchange friendship rings had been hatched while they were in sixth grade. Geoff had been working his way through

166

the Tom Sawyer and Huck Finn stories. He'd been intrigued when the boys pledged friendship by pricking their fingers to mingle their blood. When he'd proposed the ceremony, Ryan, who had recently witnessed his cousin's marriage, had suggested they exchange rings as well.

"But where will we get rings?" Geoff had asked. "You know our parents don't wear jewelry except for their wedding rings. They certainly won't let us buy rings."

"We can make them," Ryan had said. "Have you seen that shiny silver ring Frank Crisler wears?" Frank drove them to school in the bus every morning, then spent the day wrenching in his machine shop before driving them home at four o'clock.

"What about Frank's ring?"

"He told me he made it himself—he filed out the centre of a big nut. It's easy to do with a rat tail file."

And so they'd set to work in Ryan's dad's shop. Just in case questions were asked, they pretended they were customizing a repair for the go-cart they'd built when they were in fourth grade.

When the rings were finished, they'd hiked down to the creek. Using a thorn from the wild hawthorn bushes, they pricked the tips of their index fingers. They touched the droplets of blood together, then anointed the inside of each ring.

"I pledge to be your friend forever and a day," Ryan had said as he slipped the ring onto the fourth finger of Geoff's left hand.

"And I pledge to be your buddy forever," Geoff had said.

Ryan had leaned forward, thinking they might kiss like people did at weddings, but Geoff cuffed him on the ear, then turned and ran down to the creek where he stepped out of his shorts and dived into the swimming hole.

"I think it's neato that you still have this ring," Geoff said.

Ryan looked Geoff in the eye. "Do you want me to make you another one?"

"No need. I'll soon have my wedding ring. Now I better get over to Coralinda's before she comes looking for me. Both she and Wing Commander Ronson are big on punctuality." He tossed the ring back into the box. "Coralinda will be happy to know you'll play for the wedding. I'll tell her you'll phone soon as you have the music picked out."

Ryan sat down at his desk and reread the math problem. He reached into the waste basket for the scrunched up diagram and smoothed it out. He tried moving the cars along the line, but couldn't keep his mind on them.

What difference did it make whether he passed math or not? Suppose he did go to college, he wouldn't be rooming with Geoff. He'd be all by himself, or with some horrid stranger who never bathed, always snored, and flung his stinky clothes all over the place. And when he came back from college, Geoff wouldn't have any time for him—for riding their bikes out to the big railway trestle, for camping beside Cottonwood Creek like they'd done every year since they'd been big enough to pitch the tent.

Geoff and Coralinda would be away on their honeymoon for two weeks. When they came back they'd have to find a place to live. Geoff would be busy during the day working the Skarnilatti place. Evenings he'd be teaching Wing Commander Ronson how to farm or spending time with Coralinda. If they did go camping, Geoff would probably want to bring her. There wouldn't be room in the tent for all three of them.

The previous August he and Geoff had enjoyed three whole days camping. They'd pitched the tent in their favourite spot beside Cottonwood Creek—a meadow lush with sweet grass, cowslips and tiger lilies—directly beneath the railway trestle. They'd spent their days setting snares for gophers, though the sly little beasts always outsmarted them. They dragged windfalls from the woods and chopped them up for firewood. They floated butt naked in the swimming hole, imagining the passengers' shock when Canadian National's *Super Continental* rolled across the trestle. One afternoon they watched Robbie McLeod and his crew arrive on the jigger to pound spikes and tighten track bolts. They scrambled up the embankment to talk to them during their lunch break. At the end of the workday Robbie had hailed them from above. "Yon fine lads, you fancy a ride?"

He didn't have to ask twice. They scrambled back up the embankment and took their places on the jigger's hard wooden bench. Robbie started the motor and putt-putted them back and forth across the trestle several times, the wind cooling their sun-burned foreheads.

Nights they sat around the campfire eating beans and bannock, just like the early explorers. They roasted marshmallows and mapped out plans for the future.

It was one of those nights when the fire blazed high, casting a ruddy glow over his features, that Geoff announced, "I'm going to be an engineer."

"You mean drive trains for CN?" Ryan tossed another log on the fire, sending a shower of sparks heavenward to join the stars.

"No, not a railway engineer, a civil engineer. Remember that guy who came and talked to us in guidance class? He said a professional engineer designs hydro dams and water systems and factories and bridges. You have to know all about the strength of materials, loads and stress points, stuff like that. That's the sort of work I want to do. Maybe I can work for the railway and design trestles like this. That guy said you need to be good in math and physics. Those are my favourite subjects so I shouldn't have any trouble."

"If I get a job in government maybe I can hire you to design something," Ryan had said. "The government's always needing something built, like that new water system they're putting into Twin Meadows, and someone should redesign that roller coaster road that flies up and down the hills south of town."

They had talked about where they'd go to college. Geoff had said Toronto would be better than Winnipeg because there'd be more opportunities for engineering work.

"Aunt Vivian lives in Toronto," Ryan had said. "She might rent us a room."

"Will you keep on going to church on Saturday when you leave home?" Geoff poked at the fire, sending another shower of sparks heavenward.

"Probably. It should be fun going to a big church where they have a grand piano instead of that boring upright in our little church in Sprucegrove. How about you? Will you still be a Tabber?"

"Don't know. Sometimes I think Brother Tingley was just a crazy old man, should have been locked up in the loony bin. Still, there's a lot of good things about being a Tabber. Should I get my Bible and we'll read something before we go to bed?"

"You brought your Bible camping?"

"Of course. Apostle Lawrence says we should read it every day."

Geoff read about the children of Israel camping in the wilderness. The two boys talked about what it must have been like to have God with them—a pillar of light hovering over their tents. "You'd think the tents would have burned up," Ryan said.

"The branches didn't burn up when God spoke to Moses out of the burning bush. Maybe God's fire isn't hot, just sort of cozy like a flannelette-lined sleeping bag." Geoff closed his Bible and tucked it into his backpack.

"Maybe God's fire is ice cold. Maybe it kept them cold in the desert, like air conditioning." Ryan yanked off his T-shirt. "I'm too hot and sweaty to sleep. Race you to the far side of the creek."

Stripping off the rest of their clothes, they ran down to the swimming hole that lay like a silvery blob of mercury beneath the full moon. After diving towards the bottom they swam for the far bank, turned back and stopped to rest in the centre of the pool. They lay floating on their backs, the cool water soothing their sunburned skin. Geoff pointed at the Milky Way, stretched like a blazing banner above them. "Brother Tingley said he travelled along the Milky Way to the heavenly country."

"Our prophet, Ellen White, did that too," Ryan said. "She wrote about going through the corridors of Orion, whatever that means."

"Was she in a rocket?"

"Hardly. Rockets hadn't been invented in the 1800's. She never said how she got there. It seemed she just went into some sort of trance and suddenly she was there."

"Brother Tingley got to eat with Jesus and the angel, Gabriel," Geoff said. "They had figs and grape juice."

"Ellen White was taken into God's throne room," Ryan said. "There were zillions of angels."

"Brother Tingley wrote fifteen books."

"Ellen White wrote forty books and thousands of magazine articles."

"Brother Tingley walked the streets of gold." Geoff cuffed Ryan on the ear.

"Ellen White visited other planets. She saw people gardening, though she said they weren't doing it the same as us, whatever that means." Ryan poked Geoff in the ribs.

"Brother Tingley wrote that just before this world ends, animals will turn on people. Dogs, cats, even pet birds will attack their owners." Geoff punched Ryan's shoulder.

"Jesus told Ellen White there'll be terrible earthquakes and storms. Whole cities will fall apart and governments all over the world will force people to attend church." Ryan grabbed Geoff's muscled shoulder and shook him. "The government will say, '*Go to church or I'll drown you.*'" He shoved Geoff under the surface.

He came up spluttering, grabbed Ryan by the ankle and pulled him under. They thrashed around until both were gasping for air. Once again they lay floating on their backs.

"What good will forcing people to attend church do?"

"Who knows? Maybe governments are superstitious like some people. They think if people start praying and singing hymns the tornadoes and earthquakes will stop."

"Hey! Get away from me, Mr. Mosquito." Geoff swatted at the insect. "Come on. Let's get into the tent before we get bitten. I'll race you." Geoff twisted onto his belly and headed for the shore.

Inside the tent, it was still too warm to be comfortable, so they lay listening to the trains hammering across the creek. As the locomotives rolled over the valley the big, steel trestle groaned and made pinging sounds as though the rivets were popping out. The steel wheels squealed and thumped against the rails. "Sounds like World War One," Ryan had said.

"How would you know what World War One sounded like?"

"Vincent Skarnilatti told me. You know he's my dad's third cousin. He's always telling stories about the trenches at Vimy where he was wounded. Every time the big guns opened up the men would do whatever their commanders ordered. It was just too damn noisy to think for themselves." Ryan wouldn't ordinarily have said *damn* because he knew it was a bad word, but that's the word Vincent always used.

"How was he injured?" asked Geoff.

"A big hunk of shrapnel buried itself in his head. If his mates had pulled it out he'd have died, so they left it in until he got to the field hospital. Now he's got a steel plate in his skull."

"My dad says Vincent Skarnilatti is bone lazy. That's why his fields are full of weeds and his barn's falling down."

"He's not really lazy, just starts things and never finishes them," Ryan said. "Vince says he's going to sell out next year, move into town."

"Who would want to buy that rundown place anyway, but never mind. Let's get some sleep before the next train pounds across the trestle." Geoff whacked his pillow into shape before lying down again.

The second night was just as warm, but the third evening a weather system blew in from the northwest. It brought cooler temperatures and at dusk fog stole up the hillside from the swimming hole. Its damp fingers circled the tent and poked inside. Towards morning Ryan awakened shivering, his teeth chattering and his bladder full. When he sat up to pull on a T-shirt and shorts, Geoff woke up too. "Why are you getting up?"

"Stepping out for a leak."

"Why the shorts? You think the coyotes will bite it off?"

"I'm freezing. This old sleeping bag isn't very warm."

"Want me to warm you up?"

Ryan peered through the darkness at Geoff's stocky body stuffed into his sleeping bag. "Is there room for both of us in there?"

"I didn't mean you should get inside with me, but we can open our bags up, lay yours on the floor of the tent, put mine over us, and spread our clothes on top. Then you should be warmer, though no cuddling. I'm not funny or anything."

Warmed more by the thought of lying next to his friend than by the heavier sleeping bag, Ryan had fallen back to sleep. When the next train awakened him he was lying with his back snugged against Geoff's cozy flank. He didn't want Geoff to think he was funny either, but he was afraid if he moved he might disturb him, so he lay still. Instead of falling back to sleep he'd lain awake, imagining their future together.

In Ryan's imagination they both had jobs in Winnipeg. Geoff was a civil engineer. He worked in an office on the top floor of a downtown office building. Ryan would have a job in the Legislative Building on Memorial Boulevard. He imagined carrying an attaché case filled with important documents and walking up the steps below the six tall limestone columns at the main entrance.

He and his dad had once toured the building while his mother shopped. They had ascended the grand staircase flanked by the two bronze bison, stared dizzily up at the inside of the dome, and then climbed another stairway to the visitor's gallery. He had admired the pages in their smart, blue uniforms, and the way they could walk up to any member of the assembly to deliver a message.

But Ryan didn't want to be a page, nor a politician. He dreamed of being a policy advisor to one of the cabinet ministers. He'd be one of the guys dressed in a chalk-striped blue suit standing behind the Minister of Culture when he made an important announcement. He'd help plan special events—art shows and concerts.

After work he'd walk downtown to meet Geoff. They'd have dinner in Eaton's Georgian Room with its thick, maroon carpet and sparkling chandeliers. In the evening they'd attend a symphony concert or stroll through the art gallery. Late at night they'd return to their apartment, enjoy a mug of hot chocolate, then prepare for bed. Finally they would kneel beside their king size bed, hold hands and pray, and then snuggle up together for the night.

None of those fantasies would come true now. Geoff's surprise wedding announcement had derailed any chance of a life together. Ryan should have seen it coming. Until the end of January they had sat together on the school bus. They'd helped each other with homework, or just yakked during the thirty-five minute ride to and from the big consolidated high school in Sprucegrove.

Things began to spoil in February when Wing Commander Ronson bought the farm from Vincent and Olive Skarnilatti. Coralinda and her brother started taking the bus to school. Ryan remembered the betrayal he'd felt that first afternoon when Geoff had sidled across the aisle to sit with Coralinda. Ryan had comforted himself with the thought that it was just a phase Geoff was going through. He'd soon tire of the little Jezebel's high-pitched squeals about The Beatles' latest song. He'd get fed up having her long, blond hair flipped into his face every time she flicked it out of her purple-shaded eyes.

Just to show that he didn't really care, Ryan had moved to the back of the bus. He sat with Shirley Morguard. They reviewed their homework and exchanged the latest Kennedy news, but it wasn't enough to distract Ryan from what was going on between Geoff and Coralinda at the front of the bus.

It was Easter of that year when Geoff bought the '56 Ford Crown Victoria Skyliner off Frank Crisler, the school bus driver. Ryan spent many evenings with Geoff, chipping years of dusty oil buildup off the block and valve covers. He helped Geoff replace the spark plugs, flush out the radiator, change the transmission fluid and install new tires. Together they washed and polished the red and white exterior until it shone like it had just rolled out the factory door.

While working on the rare classic, Ryan and Geoff had talked of the trips they might take. Once warmer weather came, they could drive up to Riding Mountain National Park and camp on the shores of Clear Lake. They might head south of the border to explore North Dakota's Black Hills, or even drive to Alberta—see the Rocky Mountains, camp at Banff and Lake Louise.

Those plans withered away like wheat in a summer drought the day Geoff started driving to school. Instead of offering his best friend a ride, he'd stop for Coralinda at the end of her lane. Just before reaching Sprucegrove, Ryan would hear above the rattle and bounce of the bus, the roar of twin Hollywood Mufflers. A horn would blast, and the Crown Victoria would overtake them. Ryan struggled to keep his eyes on whichever assignment he was reviewing, but couldn't help glancing down through the car's glassed-in roof. There he'd see Coralinda snugged against Geoff.

Ryan still sat beside Geoff in most of his classes, but his friend was too busy drawing hearts and doodling his and Coralinda's initials in the margins of his notebooks to pay him any attention. At the class bell, Geoff brushed right past Ryan as he dashed into the hallway to meet up with Coralinda so he could carry her books to her next class.

Ryan wondered if the distance between them was partly his own fault. On New Year's Day of that year, they had tossed their skates over their shoulders and hiked down to the frozen swimming hole. While tying on his skates, Geoff had yanked out of his pocket a tatter of centerfolds from *Playboy*. He'd handed them to Ryan as though he was gifting him with some prized artifact.

Ryan had flipped through the stained pages, barely glancing at the images. Beads of sweat broke out on his forehead despite the icy wind blowing down the valley. "You're bad, Geoff. You're bad. These are evil. We shouldn't be looking at these pictures."

"Why not?"

"Well, because we're not supposed to look at naked women. Didn't Jesus say— "

Geoff grabbed the pages out of his hand and shoved them back into his pocket. "There's nothing wrong with looking."

"Jesus said looking at women lustfully was the same as committing adultery."

"That's only if you're married. We're not married and we don't know if these chicks are married. What's the harm? Besides, what's the difference between admiring naked women or that red fox watching us from inside the thicket over there?" He pointed to a clump of willows on the far side of the swimming hole. "Women are God's creation too. They're meant to be admired—just like that fox."

"You're wrong."

"Fine. Forget it then." Geoff finished tying his skates. "I'll race you up the creek." He took off without waiting for Ryan.

They'd skated up the creek until the ice was blocked by a downed cottonwood. When they got back to the swimming hole, instead of building a fire and spending the whole afternoon skating and warming up as they often did, Geoff called it quits. "I want to get a head start on next term's physics textbook," he had said, untying his skates.

At the time Ryan hadn't given it much thought, but later he realized that his refusal to look at the centrefolds had offended Geoff. On that wintry day some of the life had leaked out of their friendship and was left on the frozen creek to be washed away come spring.

Giving up on the math problem of the two cars approaching each other, Ryan slammed shut his textbook. He went downstairs and began dragging music out of the piano bench. He paused at Handel's *Dead March in Saul*. Considering how Geoff had just killed their life together, it would make a perfect wedding piece. He finally settled on Handel's *Water Music* and Pachelbel's famous *Canon in D Major* for before the service. He would pound out Wagner's *Here Comes the Bride* as Jezalinda—he chuckled at the melding of her name with Jezebel's—pranced into the tabernacle. He bypassed Mendelssohn's popular *Wedding March* for the recessional in favour of Handel's *See the Conquering Hero Comes*. It would be his final tribute to Geoff—whiz at football, math, physics—hero of pretty well everything.

The sun was beating down on the tabernacle's black tin roof the day of Geoff and Jezalinda's wedding. There hadn't been a church wedding in Twin Meadows for some years, so the twelve rows of darkly stained pews were filled by the time Ryan arrived. The heat intensified the stuffy smell of the place—a spiritual mixture of lemon-scented furniture polish, slowly decaying hymnbooks, and prairie dust.

As Ryan walked to the front of the tabernacle, he unbuttoned his suit jacket and loosened his tie. He hoped Jezalinda would be on time. In this heat, people would be fainting if they had to wait while she played some foolish game of hard-to-get.

He arranged his music on the piano, glanced at his watch—a quarter to two. He began Pachelbel's *Canon in D*. As he played he struggled to keep his mind on his music, but his thoughts insisted on wandering down uncomfortable pathways. In the weeks leading up to the wedding, he hadn't had time alone with Geoff. Even if he had, he probably wouldn't have asked him about the *talk* he was hearing.

And *talk* there had been—lots of it—ugly talk that got uglier the more often it was repeated. The rawest story was that late one evening—a week before Geoff asked Ryan to play the piano for his wedding—Wing Commander Ronson had made a trip to the Stephens' farm. The family had been in bed but that didn't stop him from hollering and banging on their door until the family came running downstairs.

Some said he was wearing his blue air force uniform with gold stripes on the sleeves. Others said he was wearing battle fatigues. When Mr. Stephens opened the door Wing Commander Ronson pointed his service revolver at his head. Others said he actually wrestled Mr. Stephens to the floor. Ugly words were exchanged. By the time Wing Commander Ronson left two hours later, the marriage had been decided.

Ryan refused to believe the story. The few times he'd seen Wing Commander Ronson, he hadn't been carrying a revolver. He doubted that wing commanders carried revolvers. Why would they when they flew planes loaded with missiles and machine guns? The whole thing was probably some old gossip's fantasy.

Besides, Ryan wanted to believe that Geoff was still a virgin. Hadn't he brought his Bible along on their camping trip last summer? Hadn't he insisted they should read a chapter or two while sitting beside the campfire? Hadn't he been the one who suggested they pray before crawling into the tent for the night? There was no way he could have done anything to embarrass his parents or anger Wing Commander Ronson.

Ryan hoped that at the last moment Geoff might change his mind about this unsuitable marriage. Just as Apostle Lawrence was about to pronounce them husband and wife, Geoff might raise his hand. There would be a hushed pause before he spoke. *Coralinda, I love you too much to ruin your life by marrying you before I have my engineering degree.*

He would step over to the piano, place his hand on Ryan's shoulder. *Everyone, I want to introduce you to my best friend, Ryan McDonald. We're going to be roommates at university, just like we've always planned. There'll be time enough for marriage later.*

Everyone would applaud. Even Jezalinda, her mother and Wing Commander Ronson, would agree that it was best for Geoff to get his education first.

Ryan glanced at his watch—five past the hour. Where was Jezalinda? Just like the selfish witch to keep everyone sweating inside the tabernacle. He would run out of music if she didn't show up soon. He was on the last page when Jezalinda's brother walked up the aisle and turned to face the congregation. Ryan stopped playing. He expected to hear the usual announcement about it being okay to take photographs inside the tabernacle, but please, no confetti.

"Thanks for coming to my sister's wedding," her brother said, fidgeting with his tie, "but there's going to be a delay. In her excitement Coralinda forgot to bring her bouquet. Geoff has driven my mother back to the farm to get the flowers. Knowing how fast Geoff drives, it shouldn't take them more than twenty minutes." Everyone laughed, for both country folk and townspeople had been victimized by the roar of those Hollywood Mufflers.

"Coralinda and her attendants are hiding out in the basement where it's a bit cooler. Please step outside where there's some shade. I'm sure we'll all hear Geoff gunning it up the roller coaster road. That'll give us time to come back inside."

There were more chuckles as everyone stood and shuffled out of the tabernacle. Ryan re-arranged his music before following the others outside. His mother was standing at the bottom of the steps talking to Olive Skarnilatti who was buttoning up her suit jacket.

"I'm probably the only one who feels the cold," Olive said, holding an icy finger to Ryan's cheek as he came down the steps and gave her a hug. "I think it's my heart. I should probably see Doc Winsler, but he's at a conference in Winnipeg until Tuesday."

"Did Vincent not come with you?" Ryan asked.

"Vince isn't much for dressing up. He said something about going for a drive to see how the crops are coming along. When I left home he had his head stuck inside that old truck of his, some trouble with the motor. I don't know why he doesn't get a new one. The good Lord knows we got enough from the sale of the farm to buy a car that doesn't break down all the time."

"The truck gives him something to do," Ryan said, further loosening his tie. Then he walked over to chat with Shirley Morguard who was standing in the shade. Like Geoff, she'd been exempted from her finals, even from French.

Back in November, Ryan had been yanking books out of his locker for his afternoon classes when she'd come running up to him. "President Kennedy's been shot. He's been assassinated in Dallas."

Since that horrible day, Shirley had immersed herself in what the press was calling *the Kennedy mystique*. She pasted into a scrapbook everything printed about the Kennedys. As Ryan approached her she twirled around so he could see her from all sides. "How do you like my dress?" she asked.

"It's stunning. You look like royalty in white. Where'd you get those gloves that snake up beyond your elbow, and what do you call that hairstyle?"

"I don't know, but Jackie wore hers like this for the inaugural ball in 1961. I made the dress myself. I copied it from a photograph."

"Well, you look fabulous." Ryan bowed his head, reached for her hand and brushed his lips across the soft, white glove.

"Stop it. You'll embarrass me." She pulled her hand back. "Let me tell you about the outfits I've been making to wear at university this fall."

Ryan listened as she described each design though half the time he didn't know what she was talking about—flounce, A-line neck, raglan, leg of mutton. Finally he heard the distant roar of Hollywood Mufflers. "Sorry to interrupt, Shirley, but isn't that Geoff's car now?" He excused himself and ran out to the road. He shaded his eyes from the sun and looked south. He could see a plume of dust and then the Crown Victoria crested the distant camel's back. Sunlight flashed off the Plexiglas roof for a brief moment before it plunged into the roller coaster's next dip.

"Here they come," he called, hurrying back to the tabernacle. When he reached the steps he heard the putt-putt-putt of another motor, and glancing over his shoulder, saw Vincent Skarnilatti heading out of town in his rusty green Fargo. "Looks like Vince got the old wreck going," he said to Olive. "Sounds like a couple of cylinders are missing."

"I keep praying the good Lord will put that old rattle trap out of its misery," she said.

Everyone was now crowding the steps and Ryan turned to hurry inside when the summer afternoon was shattered by the ugly clash of metal impacting metal. There was a brief moment of silence, then a jingle-jangle as though a bucket of knives and forks had been flung from the sky.

Ryan stopped, turned around. Along with everyone else he watched Frank Crisler run out to the road. Frank shielded his eyes against the sun, against the awful silence. "Someone phone the fire department and the ambulance," he bellowed, then took off running south.

The wedding guests looked at each other, shook their heads, then hurried out to the road, a sea of flowered dresses and black suits jostling for position. They stood in the road for a moment as though willing those Hollywood Mufflers to come roaring over the last rise. But there was only the soft hum of a prairie afternoon—

bees buzzing in the caragana hedge and the click-click of a grasshopper's wings as it hovered over the middle of the road.

Those who had come to witness the wedding now set off down the road, bumping each other in their haste to catch up to Frank, who was already at the bottom of the first dip. Anyone watching from above would have been looking for the Hollywood cameras, the microphones on long booms, the trailers housing makeup and costumes, Alfred Hitchcock sitting in the director's chair.

Ryan shook himself out of his stupor and took off in pursuit of the crowd. He soon caught up with them. "Please God, let Geoff be okay. Let Geoff be okay. Let them all be okay," he prayed as he ran.

He could hear others praying and cursing as their hard-soled dress shoes skidded on the pebbles covering the dusty road. He pulled ahead of those who were pausing to hold their sides, gasping for breath. Half way up the last rise he paused to catch his own breath. Suddenly there was a massive whoomph, like a giant had shaken the sand out of his beach towel. A split second later Ryan sensed a change in the air—like someone had caressed his cheek with a warm touch.

He started to run again and when approaching the top of the hill he came upon a lone hubcap, *FARGO* embossed across the centre. There was another one, then a door handle and a strip of chrome. The air was full of crackling sounds. "Oh Lord, please, please, please let Geoff—" His prayer died on his lips as he crested the hill and saw the wreck.

It was a third of the way down the grade, an ugly knot of metal being devoured by a hungry monster of oily smoke and twisting flames. Ryan could see the back of Vince Skarnilatti's truck, but what had he hit? Was it the Crown Victoria or had someone else been on the road—another truck, or a farm tractor? The smoke made it difficult to see beyond the truck. Maybe the Crown Victoria with Geoff and Mrs. Ronson was stopped beyond the wreck.

Ryan began praying again. "Let Geoff be okay. Please God, I'll never ask for anything else as long as I live. Just let him be okay." He ran toward the fireball, pausing beside Frank Crisler.

"Who is it, Frank?" he asked. "Who did Vince hit?"

"It's Geoff's car."

"No. Please don't say that. Did they get out? Did everyone get out okay?"

Frank shook his head. "They wouldn't have had a chance. You know how fast Geoff drives and Vince takes whichever side of the road is smoothest, never mind if it's the wrong one."

"But maybe they jumped out when they saw they were going to hit." Ryan took a couple of steps forward.

"Keep back, my boy. The wind could change direction or there could be another explosion. You don't want to get burned."

"But can't we do something?" Ryan took another step towards the wreckage. Frank grabbed the tail of his suit jacket and pulled him back.

"There's nothing we can do until the firemen get here."

"But they have to come all the way from Sprucegrove. It'll take half an hour. Can't we look around? Maybe they were thrown out when they collided. Maybe they're all lying in the ditch, hidden by the tall grass. Maybe they're bleeding to death. We need to look."

Frank shook his head but followed Ryan into the ditch. The intense heat forced them to crawl through the barbed wire fence to the field beyond. On that side they were upwind of the fire, and after taking a few steps, were able to climb back through the fence, move in closer. Ryan scanned the grassy ditch, then the wreckage. Because of the smoke bellowing out of the vehicles it was difficult to see whether anyone was still inside them, but when a gust of wind blew the oily smoke aside Ryan thought he saw something on the Ford's dashboard, something skull-like, hairless, white bone glowing red hot in the flames.

Ryan doubled over, retched, threw up the cheese sandwich he'd gobbled before heading to the wedding. He wiped his mouth with his tie, straightened up, forced himself to look at the flaming wreckage again.

I've got to get him out of there, Ryan thought as he stripped off his tie and jacket. He lunged forward, not caring if he got burned during the rescue. He'd gladly wear the scars. The heat was searing hot as an iron on his face so he crouched down. He was about to make a run for it when a hand hooked his belt. Next thing, he was flat on the ground, Frank Crisler straddling him.

"Come away boy. We can't do anything."

"No. Let me up. Geoff's inside. I saw him. I have to—"

"You'll only be killed if you try to get inside what's left of that car."

"But I've got to try."

"You're not getting up until you promise me you'll come back to a safe distance." Frank eased off Ryan and began dragging him back to the fence line. He climbed through the fence, then dragged Ryan beneath the barbed wire onto the ploughed field.

"He's in there, Frank. I saw him. I saw his head."

"I saw him too, but there's nothing you can do. The three people in that wreck are tragedy enough for one day. We don't want to bury you too. Now come with me. I need your help. We need to get back on the road, stop others from seeing what we've seen. Will you help me?"

By the time they'd retraced their steps some of the women were arriving. "Go back. Go back to town." Frank held out his arms like he was herding cattle into the barn. "There's nothing to do here, nothing to see. Away you go."

Ryan saw his mother coming over the crest of the hill, one arm around Olive Skarnilatti's shoulder. He ran through the crowd.

"Ryan, what's happened to you?" His mother pointed to his clothing. "Where's your tie, your suit jacket?" He glanced down, for the first time seeing the grass stains, the ground-in dirt from when Frank dragged him away from the flames.

"Never mind my suit. You should both turn around. Olive, you mustn't come any closer."

"That is Vince's truck then?" Olive gestured toward the wreckage, clearly visible now that the oil and gasoline had burned off.

Ryan nodded and reached his arms around Olive and his mother. "They're dead. They're all dead. Vince. Geoff. Mrs. Ronson."

"Oh no, Ryan. That can't be." His mother and Olive both began to cry. Ryan let the tears flow too, the three of them standing in the middle of the road, holding onto each other, trembling with the horror of it.

"Oh my precious Jesus, no," Olive cried. "When I said I wanted that old truck to die I didn't mean for Vince to die with it. Oh Lord God in heaven, have mercy on us."

The three of them were distracted by renewed cries of, *Go back! Go back!* They looked up. Coralinda was stumbling drunkenly towards them in her high-heeled shoes. Wing Commander Ronson was on one side of her, her brother on the other. Her white dress was askew, the sequined skirt filthy with prairie dust. Her attendants in their long, pink dresses were trying to keep her white veil out of the dust as though the wedding might still go on after this interruption had been sorted out.

"Get her away from here!" hollered Frank Crisler. "Don't let her come any closer." Several of the women immediately joined hands, forming a human fence between the bride and the smouldering wreckage. Coralinda kicked off her shoes and dodged from side to side like a newborn calf separated from its mother for the first time.

Finally, her brother and Frank Crisler caught her in their arms, and between them they turned her away from the scene. Frank put his arm around Wing Commander Ronson's shoulder and said something to him. The airman shook his head, threw his arms around Coralinda and bawled like a schoolgirl.

"There's nothing any of you can do here," Frank Crisler said. "Away you go. Everyone go home. I'll stay here until the firemen arrive."

Ryan hesitated. Should he stay? He'd feel like a traitor if he left Geoff. Yet, one glimpse of that head on the dashboard was horror enough. He had no desire to see what the firemen would drag out of the wreckage once they had the flames extinguished.

As he stood in the centre of the road he saw Shirley come over the brow of the hill. Her beautiful white gown was covered with dust. She was limping barefoot, carrying her shoes, the heel broken off one of them. He ran towards her, his heart pounding, the tears pouring down his cheeks. "He's gone. Geoff's gone. Mrs. Ronson and Vincent are gone. They're all dead. Burned alive."

She held out her arms and he fell into them, howling with the horror of it all. "Come, let me help you over to the side of the road," she said. "My feet are killing me. We both need to sit down for a minute and—"

"But your dress."

"My dress is ruined, just like Jackie Kennedy's in Dallas on November 22nd, but no matter. I can make another one." They sat down on the grassy shoulder. Shirley put an arm around Ryan's shoulder and held him until he could cry no more.

Ryan didn't sleep that night, or the next, despite his parents' attempts to console him. His mother made pecan cinnamon rolls, his favourite breakfast treat—but they only reminded him how Geoff would wolf down two or three at a time. His father told him Geoff was the lucky one—he wouldn't have to put up with this life's disappointments.

The Adventist minister came by the second evening. "God's weeping with you good folks right now." He paused as he slathered margarine on his second cinnamon roll. "There's no doubt in my mind that God would like to intervene, but he can't. He has to be fair to the devil, let him show the universe what a planet under his rule of selfishness looks like. Our only hope is that when Jesus returns he'll resurrect those who have died. I'm sure your young friend will be one of those." He nodded to Ryan and smiled reassuringly before shoving the bun into his mouth.

The third night Ryan wished he hadn't slept, for he kept having fiery nightmares.

He and Geoff are driving to Alberta. The Crown Victoria is crammed with their camping equipment.

They are just past Regina when Geoff realizes he's forgotten his sleeping bag. Will they have to drive all the way back to the farm?

No. They'll buy a new one. Geoff drives into town and stops in front of the T. Eaton Company store. Ryan runs inside but can't find the sports department. He finally asks a woman for directions. When she turns around he sees that it's Jezalinda.

"Get out of the store!" she screams. "I know what you want. You want to steal Geoff from me. Get out before I call the police."

"You're the thief," Ryan bawls. "Geoff has always been mine. I've known him far longer than you. I'm the one he loves."

Jezalinda balls up her fists.

Ryan felt a hand shaking his shoulder. He opened his eyes to find his father bending over him, telling him to go back to sleep, to trust God to reunite him with Geoff on the resurrection day.

He lay awake for a long time after that, afraid to sleep, yet wanting to if he could be close to Geoff one more time. He finally nodded off.

He and Geoff are driving to Riding Mountain National Park. As they near the park gate they smell smoke. Suddenly the forest on both sides of the car is on fire. Geoff shifts into reverse. The car won't budge. "Did you fill the tranny with fluid after you drained it?" Geoff glares at him as a flaming branch lands on the Plexiglass roof.

"Yes, I did. You saw me do it."

"No, you didn't. You ran home to study math. Why didn't you fill it?"

"I did fill it. Stop yelling at me!"

Again he awakened. This time his mother was at his bedside.

"Would you like me to sing to you for awhile? Remember how I used to sing you to sleep when you were a wee fellow, when you were frightened by the thunder and lightning?" She began to sing *Jesus Loves Me* as she reached to smooth his hair.

The next morning Ryan helped his dad and Frank Crisler move the piano from the community hall to the curling rink, the only space large enough to accommodate the triple funeral. Other men brought chairs from every available source while the ladies raided their gardens to bank blooms against the bare walls.

When Ryan got home his mother told him that Coralinda had called. "She wants you to play the piano for the service."

"But the funeral's tomorrow," Ryan said. "How can she ask me to play on such short notice? I'd need to dig out a bunch of funeral music and practice."

"She wants you to play the same things you were going to play for their wedding."

"What if Geoff's mom and dad, and Olive don't want wedding music at the funeral?"

"Coralinda has talked to the Stephens and to Olive. Everyone's agreed to the wedding music."

"But how can Coralinda expect me to play for my best friend's funeral? We were practically brothers."

"All the more reason for you to take part in the service."

"Oh Mom, I can't possibly play. I'll start crying. I won't be able to see the notes. I'll have to stop playing in the middle of a hymn and everyone will stare at me. I'll get dizzy and fall off the piano bench. I'll feel nauseous and throw up all over the—"

"Stop it Ryan. It's a terrible tragedy. I know you're sad and upset like we all are, but why must you be so dramatic about everything?"

"That's easy for you to say. It won't be you sitting at the piano while what's left of your best friend is lying in a box behind you."

"Funerals are for the living. Quit thinking about yourself and think about Coralinda. How do you think she feels? She's lost her mother and her husband-to-be. Think of Mr. Ronson who lost his wife and almost son-in-law who was going to teach him how to farm. Think of Olive who will have to spend the rest of her life alone. It's them you should be concerned about. You'll be playing for all of *them*, not for the dead."

"Okay, okay," he said, stung by his mother's words. "I'll think about it, okay?"

"Well, be quick about it. Coralinda needs an answer today."

Ryan slammed out of the house and set off down the lane. He paused at the road, not knowing where to go, what to do. Why couldn't his parents understand what Geoff's loss meant to him? Why did they expect him to go on with life as if nothing more important had happened than a still-born calf out in the barn? While contemplating their callousness, he heard a train horn blowing a warning before crossing the trestle over Cottonwood Creek.

He'd hike down to the swimming hole. Maybe he'd feel close to Geoff there and he'd be able to decide whether to play for the funeral. He crossed the road, climbed through the pasture fence, and set off down the trail. In ten minutes he reached the spot where another trail ascended the hill to the Stephens' farm. He and Geoff always met at that spot, but never again. There'd be no more swimming on hot summer days, no more camping, no more skating when the creek froze.

Ryan kicked at a dried cow pie in the pathway. So what if God had to let the devil display his system of government. Couldn't he have interfered just a tiny bit? Couldn't he have whispered in Vince's ear, told him to get onto his own side of the road? If he didn't want to prevent the crash, couldn't he have ordered the guardian angels to fling Geoff and the others out of their vehicles? Couldn't he at least have let them break their necks and die in the ditch instead of being cremated alive?

In fifteen minutes Ryan was at the swimming hole, standing in the meadow where he and Geoff had pitched their tent many times—where they'd have pitched their tent this summer if Jezalinda hadn't come along. With the spring and summer rains the grass had grown long and sweet. It would have provided a perfect bed for their sleeping bags.

The steel trestle pinged, the joints expanding in the afternoon heat. Ryan looked up and raised his fist. "Bring him back, God. Bring him back to life. You did it for Lazarus and others when you were walking around on this planet. I don't care what you do to me—give me cancer, let me fall into the grain auger, let it chew off my legs and arms, but bring Geoff back."

The only reply was the sighing of the wind as it blew through the crosshatch of bracings holding up the trestle. It sounded like it was mourning Geoff too.

Ryan lifted the bottom edge of his T-shirt to wipe the tears from his eyes. He looked up at the trestle again. Why hadn't he thought of it before? Life without Geoff was going to be too painful, so why stand there bawling his eyes out? He could—and he would—do something about it. Gritting his teeth he ran over to the embankment and began scrambling up to the tracks. Tears hampered his progress as he grabbed blindly at snowberry and golden rod stems. Sometimes they came out by the root, leaving him sprawled flat on his belly, his hands scratched and bloody.

Finally, he reached the top and stumbled onto the track. A striped gopher that had been feeding on spilled grain from the hopper cars scampered away. A flock of pigeons enjoying the same free meal took flight. Up top the wind was strong and warm out of the south. He braced himself against it as he started forward. Several times he almost lost his balance when he put his foot down to find nothing between himself and the ground far below. He stumbled onto the little side platform where Robbie McLeod kept a barrel full of water in case of fire. There, he braced himself against the wind by gripping the flimsy two-by-four railing.

He wiped the tears and dust from his eyes, then forced himself to look down. He was standing directly above the tenting site. What better place to end his life, he thought as he swung one leg over the two-by-four railing. If Adventist theology was right about death, he'd split his head open on the blackened rocks around the fire pit and the next moment would be the resurrection morning.

He'd pop out of the grave with a new body. He'd look across the cemetery and Geoff would be standing beside his grave. They'd run to each other, hug, and be together for eternity. There'd be no more car accidents, no more fires, no more earthquakes, no more evil, period.

And hadn't Jesus said people wouldn't be married in heaven? That meant he wouldn't have to worry about Jezalinda or anyone else stealing Geoff away from him.

He swung his other leg over the railing so now he was seated with both feet hanging over the tenting site. He leaned back against the wind which was picking up. He swiped the back of his hand across his eyes to clear the tears. He pressed his hands down on the railing, about to launch himself into freefall. He paused. Shouldn't he say something first, something significant?

Geoff, I'm doing this because I don't want to live without you. Would that be appropriate? Or should he be praying like the thief who was crucified beside Jesus? *Lord, remember me when thou comest into thy kingdom.*

Jesus had assured the thief he'd be in heaven. Of course, the thief hadn't wanted to die. Did that make a difference with God? Would God not resurrect him if he deliberately jumped off the bridge? But Samson had committed suicide. He had yanked the Philistine's temple down on top of himself and he was now listed among the saints. God would probably understand.

Ryan looked down again. He was poised directly over the fire ring, but it looked pretty small from so high up. What if the wind blew him off course and he missed it? What if he didn't split his head open and dash his brains out on the rocks? What if he fell flat on the grassy meadow, broke his neck, his back, suffered a brain injury? He might have to live at home for the rest of his life. He might be bedridden, his mother singing lullabies to him until the day she died.

The wind was strengthening again. Ryan's hands were trembling from gripping the railing so tightly. If he was going to jump he'd better do it soon.

"Yon lad, what be ye plannin'?"

190

Ryan almost lost his balance as he turned to look over his shoulder. The wailing of the wind through the trestle's spidery supports had drowned out the putt-putt of the jigger's approach. It had stopped some distance away. Robbie McLeod and one of the section men were standing on the trestle, only a few steps away. Robbie took a step forward. "You'll not be thinkin' of jumpin', are ye?"

Ryan looked down at the fire pit, then back at Robbie and nodded.

"And who are you thinkin' will be pickin' up the pieces after ye break yer bloody neck?"

Ryan shrugged.

Robbie stepped closer. "I'm thinkin' it'll be me and me lads. But we've got better things to do. Me and my lads have switches to inspect, signal lights to test and spikes to pound. If we have to climb down to scrape you off them yon rocks and haul your bloody carcass up here, there's no tellin' when we'll be gettin' our supper. Will ye no' let me give ye a hand down?"

Ryan, dizzy with fear—or was it grief—tried to respond but he couldn't form any words. The sound that came out was half moan, half plea for help. He tried to pry his hands off the railing.

"Here, my fine lad. You sit tight like you are. There now. I've got you, laddie." Robbie gripped Ryan's arm while the section man locked his arms around his waist and pulled him over the railing to safety.

"That's the good lad. Just stand steady." Robbie waved to the section man who had stayed with the jigger. He started the engine and moved towards them. "There now, up with ye onto the seat and we'll have ye back on God's good earth in no time. Why would a fine lookin' lad like ye be thinkin' of endin' his life?"

"Didn't you...Didn't you hear about the accident?" Ryan forced the words out between chattering teeth. Now that he was safe, he was shivering like it was the middle of winter instead of a hot day in July.

"Yon lad killed in the car wreck on his wedding day? He the lad ye was camping with last summer?"

Ryan nodded.

Robbie shifted the machine into gear and they put-putted off the trestle. "Surely yon friend would not be pleased to see your brains spilled out where ye had so much fun last year."

"Guess not." Ryan wiped the tears from his eyes. "I'm supposed to play the piano for his funeral."

"Well ye better be gettin' home and practicin', then, right lad?" Robbie slowed as they approached the road crossing.

Ryan nodded. Robbie helped him off the machine, patted him on the back, then sped back to where he'd left his crew.

"Where have you been?" Ryan's mother asked when he got home.

"I was out."

"I know you were out. Your father and I have been looking all over for you. Look at your clothes, all covered in dirt, and grease on your arm. Reverend Middleditch from the United Church called. They're having a meeting about the funeral. You'll be late if you don't get cleaned up and away to town right now."

Reverend Middleditch, a weary looking man several years past retirement age, hosted the meeting in the vestry at the United Church. Father Ringwold, in a black shirt and trousers, was there for the Ronsons. Young, ginger-bearded Apostle Lawrence, from the tabernacle, represented the Stephens.

The meeting got off to a bad start when Father Ringwold announced that he wanted the service to begin with the hymn, *Hail, Holy Queen.* He handed a photocopy of the music to Ryan.

"Geoff's parents will be offended if a song of praise is sung to the Virgin Mary," Apostle Lawrence said. "We Tabbers do not believe Mary is enthroned above, or anywhere else. According to our teachings, she is sleeping in her grave. The Stephens may refuse to sing such nonsense. They may even walk out if those words are sung."

"But what a comfort the words will be to those who follow our traditions." Father Ringwold raised his eyes to the ceiling and sang in a trembling falsetto.

To thee do we cry, poor sons of Eve, O Maria!
To thee we sigh, we mourn, we grieve, O Maria!

"Those words aren't comforting," Apostle Lawrence said. "Surely there are better—"

"Come now, gentlemen." Reverend Middleditch used his middle finger to push his black-framed glasses up his nose. "Surely we need not argue over this. If it's a hymn good Catholics are familiar with, couldn't Ryan simply play it on the piano at some point during the service? That way no one will be offended and those who know the words can think of them and find comfort."

After ten minutes of argument this was agreed upon, and the inoffensive *The Lord's My Shepherd* was approved as the first hymn. Apostle Lawrence said it was Geoff's favourite song. Ryan didn't believe that. So far as he knew, Geoff didn't have a favourite hymn. He couldn't even carry a tune when he whistled.

Ryan insisted the last hymn had to be *Thine Is the Glory* set to Handel's melody for *See, the Conquering Hero Comes*. It was the recessional he had planned to play for the wedding and the words spoke about Christ's victory over death. No one argued with him, so the music was settled.

The clergy then started arguing about the sermon, the talk, the homily—each had a different name for it. Father Ringwold said he couldn't, in good faith, put Mrs. Ronson in heaven because she hadn't been to confession for years. So far as the church was concerned she had died with a load of sin on her heart. "It would be a mockery to say she is with the Lord when she may be in hell for all I know," he said.

"We don't have that problem with Geoff." Apostle Lawrence picked at a pimple on his forehead. "I'll tell the people Geoff is sleeping quietly in the grave until the resurrection morning."

"I say we keep our mouths shut about where the three of them are," Reverend Middleditch said. "Doesn't the Good Book tell us not to judge folk? I saw Vince Skarnilatti in church every Sunday, but I have no idea what was going on inside that steel-plated head of his. For all I know he may have been dreaming about his Sunday dinner or how to keep that old truck running. What we do know is that all three of the poor souls are in the arms of the loving Jesus. He'll be a much fairer judge than any of us."

"That type of wishy-washy theology may be popular in this building, but it won't do for faithful Catholics." Father Ringwold reached inside his black shirt and scratched his belly. "Mrs. Ronson may not be safe at all. She may be writhing in hellfire at this very moment. It would do the people good to hear that; maybe sober them up, stop the young people listening to Elvis and The Beatles, get them back in the pew where they belong."

"In other words, you want to use this horrible accident to scare people into loving God." Reverend Middleditch frowned and glanced at the clock.

"A little fear of God never hurts." Father Ringwold sat back in his chair.

"Sounds like an oxymoron to me," Apostle Lawrence said.

Ryan didn't know what an oxymoron was, but he was beginning to wish he had jumped off that bridge. With the snap of his neck he'd have been dead, catapulted straight to the resurrection morning whether it happened in five years or five thousand years. When raised to new life, he'd be swimming with Geoff in heaven's sea of glass instead of listening to these fools argue. "Excuse me," he said, "I'd better get home and practice *Hail, Holy Queen*."

While practicing the piano that evening, Ryan could hear mutterings from his parents who were sitting in the family room. Clearly they were talking about Geoff and Coralinda. Ryan depressed the damper pedal so he could better hear what they were saying, something about Coralinda being pregnant.

"What are you saying about Geoff?" he called out.

"Nothing important," his mother said.

"If you're saying that Geoff got Coralinda pregnant, it's not true. He would have told me."

"You shouldn't be listening to our conversation. Get on with your practicing." His father switched on the television set to watch some news program.

Late that night, before getting into bed, Ryan opened the little Black Forest box his Aunt Vivian had given him. He took out the ring Geoff had made for him. He kissed it. He tried to slip it onto the fourth finger of his left hand but his finger had grown too large.

He got into bed but couldn't sleep. Tears spilled onto the pillow as Ryan thought of those snug nights in the pup tent. He had felt so safe and warm, so protected and hopeful for the future, especially that last night when he had snuggled up to Geoff to keep warm. Now he would be alone for the rest of his life. He would never find another friend like Geoff, a friend who wouldn't make fun of him for going to church on Saturday, for saying no to booze and cigarettes, for being a vegetarian.

He finally fell asleep, but like the previous night, he got no rest. His brain kept kicking into nightmare mode.

Ryan is seated in the Crown Victoria's back seat, directly behind Geoff. Mrs. Ronson is in the front passenger seat, holding Coralinda's bouquet on her lap. She tells Geoff the roses are fading and urges him to drive faster. Geoff takes his eyes off the road to look at the bouquet.

"Look out! Look ahead!" Ryan yells, but his warning comes too late. Before Geoff can react there is that awful crashing sound and everything inside the car explodes. The mirror pops off its anchor over the windshield, the door handles fly off, the radio bursts out of the dashboard.

The queer thing is that none of them are injured. When everything settles, Vincent Skarnilatti lies sprawled on the Crown Victoria's hood. He peers through the cracked windshield, bangs on it with his fist, and shouts something about having lost the steel plate from his head.

"We can't help you look for it now," Mrs.
Ronson says. "Coralinda's flowers are wilting."
Ryan says, "Don't worry, Vincent. I'll come
back and help you look as soon as I've played for
the wedding."
And then Ryan sees a lick of flame coming out of
the Crown Victoria's hood. He yells, "Get off the
hood, Vince. Get off the hood!" The old man just
waves to them with that funny way he has of
opening and closing his fist.
"The roses are wilting. The roses are wilting,"
Mrs. Ronson yells. Geoff tries to open his door but
it's jammed. He reaches across Mrs. Ronson but
her door is jammed shut too. He tries to start the
car so he can back away from the flames.

Ryan woke up. He was sitting up in bed, his pillow and
pajamas soaked with perspiration. He flipped his pillow over, then
lay awake wishing he really could have been in the Crown Victoria
with Geoff. Perhaps if he'd been sitting in the back seat he
wouldn't have been injured. He could have reached forward and
helped Geoff and Mrs. Ronson escape before the fire started. Even
if that had not been possible, he could have touched Geoff, held his
hand while they burned up together.

Ryan arrived at the rink twenty minutes before the funeral
service was to begin. Sprucegrove High's football team and
cheerleaders were already seated in the second row from the
front—a solid line of blue and white jerseys.

The three caskets were lined up across the front of the rink, a
spray of white lilies on top of each along with a framed
photograph. Ryan paused at Geoff's casket. Geoff was pictured
wearing his football jersey, his helmet under his arm. He had a big
smile on his sweat-slick face, his curly blond hair matted down.
Ryan had thrilled to that smile so many times over the years—
when they'd raced each other across the swimming hole; pounded

their bikes up and down the roller coaster road like their lives depended upon it; playfully body-checked each other when skating around this very rink; played one-upmanship with the details of their queer religious beliefs.

Ryan might have stood there for the whole service if Shirley, wearing a black dress and a single strand of pearls, hadn't come along. Gently she took him by the arm and led him over to the piano. "I'm going to sit beside you," she said, pulling an extra chair from the end of the front row. "I'll turn pages for you."

Ryan thanked her, then arranged his music on the piano, sat down and began to play Pachelbel's *Canon in D*. As he played he could hear a great rustling of paper tissues and blowing of noses among the football players and cheerleaders. In the mirror on top of the piano he could see the fellows patting each other on their shoulders and the girls embracing each other.

At two o'clock the long train of mourners filed into the rink and took their places in the front row. Coralinda was wearing her wedding dress, the veil over her face. The opening hymn was announced. Ryan played the introduction. He was doing fine during the singing until the third stanza when he choked up over the words, *Yea, though I walk in death's dark vale.* The thought that his faithful friend, Geoff, was now in that dark vale, brought a gush of tears to his eyes. The notes blurred on the page and he started to panic. He felt dizzy. He might have collapsed on top of the piano's ivories if Shirley hadn't, at that moment, put a comforting hand on his shoulder.

"Remember Jackie Kennedy," she whispered. "She didn't cry once during The President's funeral."

After the devilish arguments during the clergy's meeting the day before, the funeral service was anticlimactic. Prayers were said. Scriptures were read—thankfully none about the horrors of everlasting fire. In fact, the clergy behaved themselves, only reminding the congregation of the uncertainty of life and how everyone should be ready to meet God with a clear conscience at every moment of every day.

After Reverend Middleditch concluded his remarks, Ryan played *Hail, Holy Queen,* as the captains of the football and cheerleader squads carried wreaths forward and placed them in front of Geoff's casket. Then Apostle Lawrence invited people to come forward to say a few words about the deceased.

Half the football squad jumped to their feet and jostled their way forward, but after the first two broke down while describing some of Geoff's memorable plays, the others shuffled back to their seats. A couple of cheerleaders told how Geoff was a true Christian. He had helped one of them sort out a tricky algebra problem. He had pithed a frog for another when she was too frightened to do it herself.

Several women who worked at the IGA grocery store told what a fine employee Mrs. Ronson was. She always arrived at work a few minutes early; she told interesting stories of the family's time in Germany; she taught them all a few words in French and German.

No one said anything about Vincent Skarnilatti until Ryan's dad, Vince's only relative, walked to the microphone. "Vince was always happy to help me with chores," he said. "He mixed cement for that addition I put onto the barn. He served on the board of the Wheat Pool, and every spring he helped clean out the elevator's bins."

There was a hush when Coralinda walked to the microphone. After thanking everyone for coming, she said, "I want everyone to know how proud I am to be carrying Geoff's child." She paused until the murmurings and program rustlings died away. Ryan watched as Mrs. Stephens, who until then had been sitting ramrod straight on her chair, slumped down a wee bit. Mr. Stephens reached for her hand.

"I know what you're thinking," Coralinda went on. "You think that's very wicked, but Geoff and I loved each other. We really and truly and definitely loved—" She paused, unable to complete her sentence. Wing Commander Ronson stepped forward to hand her his handkerchief, then stood with his arm around her until she was able to compose herself.

"I'm happy—I'm so happy to know Geoff will live on in the life of our child, our precious love child. I don't know yet, but I'm hoping, and praying," she looked directly at the Stephens, "that the baby will be a boy who looks exactly like his daddy, exactly like—" Once again emotion overwhelmed her. Wing Commander Ronson helped her back to her seat.

After that revelation no one else cared to say anything, so Father Ringwold announced the last hymn. Ryan turned to the piano and pounded out Handel's magnificent melody. The congregation sang the words printed in the order of service. *Thine is the glory, risen, conquering Son,* but Ryan was playing for Geoff and mouthing Handel's original words – *See, the conqu'ring hero comes! Sound the trumpets! Beat the drums!*

Those words suited Geoff so well: Sprucegrove High's star football quarterback, winner of ten ribbons at the previous summer's 4-H fair, restorer of the Crown Victoria. If only he'd never bought that Crown Victoria, Ryan thought. He would never have started taking Coralinda to school. He would still be alive and instead of being at a funeral, they might be camping down by Cottonwood Creek.

After the benediction Ryan played *See, the conqu'ring hero comes,* a couple more times while the caskets were wheeled out. Then he joined his parents and Shirley for the trip to the graveyard. The only access was by the roller coaster road, past the spot where the rain was turning the accident site into a sad, black blot on the prairie landscape.

At the cemetery Ryan and his folks hurried over to where Vince was being laid to rest. Reverend Middleditch consigned Vincent to the heavenly country, perhaps driving one of God's fiery chariots at that very moment. It was a poor choice of phrase, considering the mayhem Vince had caused. It set Olive to weeping and crying out once again that when she prayed for the old wreck to be disabled she hadn't meant for Vince to die.

When the casket had been lowered, Ryan slipped over to the Stephens' plot where Apostle Lawrence was laying Geoff firmly in the grave. The apostle took a small silver vial from his pocket and sprinkled two lines of dust on the casket's lid to form a cross. "Dust to dust and ashes to ashes," he said. That didn't seem appropriate either, considering how Geoff had died. "And now Lord, we commend our son and friend Geoff Stephens to your care. May you bring him forth alive when you return to take all of us home to the heavenly country. Amen."

The undertaker stepped on a small lever sticking out from the brass frame around the grave, and the casket, with a gentle whirring sound, descended. Ryan wondered what was inside. Ashes? A few blackened bones? The remains of the flaming skull he'd seen on the dashboard? Frank Crisler hadn't described what the coroner found after the firemen cooled down the heat-twisted wreckage. Ryan hadn't asked either. It was better not to know.

Ryan shook hands with Mr. and Mrs. Stephens. "Don't forget us," Mrs. Stephens said, hugging him. "You've always been like a second son to us. Come over as often as you like."

"I will. I will." Ryan hugged her back.

He watched as the Stephens said a few words to the football and cheerleading squads before getting into the limousine. Then he hung behind, watching the undertaker remove the brass frame with its webbed straps from the grave. Ryan helped him roll up the green rugs that had been covering the mounds of soil, then stood alone by the open grave.

He fished from his pocket the ring Geoff had given him. He turned it over, tried it on his fourth finger again. Should he use the rat-tail file to ream it out, make it fit again? No, that would spoil it. It would no longer be the same metal Geoff had touched.

Ryan brought it to his lips, then held it over the grave. "Geoff, I'll always love you." He was about to let the ring drop, when he felt a hand on his shoulder.

Coralinda was standing behind him, her wedding dress stained where it had dragged over the wet grass. She held her veil bunched up in one hand. "Geoff heard what you said."

Ryan shook his head as he pocketed the ring. "Probably not, but God heard me."

"I'm sure he did," Coralinda said, flipping her hair away from her eyes, swollen and red from crying. "I want to thank you for playing the piano for our wedding—"

"What do you mean?"

"I know you practiced a lot, and from where I was in the tabernacle's basement, I could hear you playing. And thanks for the funeral music too. It must have been difficult for you, being Geoff's best friend for so many years."

Ryan shrugged his shoulders, afraid to say anything in case his voice broke.

"I have a question for you, and I hope you'll say yes."

"What's that?"

"I know you were Geoff's best friend so he'd approve of what I'm asking you." She paused, wiped a tear from her cheek.

"What is it, Coralinda?"

She placed her hands gently over her tummy. "Will you be godfather for our child, for Geoff's child?"

Ryan hesitated. He'd heard the word *godfather*, but he didn't know what it meant. "I'm not sure what a godfather does."

"He's sort of like a favourite uncle. You'd come to his christening and promise to help him grow up to be a good person. You'd be someone little Geoff could talk to if he had some problem he didn't want to discuss with me. You could help him celebrate his birthdays and other special days—sort of look out for him, make sure he grows up proper."

"But I'll be away to university in September. I won't be around to—"

"But you'll be coming home some weekends and holidays to visit your parents, won't you?"

"I suppose so."

"Then there's no problem. I think it would be nice if Geoff's best friend could be little Geoff's godfather. You could tell him about his daddy, about all the things you and Geoff did when you were little."

"I guess I could tell him how we camped under the train trestle, maybe even take him camping when he gets older. Would a godfather do that?"

"Oh yes, and I'd like that. I'm not much of an outdoor person, but Geoff was always talking about the fun you guys had down at the swimming hole."

"Okay, I guess it's something I could do then," Ryan said.

"Thank you. If Geoff's watching and listening, I'm sure he's pleased." Coralinda threw her arms around Ryan and kissed him on the cheek, then hurried over to where her dad was waiting.

Ryan reached into his pocket for the ring. He pulled it out and turned back to the grave, was about to drop it, then changed his mind.

"Geoff, I'll keep your ring for now, but one day I'll give it to your son. I'll tell him you made it, and when he wears it, he'll remember what a fine man his daddy was."

Together Forever

"Willie *is* coming!" The news spread quicker than the Dee leaps its banks after a summer storm. Everyone had been praying Kaiser Bill wouldn't come. But why should this be any different than all the other times he'd invited himself to Balmoral?

"The wicked reprobate should stay home." Cook took her place at the end of the table in the servants' hall.

"Ach, ye'll not be understandin' the politics of it," said Mr. Miggs, the butler. "The Prime Minister wants the old Queen to talk some sense to him, warn him against building up his navy."

"He better leave his beast at home," said Collins, the Head Footman. "One piece out of my backside is enough, and I refuse to valet for him."

"Don't look at me." I helped myself to the cold venison. "I'll have plenty to do, valeting Lord Edward."

"Neither one of you'll be seeing to the naughty nipper. He's bringing his own man." Mr. Miggs waved a butter-slick finger at Collins and me. "Mind when serving at dinner you don't stare at that shrunken arm of his. Don't want to start a war."

I was Second Footman at Balmoral that summer of 1900, having started at the castle a year previously. Papa, looking at my slim build, said I was more suited to be a footman than helping him in the smithy. Working inside wasn't easy either. I was forever running up and down stairs: hauling coals to stoke the fires, cleaning boots, fetching trays to those who wanted to eat in their rooms. This would be the first time I'd valeted for one of Queen Victoria's guests. "What's Lord Edward like?" I asked.

"He's the second son of the Duke and Duchess of Strathclyde. They come every season for the shooting." Mr. Miggs peered over his spectacles at the maids. "You keep out of his way. He can be too familiar with the servants."

"Is he handsome?" asked the scullery maid.

"Never mind," Cook said. "No good comes messing with our betters. When they gets what they wants, they toss you in the dustbin, so while Lord Edward's here, save your eyes for your work."

When the Strathclydes arrived the next day we lined up at the door to welcome them. Young Edward appeared to be my age—barely twenty. He was tall and solidly built with the family's rusty hair and freckles.

"Lord Edward, Andrews will look after you." Mr. Miggs nodded for me to take Lord Edward's bags.

"Does Milord wish to bathe before dinner?" I asked, leading the way upstairs. "I can arrange for water to be brought up."

"How kind, Andrews. Those railways are so filthy, aren't they?"

"Don't know, Milord. I've never had the good fortune to travel by train."

"You don't attend Her Majesty in London?"

"No, Milord. I stay here to see to things when she's gone."

"You're the lucky one. Train travel is modern and fast but filthy—smoke and cinders. Give me a horse and carriage any day. A journey may take several days instead of hours but one has time to see things. Now a steamship, there's an excellent way to travel. Have you seen one, Andrews?"

"No, Milord. I was born and raised here. Only been to Crathie with me dad."

"I was born in Ceylon," Lord Edward said. "Had a baby elephant when I was a wee one. Ceylon's a fine place. You must go if you get the chance."

"Don't suppose I shall, Milord."

"You don't have to call me Milord all the time. My name's Edward. My family calls me Eddie. What's your first name?"

"Cameron, Milord. Cameron Andrews"

"Well Cameron, you can all me Eddie."

"Wouldn't be right, Sir. Mr. Miggs would have a fit of apoplexy if he heard me call you anything but Milord."

"Very well, Cameron Andrews. We shall keep it formal, for now."

"Will I build up the fire before you bathe, Sir?"

"Please do. Mommsie warned me this castle was cold as Jack the Ripper's heart. Have you heard the latest rumor about his identity?"

Lord Edward chattered away while I set the hip bath before the fire, then unpacked his bags while waiting for the water. When the tub was full I said, "There you are, Milord. Shall I return in a quarter hour to help you dress?"

"Don't suppose you'd scrub my back, would you? I'd be ever so grateful if you would. I'm sure some cinders fell inside my collar." He rubbed his neck.

"Well, Milord, if you wish." I removed his tweed travelling jacket, then his tie, collar and cufflinks. I thought he would remove his own trousers and shirt, but he stood waiting. When he was down to his flannel drawers I turned my back while hanging his jacket and trousers in the wardrobe. When I turned around his drawers were on the floor. You can imagine my embarrassment when I noticed his member was revealing some inner excitement.

I nodded towards the tub, and after another moment's hesitation, he stepped over and eased himself into the water. He settled back, closed his eyes, and sighed.

"Do you want me to wash your back now, Milord, or would you like to soak awhile?"

"Now, please."

I slipped off my jacket, lathered the sponge with soap, and got down on my knees. "Tell me if I'm scrubbing too hard, Milord."

"That feels soooo gooooood." Lord Edward leaned forward and closed his eyes.

"Will that do, Milord?"

"I suppose you'd best leave some skin intact. Is there a chance you'd scrub the rest of my sooty bones?"

"Better do that yourself, Milord." I stood up. "I'll return to help you dress."

Without giving him a chance to say anything more, I quit the room. As I hurried downstairs I wondered if the rumors about Lord Edward's familiarity with staff were due to his attentions to footmen and boot boys rather than to upstairs maids.

More troubling was why he had sought attention from me. Could he read in my features the love I shared with Garth Campbell? Did something in my voice betray the loving words we whispered to each other in our bedroom?

When I returned to Lord Edward's room he had dried himself off and was wearing the clean pair of drawers I had laid out for him. "My back feels raw from the scrubbing you gave it, Andrews."

"Was I too rough on you, Milord?"

"No. I enjoyed it, but could you rub that into my skin?" He pointed to a bottle of almond oil he'd set on the dresser.

"Very well, Milord." I thought he'd simply turn his back to me while remaining erect, but he leaped onto the bed and lay face down. "You'll have to move closer to the edge of the bed if I'm to reach you, Milord."

"I thought you might straddle me."

"It would be more comfortable for me to stand, Milord." I poured oil into the palm of my hand as he wriggled over to the bedside. "That's good. I can reach you now."

As I worked the oil into his flaming red skin, he wriggled deeper into the bed clothes, arching his well-formed arse now and again.

"You can go lower if you like, Andrews. Shall I remove my drawers? Would that make it easier for you?"

"The skin's not so red down there," I said after briefly lifting the waistband. "I think this will do nicely, Milord."

"Are you a prude, Andrews?"

"I'm not familiar with the word, Milord."

"Never mind."

When I had finished, he extended a leg over the side of the bed and stood up. "That feels good. Let's get me dressed and downstairs. I feel in need of my dinner. Mommsie says Mrs. McLeod's aspic is worth the journey. Is she still in the kitchen?"

"Yes, Milord. She and the man from India see to the cooking." As I fidgeted with his tie, his eyes, sparkling blue-as-the-Dee on a summer's day, locked on mine. I blushed, wondering what he saw in my face, and questioning whether I would have responded to his flirtatious ways if I didn't love Garth. I could understand how a lonely footman would react to his mischievous grin, to the little-boy freckles raining down his forehead onto his nose and cheeks. If I had been yearning for love I might have leaned forward to taste the welcoming red of his lips.

"There you are, Milord."

He looked in the mirror. "A very fine piece of work, Andrews. I'm glad you're looking after me. I hope we shall become friends." He laid his fingers upon my hand as he passed into the hallway.

Prince George was seated at dinner beside his grandmother, Kaiser Bill on the other side. He spoke with a thick German accent, boasting about his new dreadnoughts—their speed, the size and number of their guns. I followed Mr. Miggs' advice not to look at his withered left arm until I was serving the aspic to Princess May who was seated across the table from him. I risked a glance. He was eating with his right hand. The left hung at table level, a pitiful, useless claw.

It was past midnight when the gentlemen retired. I followed Lord Edward upstairs to help him change for the night. I had to steady him a couple of times along the way, and once in the room, guided him to the bed.

"I put myself entirely in your hands, Andrews, my good man. You may do with me whatever you like." He leered and fluttered his eyelids in a drunken approximation of a wink.

I reached to loosen his tie but before I could touch it he flung his hands around the back of my head and planted a sloppy, whiskey-soaked kiss on my lips.

"Please, Milord, you're making it difficult for me to remove your tie."

"Pardon me, Andrews. Far be it from me to get in your way. Here I am." He took a wobbly step backwards, then spread his arms. "Undress me. Lay me out on the bedclothes. Do with me as you see fit."

Jacket, tie, and collar removed, I bent down to take off his footwear. I placed his shoes by the door. I would take them downstairs with the others from the Bachelor's Wing, to be blackened before I took to my own bed.

When I straightened up, Lord Edward had fallen on the counterpane, snoring like a spent stallion. Free of further flirtations, I completed my task, stripping him naked. He was well-formed back and front, his chest, belly, and legs peach-fuzzed with that rusty coloured hair for which the Strathclydes were famous. If I hadn't had Garth waiting for me, I might well have taken liberties with his soft, but still large, member. Close up, I could see that the shaft, like his arse, was spattered with freckles. I watched for a moment as it lay twitching with each snore, reached to stroke it, then thought of Garth and straightened up. I yanked the bedclothes up to Lord Edward's chin and quit the room.

The clock chimed two by the time I finished cleaning the boots. Garth was sleeping, so I tiptoed into the room before crawling into bed beside him. He grunted, then turned onto his side, stretched a furry thigh and arm over me, and snugged me in close to his chest before kissing me on the cheek. I felt his manhood hardening, but except for a light caress, I let it be. Garth was a morning person. I knew, come morning, he'd want to rut like a stag.

I woke with his mouth sucking at my swelling root. As I shifted, Garth moaned. "Mmmm. My wee footman feels big and strong and full of juice this morning." He kissed the crown of my member, then came up for air and started on my mouth.

Garth was a big fellow, easily manhandling the four-footed residents in the Queen's stables, and I loved it when he manhandled me. During the next half hour Garth flipped me over several times, covered my body with kisses, massaged the muscles in my chest with his powerful hands, then my arms, my calves, thighs, and finally my arse.

When he had satisfied his hunger for skin, he lay behind me, his massive chest to my back, and after gently preparing me with a healthy dollop of Dr. Backmon's Celebrated Horse Salve, began loving me as only a man can. When about to spill his seed inside me, he wrapped his salve-slick fist around my own manhood and brought us both to that place where *I love you* felt inadequate to express our feelings for each other.

While he cleaned up and dressed, I fell asleep with the warm satisfaction that always came after Garth and I enjoyed ourselves, only wakening briefly when his lips gently touched mine before he went down to feed and water the horses.

An hour later I got up and set to work coaling the fires and setting the polished boots outside each owner's door. After breakfast I prepared Lord Edward's tray. I knocked on the door before entering his room. He was lying on his back, the bedclothes thrown aside, his fist closed around his greatly swollen member.

"I'm sorry, Milord. I'll come back later." I began to close the door.

"Please, don't go, Andrews. I was hoping you'd help me with this."

"With what, Milord?" I slowly stuck my head around the door.

Lord Edward squeezed his large root, forcing a drool of juice out the slit. "I thought you might help me get rid of this." He pointed to the open bottle of almond oil on the bedside table. "A few drops of that in your gentle hands should work magic."

"I'm sorry, Milord. I can't do that. I'm already spoken for."

"Spoken for?"

"Yes, Milord."

"How unlucky for me. Who is the fortunate one you're walking out with?"

"The groom, Milord."

"That big fellow with a lion's mane of hair who drove us from Ballater yesterday?"

"Yes, Milord. We have promised each other."

"Does the old Queen know?"

"She has spoken of giving us the wee cottage beside Smithy Cottage, beside the one where me dad and mom live. If you'll excuse me, Milord, I'll get on with my duties and come back later to help you dress."

"Very well, Andrews." He pulled the sheet to cover his nakedness. "Best wishes to you and the groom. I yearn to be so fortunate. Among my people such friendships do not rate a cottage—more like a one-way ticket to the colonies. There are times I wish I'd been born in a wee stone cottage instead of in a castle."

"I'm sorry to hear that, Milord."

"All I get is a quick fondle behind closed doors or a wee scrum in the bushes after a cricket match. I envy you. I apologize if I've offended you." Holding the sheet around himself he sat up. "I'll have my morning tea now. Come back in a quarter hour to help me dress."

I pitied Lord Edward. Considering Oscar Wilde's recent sentence to hard labor, he was right that a life like mine with Garth was impossible for him. It would have been impossible for me too if the old Queen hadn't been such a romantic, never happier than when encouraging love matches among her family and retainers.

The rest of Lord Edward's visit passed amiably enough. I would have believed we were becoming friends if I hadn't been aware of my position as a footman. He quizzed me about my life with Garth. How long had we lived together? Did our parents understand the nature of our love? Did they approve? How had the old Queen found out?

I summed it up on the last morning as I packed his bags. "Ach, Lord Edward, so long as no one speaks of it, like me and you are doing, it don't happen, and no one fusses."

It had been a treat to talk openly of my love for Garth. I would miss Lord Edward. I gallantly accepted his good-bye embrace and kiss on the cheek before I saw him out the front door. Garth was waiting with the team and carriage to drive the Strathclydes to the station. Unfortunately, Kaiser Bill decided to stay a few more days.

The old Queen was feeling poorly Saturday night and announced she wouldn't attend church on the morrow. There would be no need for the carriage, so Sunday morning Garth and I were enjoying a cuddle after our morning lovemaking when Collins pounded on the door.

"Her Majesty wants the carriage brought round. She'll be going to church after all."

Garth leaped out of bed, pulled on his livery, and hurried down to the stables. From the warmth of our bed I listened to the familiar sound of hooves on cobbles, the rattle as he shook out the harness, a dog barking, and then Garth hollering at someone. I threw back the bedclothes and ran to the window to see what was upsetting him.

Kaiser Bill was standing below, his foul dachshund nipping at the team's heels. I watched Garth kick at the dog, which raised a roar of protest from Kaiser Bill. This further inflamed the dog's evil temper. He fastened his teeth into old Jessie's left hock. She kicked. The carriage jerked forward. The whippletree caught Garth behind his thighs.

"Oh God, no," I shouted as he tumbled forward, smashing his face on the cobbles. The team bolted, pulling the carriage—a heavy landau—overtop Garth, arse to head. With the sound of breaking bones in my ears I raced barefoot down the stairs in my nightshirt. I shouldered my way past Kaiser Bill who had finally grabbed his killer dog by the collar.

"Garth. Talk to me. Talk to me." I ran my fingers over his cheek, along his neck which was bent at an unnatural angle. "Garth, don't leave me, my love. Don't die."

I scented a sharp, metallic odor, felt a sticky dampness around my knees, and looked down to see a river of blood filling the space between the cobbles.

"Get the doctor!" I howled at Kaiser Bill. "Don't just stand there, you bloody fool. Get the doctor."

I gently turned Garth over. His white breeches were crimson from the waist to the crotch. I unbuttoned his coat and shirt, exposing a sight I'd seen only in the butcher's shop or on the hunt—the bloody ends of three ribs piercing his skin.

"Please, God, don't let Garth—" But I knew from the blood, the shattered ribs, and the twisted neck that my love was beyond help.

The story of how Kaiser Bill *murdered* the old Queen's groom spread to all the great houses. The day of Garth's funeral, I received a letter in a black-edged envelope from Lord Edward.

My dear, dear friend. I pray that I may call you my friend. Since we shared our private lives such a brief time ago, I may be the only person who fully understands your loss. I want you to know...

Lord Edward was right. Everyone else thought I should get on with life. They said working with horses was a dangerous business. Grooms were maimed or killed all the time, so I should quit moping about like an orphaned lamb. Collins was especially cruel, jabbing me in the ribs and saying, "Snap out of it, Andy Pamby. Quit the tears before your head shrinks."

Some said the old Queen's death, a few months later, was hurried along by the guilt she felt for changing her mind about church that Sunday morning. I don't know if that's true, but whenever I saw her afterwards, she asked how I was doing and kindly touched my arm.

Upon her death my position became uncertain. Bertie, or King Edward VII as he was known, had his own staff. After some weeks, Collins and I were assigned to the Duke and Duchess of Cornwall and York, Georgie and May, who were living in creakingly cramped quarters in St. James Palace.

I was excited about going to London. I'd never dreamed I'd set foot on its streets, but I wished Garth were alive to go with me. My last evening at Balmoral, I stood near his resting place. I shed some tears and kissed his gravestone, never dreaming it would be the last time I'd be close to him.

Next morning Collins hooted when I shrunk back as the train chuffed into Ballater station. I had never been that close to a Puffing Billy and I was a-feared the steam jetting across the platform would burn me. Of course it didn't, and soon, we and our bags were stowed inside the carriage and away we went.

I couldn't believe the speed. The guard said we were doing forty miles an hour. I had never before travelled so fast or so smoothly. We seemed to float through The Highlands, the hills skipping above us, the valleys diving below as we sped along the iron roadbed. I well understood why doctors ordered some women not to travel. Such excitement would surely affect an unborn child.

London was noisy and dirty. Carriages thronged The Mall at all times of the day and night. Adding to the clatter of the horses' hooves and the scrape of metal tires on cobbles were the shrill cries of trains arriving and departing from Victoria Station across the park. I yearned for the clean, fresh air and quiet of The Highlands.

Collins was more ornery than ever. He'd been to London several times before and strutted about like he was the Lord Mayor himself. My half days off, I escaped him by walking to the Thames. I watched the ships departing for the colonies. Sometimes I dreamed of hopping aboard to escape Collins' ribbing and London's clamor. Nights I closed my eyes and clung to my pillow, dreaming I was once again snuggled next to Garth.

I had been in London only a few weeks when I heard about Lord Edward. The story was that he'd approached Lord Manchester's footman in the same way he approached me. He'd been punched in the nose and his family had packed him off to Canada with a small pension. Though he had acted badly, I understood why. I felt sorry for him. I half wished I could be there to serve him in the loneliness he must feel so far from home.

A month later I received a letter from Canada. "Has Andy Pamby got another beau?" Collins teased when I rushed to my room to read it in private.

Lord Edward was exploring Toronto. He finished by writing, *There's free land in the northwest. I may start a cattle ranch. If we are friends, and I hope we are, consider joining me. Perhaps one day you may find room in your heart to love me as you did Garth.*

I took Lord Edward's letter with me the next time I strolled to the Thames. I read his invitation while watching a ship being loaded with bundles of rails and barrels of spikes for Canada's railways. I tried to imagine how it would feel to sail across the sea to join up with Lord Edward.

But it was impossible. He was a duke's son. I was a footman, son of a blacksmith. There was no way we could enjoy a life together.

While I suffered Collins' cheek, Princess May suffered the new queen's jealousy. When the Duke and Duchess planted a tree or laid a cornerstone, crowds cheered Princess May. Queen Alexandra, hoping to reclaim popularity from her daughter-in-law by getting rid of her for awhile, decided their Royal Highnesses should spend several months touring the Empire.

Collins and I were chosen to be part of the royal suite. Mid-March we took the train to Portsmouth and boarded *H.M.S. Ophir*. After calling at Gibraltar and other Mediterranean ports, we sailed through the Suez Canal and approached Ceylon. I thought of Lord Edward playing with his baby elephant while growing up there. I fetched his letter from my grip and read it as the ship entered port.

The heat and humidity put Collins in a foul temper. I knew he couldn't swim and thought of pushing him overboard, but I had no desire to rot in jail, so I avoided him as much as possible.

Ophir's seamen were forbidden to set foot on the royal suite's deck, but Collins didn't mind bending rules. One evening, after serving at dinner by myself because Collins claimed to be suffering *mal de mer*—more like *mal de rum*—I cracked open his cabin door to see if he was alright. He was lying sideways on his bunk, his fat legs in the air, an able seaman with a stiff root as thick as a fire hose, pounding his arse hard enough to capsize the ship.

Neither man saw me. My instinct was to slip away unnoticed, but then thought it might be good for Collins to see I knew he wasn't the ladies' Lothario he claimed to be. I cleared my throat. His head couldn't have snapped up faster if I'd packed his pillow with dynamite. I wagged my finger at him and shut the door. From that moment he quit scoffing at my love for Garth, but his temper and drunkenness only got worse.

The mails were delivered as we were about to leave Africa for Canada, and to my delight there were letters from Lord Edward. He had taken up something called a homestead near a town named Calgary. He was buying cattle and horses. Some friends had settled nearby and they were building cabins before winter set in. His cabin had a view of the Rocky Mountains, which were snow-capped all year.

Mommsie wrote that you are on tour with Their Royal Highnesses. I'll be in Calgary the day they visit. It will do my lonely heart good to cast my eyes upon your handsome face, and once again hear the love and kindness in your voice, even if the words are not meant for me— yet.

I hoped to see Lord Edward, if only for a few moments. However, as we neared Canada, word came of the assassination of American President McKinley. There was talk of cancelling the tour, but to my relief, Their Royal Highnesses decided they could not disappoint so many loyal Canadians who were preparing to see them.

We docked at Quebec and a few days later set out by train. With official duties in several cities along the route, it took many days to reach the northwest. Finally on the 28th day of September, almost seven months after leaving England, the royal train approached Calgary. A mist covered the land, but just before our arrival it cleared and straight ahead were the snow-capped mountains Lord Edward had mentioned in his letter. As the train's brakes squealed, I scanned the crowd, but how could I possibly find Lord Edward in that cheering throng?

"Get your ugly face out of the window and get to work." Collins poked me in the arse. It was true. We had work to do. As soon as Their Royal Highnesses had left the train, I rushed the royal party's soiled clothing across the street to a Chinese laundry. It wasn't until mid-afternoon when our work was completed that we were allowed to ride in a carriage to Shagannapi point, a rise overlooking the city. Thousands of Indians in feather headdresses and buckskin clothing were camped there in tipis.

We were shown to seats next to the royal enclosure where the chiefs addressed the Royals before dancing began. I scanned the crowd for one familiar face. I was about to give up when I heard someone call my name. Turning around I saw Lord Edward making his way towards our enclosure.

Saying a word to the scarlet-coated Royal Canadian Mounted Policeman at the entrance, I made my way over to where Lord Edward was standing. I might not have recognized him if he hadn't called my name, for he looked a savage himself: his face and hands dark brown from the sun, his clothing a queer costume of light brown buckskin and leather. He threw his arms around me, and ignoring the stares of those closest, kissed me on both cheeks.

I had been nervous about meeting Lord Edward, but because of the letters we had exchanged, within moments I felt I was meeting a dear friend. He led me to a place where we could talk, away from the Indians' pounding drums and excited war cries. His words tumbled out like the Dee in flood as he told me about his ranch, his herd of cattle, his team of Clydesdales.

"And that's just the beginning," he said. "Once I've proved up this quarter section of land I'll buy more. Mommsie and Papa have sent the money."

"Tell me about your cabin," I prompted.

He touched my arm. "I wish you had time to see it. It's all closed in. When I head home with the team, I'll be hauling a cooker that'll keep the place warm all winter. There's a wee burn runs through the property. It's treed, so there's firewood to be had—and the neighbour says there's coals, free for the digging, in the hills."

He touched my hand. "This country is wonderful, Andrews. If a man's willing to work he can make a go of it, be his own boss. No more *Yes, Your Royal Highness. No, Your Royal Highness.*"

He looked around, saw all eyes were on the Royals and Indian dancers, and took my hand in his. "How about it, Cameron? Will you join me?"

"Oh, Milord, I don't –"

"Forget the *Milord*, Cameron Andrews. There's no green baize door here. When we're plowing the field or squaring logs we're all the same. Call me Eddie. Will you join me in this great country?"

I'd thought about Lord Edward's written invitation all the way to Australia, to Africa and as we approached Canada. I had lain awake wondering what I would do if fortune brought us together again. Some nights, especially after suffering Collins' bad temper, I wanted desperately to up sticks and throw my lot in with my new friend. But could I abandon the only life I knew for a man who was so far above me? Was it possible for someone of noble birth to love me?

If I accepted, there'd be no turning back. The Royals would never have me back if things didn't work out. I'd be too ashamed to return to my own people. I'd have to stick with Lord Edward no matter what. I needed time to think, but there was no more time. I could hear Prince George thanking the Indians for their display.

"My dad and grandfather proudly served the Royals ever since Prince Albert bought Balmoral," I said. "How can I abandon them in this…this wilderness?" I gestured toward the valley. Except for scrubby bushes along the riverbank, there wasn't a tree in sight.

"But don't you see, Cameron? It's a wide-open country, full of possibilities. Do Their Royal Highnesses know your birth date? Do they know anything about you, or care so long as you turn up every day to serve them their meals and iron their newspapers?"

Lord Edward squeezed my hand. "The real question is, do you think you could love me like you loved Garth? Could we build a life together?"

I looked into his eyes as he brushed a lock of his rusty hair from his forehead. "What do you say, Cameron? Will you come with me now?"

"Lord Edward –I mean Eddie—I'm afraid I'm going to say…*Yes*. Is that foolish of me?"

"You won't regret it, my friend." He smiled. "Will you tell Their Royal Highnesses?"

"I cannot leave without explaining. Let's go back to the train. I'll write a letter."

Grabbing hold of my hand he led me to where several horse-drawn hacks were waiting. "To the station, and be quick about it!"

On board the train, I scrawled a note and placed it on Prince George's desk, then ran back to my compartment, grabbed my grip and exited on the far side of the train as distant cheering announced the return of the cavalcade. Lord Edward and I pushed our way through the crowd to his hotel. From the third-floor window we watched the royal suite arrive in their carriages, Collins swaggering along the platform like always. No doubt he would feast on *Andy Pamby's* irresponsible character for years to come, but with Lord Edward standing behind me, his arms wrapped around my chest, his lips nuzzling my ear, all my fears vanished.

The band struck up *God Save the King*, the whistle toot-tooted, and the train, with its royal visitors on board, chuffed out of my life forever.

Lord Edward closed the curtains and led me to the bed where he enfolded me in his arms, brought his lips to mine, and gave me a real kiss that seemed to last forever.

"Remember that back scrub you gave me at Balmoral?"

I nodded.

"Now it's your turn."

"But where?"

"This hotel has two rooms with private bath. We've got one of them, so we'd better use it. Stand up, Cameron Andrews." He tossed my coat on the bed and began unbuttoning my shirt.

I shook my head and stepped back. "This is wrong, Milord. I'm supposed to be undressing you."

"No more *Milording*. We're starting a new life." He leaned in for another kiss before lifting my suspenders and removing my shirt. "Just relax while I undress you. I've dreamed of doing this since that night at Balmoral when I first laid my lonely eyes on your handsome face."

He kissed me again, then tongued the sensitive skin on my neck. A moan escaped my lips. I hadn't been touched in this way since that dreadful morning when Garth was killed.

Lord Edward ran his fingers through the hair on my chest. "I wondered what was beneath your footman's livery."

"You like what you see?"

"I like this," he said, brushing his hand over my chest.

"Thank you, Milord."

He put both hands on my shoulders and looked me in the eye. "Did you hear what I said, Cameron Andrews? No more Milording. We've left all that behind. From this moment it's just you and me, Cameron and Eddie. Cameron and Eddie, together forever."

"Yes, Eddie," I said. "You and me, together forever."

We were no more valet and Lord. We were just two men who loved each other the way only two men can. I closed my eyes and snuggled into his embrace.

If you enjoyed this book, I'd appreciate it if you would write an online review.

Made in the USA
Middletown, DE
12 April 2019